THE IRON WAGON

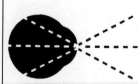

This Large Print Book carries the
Seal of Approval of N.A.V.H.

RETURN OF THE STRANGER, BOOK 3

THE IRON WAGON

AL LACY AND JOANNA LACY

THORNDIKE PRESS
A part of Gale, Cengage Learning

GALE
CENGAGE Learning™

Detroit • New York • San Francisco • New Haven, Conn • Waterville, Maine • London

GALE
CENGAGE Learning™

LIBRARY OF CONGRESS CATALOGING-IN-PUBLICATION DATA

Lacy, Al.
  The iron wagon / by Al & JoAnna Lacy.
    p. cm. — (Thorndike Press large print Christian historical fiction) (Return of the stranger trilogy ; bk. 3)
  ISBN-13: 978-1-4104-3415-9 (hardcover)
  ISBN-10: 1-4104-3415-X (hardcover)
  1. United States marshals—Fiction. 2. Prisoners—Transportation—Fiction. 3. Women pioneers—Fiction. 4. Apache Indians—Fiction. 5. Frontier and pioneer life—West (U.S.)—Fiction. 6. Large type books. I. Lacy, JoAnna. II. Title.
PS3562.A256I76 2011
813'.54—dc22   2010045474

Published in 2011 by arrangement with Multnomah, an imprint of Crown Publishing Group, a division of Random House, Inc.

Printed in Mexico
1 2 3 4 5 6 7 15 14 13 12 11

We dedicate this book to our dear friends
Jerry and Linda Weddle
(whom Al had the joy of
personally leading to the Lord),
who have been such a blessing to us.
We love you!
Al and JoAnna
Hebrews 13:20–21

FOREWORD

The Return of the Stranger trilogy is a follow-up to the Journeys of the Stranger Series and Angel of Mercy Series written for Multnomah Books by Al Lacy between 1994 and 1997.

In 1997, Multnomah's president hired JoAnna Lacy as coauthor with her husband, and they began the Hannah of Fort Bridger Series that same year. Since then, JoAnna has coauthored every book with her husband that has been published by Multnomah Books and the new WaterBrook Multnomah Publishing Group.

Since Al ended the Journeys of the Stranger and Angel of Mercy Series, which centered on John "the Stranger" Brockman and Breanna Baylor, who married in the second series, Al and JoAnna as well as the publisher have received repeated letters, e-mails, and calls asking that Al write another Stranger series. This trilogy is in pleasant response to those welcome requests.

Al and JoAnna hope that fans of the Stranger will enjoy this new trilogy and that many new Stranger fans will as well.

ONE

On Monday, August 20, 1888, Meggie Brockman's birthday party was held as planned at the Brockman home. Dr. Matthew Carroll and his wife, Dottie — Breanna's sister — were there, as well as the Brockmans' close friends deputy U.S. marshal Whip Langford and his wife, Annabeth, and Pastor Robert Bayless and his wife, Mary. When dinner was over, it was time to go to the parlor for the party.

"John," Breanna asked, loud enough for everyone to hear, "would you take me up to the master bedroom so I can rest a little bit?"

As John took hold of the handles on the back of the wheelchair, Meggie turned to her mother. "I'll wait to open my presents, Mama, until you get some rest and come back down to the parlor."

When John wheeled Breanna out of the dining room, everyone went to the parlor and sat down, with Meggie sitting by a stack of brightly wrapped birthday presents. A short while later, everyone was pleased when they heard John call from the hall that he and Breanna were back.

All eyes went to the parlor door and widened quickly when Breanna entered the room — *walking!* She held a cane in one hand, and John steadied her by holding her other hand.

Fifteen-year-old Paul, thirteen-year-old Ginny, and ten-year-old Meggie rushed to their mother, smiling broadly, their arms wide open to hug her. One at a time, they each gave her a delicate, heartfelt hug as their father continued to steady her by holding her hand.

Tears misted Breanna's eyes as she was being hugged. Everyone else jumped to their feet, staring in stunned silence, hardly able to believe their eyes.

Meggie looked toward heaven. "Thank You, Lord Jesus! I know I will like all these presents in the packages, but this is my favorite birthday present. *My mama is walking!*"

Breanna sat on a soft chair with John's help. More tears were shed as Meggie leaned over carefully and wrapped her arms around Breanna's neck, sobbing joyfully. "I love you, Mama! I love you so much! I'm so happy you can walk again!"

As Meggie eased back and smiled at her mother, Breanna looked lovingly at her little adopted daughter, her own cheeks shining with tears, then embraced her. "Oh, sweetie, I love you so much too!"

John Brockman, the Carrolls, the Baylesses, and the Langfords all smiled through their tears as they observed the scene.

Tall, dark-haired Paul now stood in front of his mother's chair with Ginny beside him, and they both poured out words of love to her as they wiped their tears, saying how happy they were that her legs had regained so much strength.

Ginny and Paul bent down and embraced their mother. Breanna's tears flowed freely down her cheeks as she told Paul and Ginny how very much she loved them.

A small frown creased Meggie's brow. "Why didn't you tell us you were able to walk again?"

Breanna smoothed a hand over Meggie's blond curls, then clasped her hands in her own. "Just because I was getting feeling back into my feet and legs, Papa and I weren't sure it would mean I could walk. It's been a hard and sometimes discouraging struggle . . . and well, we didn't want to disappoint everyone if the attempt to get me walking again wasn't successful. So every night after you children were in your beds, Papa and I went to work on the therapy recommended by your uncle Matt."

Breanna released Meggie's hands. "Honey, I've been doing some small exercises on my own when Papa was at work and you, Ginny, and Paul weren't home." She looked at her ruggedly handsome husband as he stroked his well-trimmed mustache. "Papa and I really wanted to surprise everyone once we knew God had healed me and helped me get to this point. I still have a long way to go, but thankfully, the Lord indeed *has* healed me and given me the grace and strength to come this far."

Meggie gently wrapped her arms around her mother's neck again and held her for a few seconds. A crooked smile lit up Meggie's face. "I guess it's okay you kept this secret as long as you did, but now that we all know, we can help you with your therapy, and maybe you can get all well quicker."

Breanna tenderly placed her palms on Meggie's cheeks and smiled. "Maybe so, sweet one, but I can only do so much exercise in a day!"

Meggie giggled. "Okay, Mama, we'll do it your way. Just give a holler when you want our help."

"I'll just do that, Meg. Now, I think you need to put your attention on these birthday gifts that have been sitting here waiting for you to open them."

"Oh my, yes!" Meggie squealed, her dimples flashing as she moved to where the brightly wrapped presents were stacked.

As Meggie opened her presents, one after another, her eyes widened with joy. When she had finished, she went to each and every person at the party, hugged them, and thanked them for her gifts.

Meggie then positioned herself before her family and the guests. "Oh, this has been such a wonderful birthday party!"

John stepped over to her and placed his hands on her shoulders. "Well, my sweet, you've got a long line of birthday parties in the future."

Meggie looked up and smiled. "But this one will always be extra special, Papa, because God answered my prayers and made it so Mama could walk again!"

"Amens" were spoken by everybody.

Meggie glanced at her family and choked up a bit as she said, "Papa, Mama, Paul, Ginny . . . thank you for taking me into your home and giving me the happiness I've had ever since I was adopted. I love you!"

John hugged Meggie; then Paul did the same, followed by Ginny. Breanna opened her arms, and Meggie went back to her. They kissed each other's cheeks, then embraced for a long moment.

Realizing it was time for the guests to leave, Pastor Bayless said, "Well, since the party is almost over, let's bow our heads and thank the Lord for Breanna's healing and that Meggie has had such a happy birthday."

Heads were bowed instantly, and the pastor led them in prayer.

The guests all spoke their joy to Breanna again concerning her regaining the use of her legs, wished Meggie "Happy Birthday" once more, and then left. As they were walking out the door, Breanna said, "Pastor, I'm planning to be at church Sunday morning."

Pastor Bayless paused and smiled. "Great! It will be good to have you."

After John closed the door behind them, he turned to his family and smiled. "Before we all head for our bedrooms, let's pray together. I want to just thank the Lord together once more for making your mama well enough to walk again."

The family joined hands in a circle, bowed their heads, and John said, "Dear Lord, my mind goes to verses 6 and 7 in Psalm 28 as

David wrote: 'Blessed be the LORD, because he hath heard the voice of my supplications. The LORD is my strength and my shield; my heart trusted in him, and I am helped: therefore my heart greatly rejoiceth; and with my song will I praise him.' "

By this time, tears flowed from the closed eyes of the parents and the children, and a few sniffles were heard.

John went on. "Dear Lord, we can all say with David in that seventh verse, 'my heart trusted in him, and I am helped.' " And this makes me think, heavenly Father, of the psalmist's words in Psalm 121:2: 'My help cometh from the LORD, which made heaven and earth.' Thank You, precious Lord, for healing these children's wonderful mother and my wonderful wife. Thank You that she is indeed walking again!"

There was a chorus of "amens," which were repeated when John closed off his prayer in Jesus' name.

Paul, Ginny, and Meggie hugged both parents before mounting the stairs to the second floor of the ranch house. John lifted Breanna into his strong arms. "Sweetheart, I'll carry you up the stairs for a while yet before you try climbing them on your own."

Breanna kissed his lips and smiled. "I just love being carried by you, darling. Maybe

I'll just let you carry me up the stairs from now on."

Laughter burst forth from the top of the stairs; then Paul called down, "What about when Papa isn't here, Mama?"

Breanna giggled and looked up at her three children. "Well, I guess I'll have to climb up there on my own. But don't tell your father. I want *him* to carry me up these stairs when he's home for as long as I can get away with it."

John laughed as he started up the stairs with Breanna in his arms. "Sweetheart, you can *always* get away with it!"

During lunch at the Brockman home on Wednesday afternoon two days later, Breanna, Dottie, Ginny, Meggie, and Paul sat at the table.

"Aunt Dottie," Paul said as he rubbed his stomach, "I really appreciate your being here so often to help my sisters with the cooking."

Dottie smiled at him. "It's my pleasure."

Paul put a heckling grin on his lips and looked at his sisters. "Well, Aunt Dottie, if it had been left up to Ginny and Meggie, we'd probably all be malnourished by now!"

Ginny glared back at Paul in a teasing way, her sky blue eyes sparkling. "Now, wait a minute, big brother. Meggie and I are right good cooks." Still grinning, she looked at her mother. "Aren't we, Mama?"

"Well, you both *should* be good cooks. Remember who taught you!" Breanna pointed a finger at herself.

This drew laughter from around the table.

"I was just kidding and having a little fun with my sisters, Mama." Then Paul looked at his aunt. "I really do want to thank you *so much* for all your help and encouragement to us, and especially to Mama."

Dottie ran her twinkling gaze around the table. "I wouldn't have it any other way."

"Mama," Paul said, "since school will be starting in just over two weeks, I want to ride to town later this afternoon and buy myself some new clothes."

Breanna nodded. "That's fine, son."

Paul smiled. "Okay, Mama. Just before five o'clock, I'll go to Papa's office so I can ride home with him."

"Well, that will make your papa very happy."

"Tell you what. I'll ride Papa's aging horse Chance to town today and give the old boy a little exercise."

Breanna chuckled. "I guarantee you that will make Papa very happy also."

"It sure will," Ginny piped up. "Papa still

loves to see Chance ridden now and then."

When lunch was over, Paul excused himself, saying he had some work to do at the barn, as Aunt Dottie and his sisters prepared to wash and dry the dishes.

Just after three o'clock, Paul swung into the saddle on Chance's back and waved at his mother, his sisters, and his aunt on the front porch. He trotted the black stallion up the lane toward the road, then guided Chance toward Denver from the west. Twice Paul met up with neighboring ranchers returning from town and stopped to chat with them for a few minutes.

As he was drawing closer to Denver, Paul guided Chance to the bank of the Platte River. After letting him take a good drink, he put the horse back to a trot. Exactly six weeks from today, Paul would turn sixteen. He couldn't wait until he turned twenty-one so he could become one of his father's deputies, fulfilling the strong desire he'd had ever since he was a child to become a lawman.

At a small cabin on Denver's east side, aging widower Chad Marks sat on the sofa in his parlor, just resting after mopping the kitchen floor. The silver-haired man had his head laid back with his eyes closed when he heard the sound of horse's hoofs approach the front of the house and stop. Seconds later, footsteps sounded on the front porch, followed by a knock at the door.

With effort, Chad made his way off the sofa and moved slowly out of the parlor. Before he reached the door, there was another knock.

"Uncle Chad! You in there?"

Drawing up to the door, Chad thought, *Oh no! It's that nephew of mine, Kail Gatlin.*

Kail, in his early forties, was well known as a gunfighter in Nebraska. Chad hadn't seen Kail since Chad and his wife, Martha, had moved to Denver from North Platte, Nebraska, some six years previously.

Bracing himself and knowing he must show himself friendly toward his violent nephew, Chad opened the door. He managed a smile. "Well, howdy, Kail. I thought it was your voice I was hearing, but I wasn't sure."

"Howdy, yourself, Uncle Chad."

Chad swung the door wide. "C'mon in."

Kail extended his hand as he stepped into the cabin, and Chad grasped it in a weak handshake. He led his nephew into the parlor and sat on the sofa. Kail eased onto an overstuffed chair, facing his uncle from some six feet away. "Are you still having

19

heart problems?"

Chad nodded. "I am, but I have a good doctor here in Denver who so far has kept me alive."

"I'm glad for that."

Chad sat in silence, thinking about his situation. Even though his heart was declining almost daily, he was still able to live alone in his quiet, peaceful cabin at the edge of town. His wants and needs were small, and he enjoyed awaking each morning, knowing he had made it through another night. The medicine the doctor gave him did help some, and his sedate lifestyle added to his stability.

Chad had always been a farmer, but recently he had sold off his acreage, along with his house and barn, and now lived in this small cabin, which was just the right size for him since his beloved Martha had died nearly two years ago.

Because of this surprise by his wayward nephew, Chad sat on the sofa feeling some stabbing pains in his chest and became aware of some shortness of breath. After nearly five minutes of silence, Kail took a deep breath and let it out slowly. "Uncle Chad, I have something to tell you."

Chad looked at him and nodded. "All right."

"I didn't really come here to see *you*, but since I was coming to Denver anyway, I thought I'd stop by. When I got into town, I asked around and was told where you lived."

Chad frowned. "So, why did you come here?"

Kail cleared his throat and adjusted himself on the chair. "Remember how the man called the Stranger killed my brother, Kent, in a quick-draw shootout over twenty years ago on Main Street in Grand Island, Nebraska?"

Chad took a deep breath and rubbed his chest. "I remember it well. I know Kent had been a successful gunfighter for a few years, but he *never* should have challenged the Stranger, who was well known for his exceptional drawing speed and accuracy with his gun."

Kail shrugged. "Well, Kent was only trying to make a name for himself by taking out the legendary John Stranger."

The old man shook his head, once again rubbing his chest. "Kent only played the fool by challenging him. Everyone who knew about John Stranger also knew that whenever he was challenged to a fast-draw shootout on a busy street in town, he would shoot to kill — because if all he did was wound a challenger, the challenger's gun

21

could go off and hit one of the spectators."

Kail sighed. "Yeah, I know. But he still killed my brother."

Chad's brow wrinkled with another frown. "Why have you brought up that incident of Kent challenging the Stranger?"

Kail scooted forward a bit on the over-stuffed chair and looked his uncle square in the eye. "I just learned a few weeks ago that the Stranger is now chief U.S. marshal John Brockman, whose office is here in Denver." He pulled a paper from his shirt pocket, unfolded it, and waved it before his uncle's eyes. "See this?"

Chad squinted, focusing on the image. "Yes. It's the front page from the *North Platte Daily News.*"

"Right. As you can see, there are two photographs of Chief Brockman on this page, along with an article about him."

Chad nodded. "Mm-hmm."

"Well, the article is about what they call his tremendous work as head of the federal office in Denver, which makes him the top U.S. marshal of the Western District. As you can see, one photograph is of Brockman standing in front of Denver's federal office building downtown on Broadway."

"That's right."

"And some of Brockman's deputy marshals are standing with him while Brockman towers over them."

"Yes, I've seen him many times. He is very tall — well over six feet."

"Yeah," said Kail. "And this other photograph on the front page shows Brockman at his desk in the Denver office."

Chad nodded again. "Mm-hmm. Handsome fella, isn't he?"

Kail gritted his teeth. "He killed my brother. As far as I'm concerned, he's the ugliest man I've ever seen. This article goes on to give a brief history of Brockman. It says how for several years all over the West, the Stranger helped people in various kinds of trouble and also aided the law by bringing many outlaws to justice."

Chad smiled. "Uh-huh. He's really a good guy."

A sudden scowl twisted Kail's features, and his eyes blazed with wrath. "I don't care how good a guy Brockman is in the minds of the people of the West. I'm gonna kill him!"

"I warn you, Kail, if you challenge Chief Brockman to a quick draw, you'll lose."

Kail sneered. "I know better than to do that, Uncle Chad. I would never make that challenge. I'm gonna find a way to sneak up on Brockman and shoot him in the back.

I'll put a bullet right through his heart."

The old man turned pale, shaking his head. "Don't you do it! It was Kent's fault he got killed."

Through clenched teeth, Kail hissed, "I *have* to kill him! I've got to pay him back for taking my brother from me!"

The old man clutched at the left side of his chest, and he could hardly get a breath at all. His face went white as he gasped, "I — I've got to take some of my medicine."

A worried look framed Kail's face. "Can I get it for you?"

Struggling to move off the sofa, Chad said weakly, "No. Just help me into the kitchen, please."

Kail stood and helped his uncle to his feet. He gripped the old man tightly as he staggered toward the kitchen.

"Please, Kail, just leave town and forget about killing John Brockman," Chad wheezed. By the time they entered the kitchen, the pain in Chad's chest had increased, and he could hardly get his breath at all.

He pointed to a small cupboard. Kail guided him to it and steadied his uncle as Chad removed a bottle of pills. With shaky hands, he opened the bottle and shook out two white pills into his trembling left hand.

He popped them into his mouth, then picked up a water pitcher from the counter, poured a cup about half full, and drank it down.

Kail frowned. "Is it your heart?"

"Oh, just a touch of indigestion. Like a boiling pot in my stomach that's sending the pain up into my chest. I'll be all right once those pills get into my system."

Chad was doing his best to disguise the pain in his chest, not wanting his nephew to know the seriousness of his heart problem.

"Oh. Okay. I just don't want you keeling over."

Chad forced a grin. "Not a chance. But . . . but —"

"But *what?*"

"I really think you should leave town and forget this revenge against Chief Brockman you've got in your head."

Kail frowned fiercely. "Like you just said, Uncle Chad. *Not a chance!*" Then he helped his uncle settle himself back on the parlor sofa.

Several hours later, when the clock on the wall neared four o'clock, Kail got up from the overstuffed chair, woke his uncle, and told him he had to leave.

Chad blinked. "I'll walk you to the door." He decided to try one more time. He

25

gripped Kail's upper arm with a trembling hand. "Please, Kail! Don't kill Chief Brockman! That's not going to bring Kent back."

They drew up to the door. Kail yanked his arm from his uncle's grip, opened the door, and looked into his tear-filled eyes. "No, killin' Brockman won't bring my brother back, but it'll sure make me feel better!"

As Kail headed toward his big, black-maned, gray-bodied horse tied to the small hitching post in front of the cabin, Chad silently told himself that as soon as Kail rode away, he would go to the nearest neighbor's house and ask if he could borrow one of his saddle horses. He would take a shortcut, gallop to the federal building, and warn Chief Brockman about Kail's plans.

Kail swung atop his horse and with bulging eyes stared back at his uncle. "I've *got* to do this, Uncle Chad."

He dare not let Kail suspect that he was going to leave the house at that moment. He gave Kail a dull look, stepped back, and closed the door. He stood there until he heard the horse trot away.

Suddenly Chad clutched his chest, gasped for breath, and collapsed on the floor. He breathed hard for several seconds, then stopped breathing altogether.

He was dead.

Two

At four forty-five that warm afternoon, Paul Brockman turned Chance onto Broadway Street, a block south of the federal building. With his shopping parcel tied to the saddle horn, he figured that instead of riding Chance to the rear of the building, where his father's horse Blackie was in the small corral, he would just pull up to one of the hitch rails in front. He would wait inside and chat with some of the deputies until his father was ready to head for home.

As Paul drew nearer to the federal building, he saw that the hitch rails directly in front of the building were full. He'd need to use an open spot a few buildings down. Just as he was dismounting, about twenty-five yards away from the front door, he saw deputy U.S. marshal Whip Langford exiting. Paul tied the reins to the rail, then smiled at the approaching man. "Howdy, Uncle Whip. How come your horse is tied out front instead of being in the corral in the rear?"

Returning the smile as he drew up, Whip said, "Well, I've been gone from the office since early morning, I returned only a few minutes ago, and now I'm going home. How come you're here?"

Paul explained; then Whip told him about his morning activity catching an outlaw. While Paul and Whip stood on the board-walk talking, Paul noticed his father come out the federal building door with Fred and Sofie Ryerson. They paused to chat for a moment. Paul loved the Ryersons and was smiling at the scene as a man on a big gray horse with a black mane and tail rode past him and Whip.

The mounted man drew his gun and aimed it at John Brockman's back. There was a quick catch in Paul's breath and a sudden rapid beating of his heart as, with lightning-fast action, he reached forth, grabbed Whip's gun out of its holster, snapped the hammer back, aimed at the rider, and squeezed the trigger.

The .45-caliber slug plowed into the man's back, ripping through his heart.

At the sound of the gunshot, John wheeled about to see a gun drop from the man's hand as he was falling out of the saddle.

John watched the man hit the ground beside the gray horse; then his son came toward him with a smoking gun in hand and Whip Langford at his side.

Paul and Whip dashed past the gunman, now sprawled motionless in the street. They glanced at him and quickly saw that he was no doubt dead.

People on the street, including the Ryersons, looked wide eyed at the scene as Paul raced ahead and reached his father before Whip. Paul was shaking badly as he threw his arms around his father.

John hugged his son until Whip drew up, then let go of Paul and looked at the gun in his son's hand that was still smoking a bit. "Son, what happened? Did you shoot that man on the gray horse?"

Unable to speak at the moment, Paul slowly nodded his head.

"Where did you get the gun?" John asked his son.

"From my holster, Chief," Whip interjected. "He did it to save your life."

John blinked. "T-to save *my* life?"

"Yes — Papa," Paul choked out. Then taking a deep, cleansing breath and running his hands over his eyes to clear away the mist that had formed there, Paul explained with a trembling voice what had happened.

His features a bit pale, John swallowed hard and nodded.

One of John's deputies, Barry Sotak, who had come on the scene only moments before, knelt beside the gunman who lay in the dust. He rose to his feet. "Chief Brockman, this man is dead."

While the crowd looked on, John, his son, and Whip headed that way.

When they drew up to where the corpse lay, Deputy Sotak said, "Some of the crowd told me what happened. They said Paul saved your life by shooting this man."

Chief Brockman nodded. "He sure did." John knelt and examined the dead man, who lay facedown. After seeing where the slug had hit him in the back, John turned him over, then looked up at Paul. "Son, you were explicitly accurate. You put the slug into the left side of the would-be killer's back, and it plowed right through his heart."

The crowd gathered in a close circle as Paul said in a tight voice, "I had no choice but to shoot to kill, Papa. I *had* to save your life."

John laid a hand on Paul's shoulder. "I know you had no choice, son. Thank you."

Many of the people in the crowd cheered Paul for what he did.

John bent over and removed the would-be

killer's wallet from his hip pocket. John removed an identification card and examined it carefully. "His name is Kail Gatlin, and he's from North Platte, Nebraska. I've heard of him. He was a quick-draw gunslinger and well known in Nebraska." John took a deep breath. "Well, he's dead now."

Paul swallowed hard. "I'm sorry I had to kill him, Papa. Since I'm too young to wear a gun, I had to snatch Uncle Whip's out of his holster and use it to keep him from shooting you." Wiping at the tears filling his eyes, Paul hugged his father again.

John wrapped his arms around his son. "Again, I thank you. You killed a man, yes. But it wasn't your choice. He was in the wrong and made a very unwise decision. It's okay, son. You did what you had to do."

John still saw the pain lurking in Paul's eyes. "Son, we'll talk more about this later. Okay?"

Paul nodded. "Sure, Papa. We'll talk more about it at home."

As the crowd was still in a tight circle, looking on and listening, John heard the familiar voice of the *Rocky Mountain News* reporter just behind him. "Chief Brockman . . ."

John let go of Paul, turned, and set his gaze on the reporter. "Yes, Bart?"

"I know of this gunslinger, Kail Gatlin. He's a nephew of Denver resident Chad Marks."

The chief U.S. marshal nodded. "I have met Mr. Marks."

"Well," Bart Gilmore said, "I have just learned from some folks in the crowd that Chad's next-door neighbors found him dead in his cabin less than half an hour ago."

John's eyebrows arched. "Oh?"

"Yes sir. Chad has had serious heart trouble for several months. It appears that he died of heart failure."

John rubbed the back of his neck. "Oh. I'm sorry to hear this. Chad was a good man."

Paul Brockman was still quite shaken when he and his father arrived home. After they put the horses in the corral, they headed toward the ranch house. They saw Breanna, Ginny, and Meggie quickly come through the kitchen door onto the back porch.

"We're sure glad you gentlemen made it home just before we put supper on the table," said Ginny.

"Yeah!" Meggie chimed in. "We were afraid we would have to eat supper without you!"

As father and son stepped up to the porch,

John said, "I have something to tell you ladies."

John and Paul solemnly moved up the steps, and then John began to explain. Breanna and the girls listened intently as John told them the story of Paul saving his life in front of the federal building.

While the girls stood in shock, mouths wide open, Breanna stepped up to Paul, placed her arms around him, and hugged him tightly while saying with a trembling voice, "Thank you, my son, for your quick thinking and actions. I'm so grateful to the Lord that you were on the scene and that the training your papa has given you resulted in your saving his life."

The girls hugged their father while Breanna hugged Paul; then they switched. As Breanna was in John's arms, tears flowed down her cheeks. Reality had set in, and she knew just how close she had come to losing the love of her life.

Pressing her close to him, John said, "Everything's all right now, sweetheart. I'm here safe and sound, thanks to the Lord's using the quick thinking of our boy."

Breanna sighed. "Thank You, dear Lord, for Your precious hand of protection on this cherished husband of mine."

While the two sisters hugged their tall

brother around the waist, Meggie gazed up at Paul, a lopsided grin lighting up her face. "You did good with Uncle Whip's gun, brother of mine!" Then she laughed. "Remind me to always stay on your *good* side."

Paul chuckled. "I'll do that."

Ginny sniffled, and Paul looked down into her tear-filled eyes. Paul gave her a good squeeze, and the three of them stood there, just holding onto each other. Each one thanked God in their hearts for His love and goodness in sparing their papa's life.

The next morning, Thursday, August 23, 1888, the front page of the *Rocky Mountain News* told the story of fifteen-year-old Paul Brockman saving his father's life the day before. As people all over the Denver area read the article, they designated young Paul a hero.

On that same morning, when Chief Brockman arrived at the federal building, having already read the *Rocky Mountain News* article before leaving home, he found Pastor Robert Bayless there waiting to see him.

They sat in the chief's office, and Pastor Bayless told John that in the midweek prayer service at church the previous night, Whip Langford had told him all about Paul saving John's life. When John gave some details about the incident that Whip hadn't mentioned, the pastor was even more impressed with Paul's courage and determination.

"Will Breanna still be coming to church on Sunday morning?"

John told him she sure was planning on it. This made the pastor happy.

Pastor Bayless rose to his feet. "Well, Chief, I'd better get on back to my office at the church. I've got some studying to do on my sermons for Sunday."

John also stood and smiled. "I want you to know how very much I appreciate the deep compassion you've shown Breanna since she was knocked down the stairs at the hospital and injured so seriously."

"Thank you, Chief. It's because I love Breanna as I love you and all of your family."

At these words, John opened his arms, and the two men embraced masculine-style, patting each other on the back. Tears misted John's eyes as the pastor left the office.

An hour after Pastor Bayless left John's office, there was a knock on the door, and the deputy on duty at the front desk opened the door. "Chief Brockman, Sheriff Walt Carter and a group of his deputies are here to see you."

John smiled. "Send them in."

When the county sheriff and ten of his deputies entered the office, they all told Chief Brockman how proud they were of Paul.

This touched John deeply. "I will most certainly tell Paul what you've said."

With a smile on his lips, Sheriff Carter held out a brand-new gun belt with a shiny new Colt .45 revolver in the holster.

"What's this all about?" John asked.

Sheriff Carter handed John the set. "We all know Paul is planning to become one of your deputies when he reaches twenty-one years of age. This is a gift from me to Paul, for him to wear and use when he becomes a lawman."

John gripped the leather and the gun, a sparkle in his eyes. His son would love this gift.

THREE

John Brockman smiled. "Walt, my friend, this is a tremendous gift. How very thoughtful. Paul is going to treasure it."

Sheriff Carter smiled back. "Well, that'll make *me* happy, Chief."

"Paul is still having a bit of a problem over the fact that he took another man's life, which is understandable, especially at his age."

"It sure is." The sheriff nodded.

"I still have nightmares at times about the first man I was forced to kill," John said.

"So do I," replied Sheriff Carter. "I'm sure all of us in this room know exactly what Paul is going through."

The deputies all spoke up, agreeing with the sheriff's statement. One of them added, "And Chief Brockman, all of us will help your son in any way we can."

John ran his gaze over the group. "Thanks, fellas. I just know Paul will make a good, sincere lawman. But he's my son first, and at times the apprehension of what might happen to him being a lawman comes to mind. As we both know, Walt, it's a hard and dangerous job. But I wouldn't want to be anything else, and neither would Paul, God bless him."

Sheriff Carter playfully cuffed the chief U.S. marshal on the chin, grinning. "You've got a fine boy there, John. I know you're proud of him."

John's heart swelled inside his chest. "I sure am."

"Paul is going to *do* all right, and he's going to *be* all right, John" said the sheriff. "He's got his father as an example."

A bit embarrassed, John's features tinted. He grinned and shrugged his broad shoulders.

At midmorning the next day, Sheriff Carter was at his desk in his office when he heard a tap on the door. "Yes?"

The door opened, and Deputy Homer Edwards stuck his head in. "Sheriff, Paul Brockman is here to see you."

Carter rose to his feet. "Send him in."

The tall young man who very much resembled his father stepped into the office and headed toward the sheriff as the deputy quietly closed the door.

The sheriff rounded his desk and met up with Paul, and they shook hands. "Sheriff Carter, I want to thank you for your generous gifts — the Colt .45, the holster, and the gun belt."

"My pleasure, Paul. What you did to save your father's life when that cold-blooded gunslinger was going to kill him was terrific."

Paul's features flushed a bit. "Th-thank you, sir. From now on, when I practice the fast draw, as I've been doing with my father's old gun and holster for quite some time, I will use my new gun, holster, and gun belt. And then, sir, I will also use them when I become a lawman!"

Sheriff Carter smiled. "My boy, this makes me very happy."

Chief Brockman was chatting with Deputy Barry Sotak in the outer office of the federal building when the outside door opened, and Barry and John's pastor entered.

Both men greeted Pastor Bayless; then the pastor looked at John. "May I talk to you for a minute in your office?"

"Certainly." John led him into his office. When John closed the door behind him, he gestured toward a chair. "Sit down, Pastor."

The preacher shook his head. "I really don't have time to sit and visit, Chief, but I stopped by on my way to make a call on a new family in town that is expecting me. I just wanted to ask you if Breanna is doing well enough that she's still planning on coming to church Sunday morning."

"She sure is, Pastor. It might be too soon for her to try both Sunday school and the preaching service, so Paul will bring his sisters to Sunday school, and I will bring Breanna to the preaching service."

Smiling, the pastor said, "Fine. I totally understand. I figured that might be the case, but I just needed to know for sure. I'd like you to delay your arrival just a few minutes so that when you and Breanna come into the church's vestibule, the service will already be in progress."

A puzzled look crossed John's face. "May I ask why?"

Pastor Bayless grinned. "You may ask, but I can't tell you. Just do as I ask, okay?"

John chuckled. "Hey, you're the pastor! Of course we'll do as you ask."

Early that afternoon, the chief U.S. marshal was at his desk doing paperwork when there was a tap on his door. Looking up, John called, "Yes?"

The door opened, and Deputy Sotak took a couple of steps into the office. "Chief, there's a man and his wife in the outer office who'd like to see you."

"Who are they?"

"Well, sir, they wouldn't tell me their names. They said to tell you that they met you many years ago when you were known only as John Stranger, and they want to see if you will remember them."

John chuckled. "All right. Send them in."

Seconds later, when the couple walked into John's office grinning, he looked at them inquisitively and blinked in surprise. "Monte Dixon! And . . . and — well, Jessie, you must be Jessie Dixon now."

The couple were in their midforties, and John hadn't seen them for some twenty years.

Monte Dixon had been a deputy sheriff in Butte, Montana, at that time, and John had led him to the Lord. Monte had served under Sheriff Lake Johnson. The Christian young lady's name was Miss Jessie Westbrook then, and she and Monte were obviously attracted to each other. Before the Stranger had left Butte, he told them he was sure they would end up getting married.

After shaking hands with them, John reminded them of what he had said would happen, and happily they told him he was right. "We got married shortly after the Stranger was there, Chief Brockman!" Monte said.

"Boy, I'm sure glad I was right!"

"We are too!" Monte grinned.

Jessie giggled. "Amen to that."

John invited the Dixons to sit on the sofa in one corner of his office, and as they were easing onto it, John sat in an overstuffed chair a few feet away.

"Well, Monte, what have you two been doing with your lives?"

"We've had the honor of being missionaries in South Africa for fourteen years.

John's eyes widened. "Missionaries. Wow! Praise the Lord!"

The Dixons exchanged happy glances.

Monte then talked about the day John Stranger had led him to Jesus. He explained that he had been baptized at the Calvary Baptist Church in Butte, where Jessie was a member, the Sunday after John Stranger left Montana.

The conversation then turned to the mysterious murderer in Butte who had left notes after killing people, calling himself the Snow Ghost. John Stranger had bravely caught the killer, whose name was Layton Sturgis.

Monte told John about his call to preach, his going to Bible college, and the Lord leading them to go as missionaries to South Africa, sent out by their church in Butte. He went on to inform John of the churches he had gotten started in South Africa and of the great number of people who had been saved . . . adding that if the Stranger had not led him to the Lord, none of this would have happened.

"Chief Brockman, you have a part in every precious soul that has been saved under my ministry."

"Praise the Lord!"

"We're on our way to our home church in Butte, Chief," Jessie said. "But Monte and I just *had* to stop in Denver to see you."

"Well, I'm mighty glad you did!"

"Our train to Butte leaves Denver at eight o'clock in the morning," Monte said.

"Well, you're going home with me for supper." John leaned forward in his chair. "I want you to meet my wife, Breanna, and our children, Paul, Ginny, and Meggie. I'll borrow a horse and buggy from a stable down the street, and you can stay all night with us too."

Jessie's brow furrowed. "Are you sure it will be all right with your wife if you just show up with two extra people for supper?"

John grinned. "No problem there. Breanna is used to my doing this kind of thing, and she always has an attitude of 'the more, the merrier'!"

Jessie's features relaxed. "Okay."

Running his gaze between them, John said, "Breanna is a nurse, and several weeks ago she was knocked down a flight of stairs at Denver's Mile High Hospital by a man who was out of his mind in pain. He didn't mean to do it. For a while there we didn't know if she would ever walk again, but the Lord, in His goodness, healed her. She moves a little slower and more cautiously than she once did, and she has pain in her lower back quite often, but other than that, she is doing just fine. Besides, both of our daughters are a big help to her, and they are learning from the best cook in the world how to cook."

John looked at Monte. "Let me get my horse from the corral behind the federal building. I'll lead him down the street to the stable as we walk together, and you can drive the buggy."

"Sounds fine to me," Monte said.

At the Brockman home, Ginny and Meggie had the table set, and chicken and dumplings simmered on the stove. The girls were making a large green salad of homegrown vegetables, fresh from the garden in the backyard. A golden-crusted peach pie cooled on the kitchen windowsill, and supper would soon be ready.

Sitting on a chair at the table and watching her daughters work, Breanna knotted her hands into fists and rubbed her lower back, making a deep sigh.

Meggie noticed this and frowned. "Okay, Mama," she said with a teasing, bossy tone, "supper is just about ready. Papa will be home soon, and Paul, I'm sure, is just about done with his chores at the barn and corral. You need to rest a bit. Why don't you go sit on the pillowed wicker chair in the shade on the front porch and give that back of yours some much-needed relief?"

Breanna managed a smile. "Oh, I'm okay, dear."

"No, you're not, Mama." Ginny move to stand beside Meggie. "Now, obey Meggie and me, and go rest till it's time for supper. The breeze out there is getting cool and will feel mighty good."

Breanna giggled as she rose from the chair, still rubbing her lower back. "I guess I've been outvoted!"

Meggie hugged her. "Yep, you have been outvoted."

Ginny also stepped up and hugged their mother. "Yes, Mama. It's time for you to relax."

Breanna made her way toward the parlor at the front of the ranch house. As she stepped out onto the tree-shaded front porch, she felt a nice breeze blowing. She sat on a white wicker chair, which had a thick, soft, blue and white pillow leaning against the back and an identical pillow on the seat.

She sighed. "Oh, this does feel good!"

Seconds later, Ginny came through the screen door, holding a glass of tea, and set it on the small table beside her mother. "You just enjoy this tea, sweet Mama. Papa will be home any minute now, so you just relax, sit here, sip on the tea, and wait for him. Meggie and I will finish up supper."

Breanna picked up the glass of tea and smiled up at her. "Thanks, sweetie. I'll do it."

Ginny hurried away, and after putting down several swallows of tea, Breanna set the glass on the table. She glanced toward the road, but there was no sign of her husband yet. She eased back in the wicker chair and closed her eyes.

Some ten minutes passed, and Breanna was almost dozing when she heard the sound of pounding hooves on the tree-lined lane that led to the road. *John's home now.*

She opened her eyes to see her husband on his horse, but a horse and buggy followed him. Rising stiffly, Breanna moved to the edge of the porch at the top of the steps and waited for John and whoever was in the buggy to pull up.

When they drew up, John smiled at his wife, then dismounted. He went to the buggy and helped Jessie down from the seat while Monte was getting down from his side. Then he led them to Breanna.

"Honey, these are missionaries Monte and Jessie Dixon. They stopped by to see me in town, so I invited them for supper and to stay the night with us."

Breanna beamed brightly at the couple. "Please, do come in."

Jessie walked up the steps. "I hope this isn't a dreadful imposition, Breanna."

"Oh, not at all! We love company, and it will be wonderful for the children and me to hear about how John met you."

As John, Breanna, and their guests moved down the hall toward the kitchen, both girls and their brother stepped into the hall at the doorway and smiled.

Breanna introduced Paul, Ginny, and Meggie to the Dixons. "Girls, set two more places at the table for our guests. Paul, these precious missionaries are staying the night with us. Would you go upstairs and open the windows in the guest room so it will cool down with the nice breeze blowing outside?"

"Of course." Paul hurried to the staircase at the front of the house, then bounded up the stairs.

Monte looked at Breanna. "By the wonderful aroma coming from the kitchen, I'm sure glad John invited us for supper!"

Breanna laughed. "Well, it's just plain country cooking, but there's plenty to eat, and I know the fellowship we have will be precious and special."

Soon, they were all seated around the large table, holding hands as John asked for God's blessing and thanked Him for their bounty of food and for allowing his friends to visit them.

The next morning, Saturday, John took the Dixons to the railroad station in Denver, and with tears running down his cheeks, he waved good-bye to them as they waved back from the window where they were seated in their coach.

FOUR

On Sunday morning, August 26, Paul Brockman helped his sisters onto the driver's seat of the ranch wagon in front of the house, then climbed up and sat beside Meggie. Paul snapped the reins to put the horse team into motion. He and his sisters waved to their parents standing on the front porch. John and Breanna waved back, and the children said they would see their parents at church for the preaching service. Then they headed for Denver.

"Whew, it sure is hot today!" Meggie exclaimed as they turned onto the road.

"It sure is." Paul nodded.

Ginny fanned her face with a handkerchief. "It's only nine fifteen, and that sun up there in the sky is already making it blistering hot!"

Meggie palmed away perspiration from her brow. "I'm sure glad I'm not going to hell."

"I'm glad I'm not either!" Ginny still fanned her face with the handkerchief.

"Me too," Paul said. "Praise the Lord for our salvation!"

Both sisters responded with an "amen!"

Ginny laughed. "Oh well, it won't be long and winter will be here; then we'll be complaining about the cold."

Gripping the reins, Paul chuckled. "You're so right, sis. We humans are never satisfied. Well, hardly ever, anyway. Just think — when we get to heaven, everything will be perfect, even the weather!"

"There won't be any complaining in heaven at all!" Meggie said, laughing.

After Sunday school was over at First Baptist Church, Paul and his sisters met in the auditorium at the pew a few rows from the front and just west of the center aisle, where the Brockman family always sat.

When it was time to start the preaching service, the church's music director opened the service by leading the choir in singing the stirring hymn "In the Cross of Christ I Glory." He then stepped to the pulpit, asked the congregation to stand, and led them in singing "Brightly Beams Our Father's Mercy."

After the song, the crowd and the choir

51

sat down, and Pastor Bayless left his chair. As he walked toward the pulpit, he flicked a glance toward the rear of the auditorium. The six ushers who would be taking the offering stood just inside the double doors. They smiled and nodded at him. This was their signal to let him know that John and Breanna Brockman were in the vestibule and ready to enter the auditorium.

Pastor Bayless reminded the church members of nurse Breanna Brockman having been knocked down a flight of stairs while on duty at Denver's Mile High Hospital on July 13. This fall was caused by an injured rancher who was out of his mind in extreme pain from broken ribs. The rancher was running down the hall on the second floor toward the staircase, and Breanna was climbing the stairs from the first floor. Just as she reached the top, the rancher collided with her and knocked her back down the stairs, which resulted in Breanna receiving spinal and leg injuries.

The pastor went on. "Shortly after the rancher knocked Breanna down the stairs, he tumbled down the stairs himself, adding to his own injuries. That rancher's name is Damon Fortney. His ranch is about twenty miles southeast of Denver."

Pastor Bayless then pointed at Barbara

Fortney, seated next to a big, silver-haired man on the second row of pews to the right of the center aisle. He reminded the church members of how Breanna Brockman had led Mrs. Fortney to the Lord on July 18 when she had visited Breanna in her hospital room. Mrs. Fortney had come to First Baptist Church the following Sunday, walked the aisle during the invitation after the sermon, gave testimony of her salvation, and was baptized.

The church members were smiling and nodding their heads. The pastor went on to tell of how he had the joy of leading rancher Damon Fortney to the Lord in his hospital room on July 14. "Amens" sounded all over the auditorium.

Beaming, Pastor Bayless said, "Damon Fortney has been in the hospital all this time, recovering from surgery, and was just released yesterday." He pointed at the man seated next to Barbara. "Brother Damon Fortney, would you please stand up so everyone can see you?"

Tall, muscular, heavyset Damon rose to his feet, smiling and looking around at the crowd.

"Just so you know, folks, Brother Fortney is here this morning to be baptized."

The crowd cheered and applauded; then

the pastor looked at Damon. "You may be seated now, dear brother."

When Damon sat down, Barbara smiled at him, then rose up far enough to plant a kiss on his cheek.

The pastor ran his gaze over the crowd. "Now, folks, I have a big surprise for you. I want to thank the members of this church for the way you have been praying for Breanna Brockman since Dr. Matthew Carroll told us she may never be able to walk again."

The pastor looked toward the double doors at the rear of the auditorium. "All right, ushers, please open those doors." With excitement showing on his face, he added, "Everyone rise to your feet, please, and look back at the doors!"

The church members complied with the pastor's request, and suddenly there were happy gasps and words of praise to the Lord filling the auditorium as John and Breanna Brockman stepped through the doors and stopped, John holding his wife's right hand.

Breanna's face was still somewhat pale, and she appeared to be a bit weary, but a smile beamed from her face as she nodded and acknowledged the crowd. She then gazed up into the face of her dear husband, where tears glistened in his eyes, and nodded.

The members of First Baptist Church looked on in amazement as Breanna began to walk slowly down the aisle beside her husband. There was loud applause and even louder praises being given to the Lord as the beloved couple made their way to the pew where Paul, Ginny, and Meggie stood. All three of them tenderly embraced their mother.

When the excitement finally settled down, everyone eased onto their pews.

An hour later, when the sermon was finished and the invitation was given, four adults and three young people came forward to receive the Lord Jesus Christ as their Saviour, and Damon Fortney presented himself for baptism.

Pastor Bayless baptized the four adults and the three young people first. Then the big rancher stepped down into the baptistry. Speaking so all could hear, the pastor told Damon how glad he was that Damon had finally healed up so he could come for baptism.

The big rancher smiled. "Thank you, Pastor, for leading me to the Lord. I'm so very glad I can finally be baptized." Damon was submerged in the water and raised up, with Pastor Bayless saying, "Buried in the likeness of His death, and raised in the likeness of His resurrection." The crowd applauded heartily.

Soon the pastor closed the service in prayer. As soon as the service was dismissed, a crowd gathered around the pew where Breanna was seated, and moving slowly in line, they shared with her their joy that she was able to walk again.

John, Paul, Ginny, and Meggie stood close by in the aisle to give people the room they needed to approach Breanna. John noticed that Barbara Fortney was standing near the platform, waiting for her husband to come from a side door after having changed into dry clothing. Just then Damon appeared and headed toward his wife, smiling.

John motioned to his three children. "Let's go meet Mr. Fortney." As they drew up to the Fortneys, John introduced himself and his children.

Damon greeted them warmly, then said with a slight quiver in his voice, "I — I want to tell you again how sorry I am that I knocked Mrs. Brockman down those hospital stairs."

John laid his right hand on the rancher's shoulder. "Brother Fortney, we understand clearly that you were totally out of your mind with pain and you didn't know what you were doing. It was not your fault."

The children all agreed.

Tears misted Damon's eyes. "I thank each of you for understanding. Mrs. Brockman has also told me she knows it wasn't my fault." He took a few seconds to wipe the tears from his eyes, then turned to John. "Chief Brockman, I am amazed at how much your son resembles you . . . with the same steel gray eyes, tall stature, and dark hair."

John smiled. "I agree. Paul is also like me in personality."

John and his children chatted with the Fortneys for a while, and when the crowd around Breanna diminished, only two people remained — Whip and Annabeth Langford.

Putting an arm around Breanna still sitting on the pew, Annabeth faced John. "Chief, Whip and I would like to invite your family to our house for dinner."

John glanced at Breanna, who instantly nodded. He smiled at Annabeth. "Looks like Breanna feels up to doing that, so your invitation is accepted!"

Paul, Ginny, and Meggie spoke their joy at the invitation. Then it was agreed between John and Paul that the son would drive the wagon and the girls would ride in the buggy with their parents.

Soon the Brockman and Langford buggies were moving side by side. They were close enough that the families could talk back and forth above the sounds of the buggy wheels spinning and the horses' hooves thumping the soft dirt as they moved along the road that led toward their homes.

The Langford place was just a few miles past the Brockman ranch, on the same road. Three small ranches were between the Brockman ranch and the Langford place. When they were passing the third small ranch, John saw the young couple who lived there out in front of their house.

John looked at the Langfords in their buggy. "Those folks are new here, aren't they?"

"Yes," Whip replied. "They moved here quite recently. Their names are Ralph and Lois Bergman. We just met them a few days ago and invited them to visit First Baptist Church. They said they would do so sometime."

Breanna noticed an elderly woman coming out the front door of the house toward the young couple. "Do you know who that older woman is?"

"Yes." Annabeth eyed the silver-haired woman. "She is Lois's grandmother. She came to visit them yesterday from her home in Wisconsin. After getting off work at the hospital, I happened to be out near the road late in the afternoon. They paused in their buggy, introduced her to me, and told me where she was from. They had just picked her up at the railroad station in Denver. She is in her mideighties, and her name is Ethel Simpson."

Breanna nodded. "I'm sure the Bergmans are happy to have her here."

"They sure seemed to be," Annabeth said.

A few minutes later, the buggies swung onto the Langford place, with Paul behind them in the wagon. As they drew up close to the house, Meggie was the first to spot Whip's pet wolf, Timber, in his fenced area next to the small barn.

Waving at the wolf, Meggie jumped out of the buggy. "Hi, Timber!"

The big gray wolf wagged its tail as it looked at Meggie and let out a friendly whine. Ginny stepped out of the buggy, stood beside her sister, and called to the wolf, waving her arms. Paul left the driver's seat on the wagon, hurried up beside his sisters, then called out to Timber and waved. The wolf responded to both Ginny and Paul in the same way it had to Meggie. The three of them ran to Timber's "yard," and reaching through the fence, they petted him.

The Brockman family had a wonderful time eating Sunday dinner at the Langford home. However, by the time dinner was over, Breanna appeared quite weary.

Annabeth left her chair at the table and put her arm around Breanna's shoulder. "Breanna, dear, this has been a big and exciting day for you, but I can tell how worn out you are. Whip and I would love to have all of you stay longer, but I think you need to go home and get some much-needed rest."

Glancing at her friend, Breanna smiled wanly. "You are just too perceptive for your own good, Mrs. Langford. I was trying not to let on."

"I'm a nurse too, Mrs. Brockman," Annabeth teased back, "and we are trained to take notice of such things in our patients, right?"

Breanna chuckled, patting her friend's cheek. "You are so right, my dear friend."

Annabeth mentioned that she knew Breanna had an appointment tomorrow morning with Dr. Carroll for a regular examination regarding her spinal injury and its effect on her legs.

Breanna nodded. "The appointment is at

ten o'clock. John is going to take me to the hospital for the examination, then bring me home. After that, he'll go to his office for the rest of the day."

"Mama," Meggie spoke up. "Ginny and I will stay and help Aunt Annabeth do the dishes and clean up. You and Papa go on home so you can get some rest. I'm sure Paul will stay so he can bring us home in the wagon after we've helped Aunt Annabeth."

"I sure will," Paul said.

"Okay, Meggie girl. We'll do it your way, then."

Meggie grinned at her mother as she left her chair, then kissed her cheek. "See? I told you."

John thanked the Langfords for the meal. Then, being aware of his wife's lagging footsteps as they headed toward the front door, he picked her up and carried her out to the buggy.

The Langfords and the Brockman children looked on as John placed Breanna on the seat, then rounded the buggy and got in beside her. Both of them waved at the group, and John put the buggy in motion.

As they turned onto the road and headed toward their ranch, Breanna laid her head on John's shoulder and snuggled close.

"Thank you for carrying me out, sweetheart. You are always so thoughtful. I don't know if I could have walked all the way outside to the buggy."

"My pleasure, sweet love. It's always my pleasure when I can hold you in my arms."

Monday was starting out to be another unusually hot day for late August in Colorado. John took Breanna to the hospital for Dr. Carroll to do the scheduled examination. John was eager to learn if his wife's spine and legs were healing all right. He would take her home after the examination, then ride his horse back into town to his office.

Late that morning, Paul was in the woods out behind the ranch house, practicing the fast draw with the new gun. Ginny and Meggie mounted their favorite horse, which Paul had bridled and saddled for them before heading into the woods.

Thirteen-year-old Ginny had ten-year-old Meggie sitting in front of her in the saddle. She reached around Meggie, took the reins in hand, put the horse to a trot, and headed up the tree-lined lane toward the road. Because of the heat, the girls had a canteen of water attached to the saddle horn.

When they reached the road, they headed

west toward the mountains. A few minutes later, when they were passing the third ranch from their own, they saw Ethel Simpson lying on the ground in the lane that led from the house to the road.

"Meggie." Ginny pulled the horse to a halt. "Mrs. Bergman's grandmother looks like she's been hurt. Let's go see if we can help her."

"Of course!" Meggie said.

When Ginny drew up to the spot where the elderly woman lay, she dismounted and helped Meggie from the saddle. They knelt beside the silver-haired woman, and Ginny said, "She's unconscious!" Ethel Simpson's wrinkled face was covered with perspiration.

"Oh!" Meggie gasped. "What do you suppose is wrong?"

Ginny studied Mrs. Simpson's sweaty face. "Honey, go get the canteen off the saddle horn! I've got to try to get some water in her mouth."

Meggie jumped to her feet, dashed to the horse, grasped the canteen, and dashed back.

"I know what's wrong." Ginny took the canteen from her sister's hand. "From studying Mama's medical books so I can be a nurse one day, I learned about sunstroke.

That's exactly what she has!"

"That's bad, isn't it?" Meggie's voice quivered.

"It could be, honey. While I'm using the water to try to revive her, will you run to the house and tell the Bergmans that Mrs. Simpson is having a sunstroke and has passed out?"

"I sure will!" Meggie ran toward the house.

Ginny pulled a cotton handkerchief from her pocket. *If I can just get Ethel Simpson to awaken,* she reasoned, *it would be easier to get some water into her mouth.*

After pouring water from the canteen onto the handkerchief, Ginny gently bathed the unconscious woman's face with the cool cloth while lightly patting her pallid cheeks with her other hand. "Mrs. Simpson, please, please open your eyes."

FIVE

At the Bergman house, Meggie knocked on the front door, but there was no response. She knocked again, only harder this time, calling out that she needed to talk to the Bergmans. Still no response.

She darted off the front porch and ran around to the back of the house. She banged on the back door. "Mr. and Mrs. Bergman! Please answer the door! Mrs. Simpson is very sick, and we need your help!"

When there still was no answer, she dashed off the back porch and ran as fast as she could toward the spot where her sister was caring for Mrs. Simpson.

Ginny still knelt over the elderly woman, but now Mrs. Simpson's eyes were open! Ginny had her sipping water from the canteen. The elderly woman's eyes focused on Meggie as Ginny looked up at her sister. "Honey, though Mrs. Simpson can hardly talk, she has been able to explain to me that

Ralph and Lois are in Denver grocery shopping. Her doctor in Wisconsin had urged her to take a twenty-minute walk every day for her health's sake. She was taking the walk in the lane between the house and the road when she grew dizzy and passed out."

Meggie nodded. "The hot sun was just too much for her, wasn't it?"

"Yes. Now, honey, I need you to stay here with Mrs. Simpson and keep helping her to sip water from the canteen while I ride home and bring Paul with the wagon so we can take Mrs. Simpson to Mile High Hospital."

Meggie smiled down at Mrs. Simpson, then smiled at her sister. "Of course, Ginny. I'll do that."

A short time later, Meggie was still giving Ethel Simpson small sips of water from the canteen when Paul and Ginny drove up in the wagon. Paul jumped down from the seat, hurried around to the other side of the wagon, and helped Ginny down.

"Mrs. Simpson," Ginny said, "Paul made a pallet in the wagon bed for you to lie on as we drive you to the hospital."

"Thank you for your help, dear children," Ethel said weakly.

With great care, Paul picked up Ethel and carried her to the rear of the wagon. Ginny had dropped the tailgate. Paul laid Mrs. Simpson on the pallet, which had a pillow for her head.

"Paul, I'll ride back here with her and keep her shaded from the sun," Ginny said as she picked up the parasol the family kept beneath the wagon seat.

"Me too." Meggie held up the canteen. "I'll give her more water. There's still enough in here for her."

When Paul's sisters had climbed into the wagon bed and Paul was closing the tailgate, Ginny said, "Don't go too fast, Paul. That would make it too bumpy for her."

Paul smiled as he headed toward the front of the wagon. "I'll be careful about the bumps."

Looking into Ethel's eyes, Ginny said, "You are going to be fine, Mrs. Simpson. I'm just so glad my sister and I noticed you lying there on the ground. From now on, you must walk only in the cool of the day, either in the cool of early morning or after the sun goes down in the evening."

Ethel's cheeks wrinkled as she smiled. "That I will do."

Late that afternoon when John returned home from his office, Breanna told him that Paul, Ginny, and Meggie had something they wanted to tell him. When John learned of what Ginny and Meggie had done for Ethel Simpson and that, with Paul driving the wagon, they had taken her to Mile High Hospital and the doctors said the girls saved the elderly woman's life, John commended Ginny and Meggie for being lifesavers like their brother.

Breanna smiled at her children, then looked at John. "Paul went to the Bergmans' after he and the girls returned from the hospital to see if the Bergmans were home yet. They had just arrived and were anxiously looking for Lois's grandmother."

"I told them the story of what happened to Mrs. Simpson, and Meggie and Ginny's actions," Paul said. "The Bergmans wanted to go to the hospital immediately, and I offered to go with them. They appreciated that."

Proud of her son, Breanna continued the story. "While they were at the hospital, Paul asked Mrs. Simpson if she would have gone to heaven had she died from sunstroke. When she couldn't answer him, Paul asked if she would let him show her from the Bible how to be saved, and she happily consented."

"Then I hurried to Uncle Matthew's office," Paul said. "I borrowed his Bible, then hurried back to Mrs. Simpson's room. There, I had the joy of not only leading Mrs. Simpson to the Lord, but Mr. and Mrs. Bergman also."

John squeezed Paul's shoulder. "I'm so proud of you. This is great news, son. Your mama and I have some news of our own. Your uncle Matthew examined your mother today at the hospital. Her recovery is coming along fine, but it will take time for her to heal completely."

Breanna smiled at John. "Due to the damage to my spine, I may never be able to work as hard in my nursing profession as I've done in the past. Only time will tell."

Paul, Ginny, and Meggie expressed their concern.

"Don't be discouraged, children," Breanna said. "Papa and I expected news like this. But God is good, and my future is in His hands."

On the following Sunday morning, September 2, the Bergmans and Ethel Simpson sat with the Brockmans in their favorite pew at First Baptist Church. When the sermon ended, they went forward and presented themselves for baptism.

When Ethel and the Bergmans gave their salvation testimonies to the pastor so everyone in the auditorium could hear, the Lord got the glory. After baptizing all three, Pastor Bayless stood in the baptistry and commended Paul Brockman for being the soul-winner he was and added that he had learned it from both his parents.

After the service, Ethel told the Brockmans that Ralph and Lois had invited her to stay and live with them, and she had decided not to return to Wisconsin. The Brockmans expressed their joy over this to both Ethel and the Bergmans.

As time went on at the Brockman ranch, Paul continued to practice his quick draw. One afternoon after arriving home from his office, John stood close by in the woods. After Paul had drawn at a target he had made, he was reloading the new Colt .45 revolver. He saw his father step out from behind a tall cottonwood tree and head toward him. Paul smiled. "Hello, Papa."

"Howdy, son. I just watched you draw and fire six times. You're really faster on the draw than ever with that new gun Sheriff Carter gave you."

Paul slipped the last cartridge into the cylinder, then snapped it shut. "Well, I'm glad to hear you say that. I've been thinking the same thing."

John chuckled. "I watched you shoot those last six bullets at the target, and you're definitely more accurate with that new revolver. You put every one of those slugs right in the center of the target. I'm proud of you."

"Papa, your noticing that pleases me very much."

"Son, it pleases *me* very much too."

On Monday, September 10, school started, and Paul Brockman was happy to be in the tenth grade, which meant he was in senior high school and now could participate in sports.

That evening at the supper table, Paul was talking excitedly about playing rugby and boxing. Looking around the table at his family, Paul said with a smile, "Boy, oh boy! I can hardly wait till the boxing season begins!"

Breanna and the girls talked about how Papa had spent time with Paul since he was twelve years old, teaching him how to box.

"Yeah!" said Paul. "And because Papa is so good with his fists when he has to fight big, bad outlaws and he's the one who taught me how to box, I'm gonna be a good boxer!"

"I have no doubt of that, son." Breanna smiled.

"Me neither," put in Ginny. "You'll be the champ of your weight division, big brother!"

"Right!" Meggie nodded. "I can't wait to see you in the ring!"

"Tell you what, son," John said. "Between now and when the boxing season begins in January, I'll teach you even more about boxing."

A smile spread over Paul's handsome face. "Thanks, Papa, for being so good to me. I want to be a champion boxer."

John reached across the corner of the table and patted Paul's muscular right arm. "You will be, son. You *will* be."

On Wednesday, October 3, Paul turned sixteen. A big birthday party was held that evening at the Brockman home after the midweek service at Denver's First Baptist Church.

It had been an absolutely breathtaking fall day in Colorado. Early that morning, snow had dusted the high mountain ranges near Denver, and the rest of the day, the sun had shone down from a cobalt blue sky. Amber, rust, red, and yellow leaves now adorned the trees in a colorful display.

Paul had been told by his parents that he

could invite some of his friends to the party. Pastor Bayless and his wife, Mary, were at the party as well as Whip and Annabeth Langford, and Uncle Matthew and Aunt Dottie. Of course, also present at the birthday party were Paul's sisters, who were showing their love and adoration for him.

After Paul opened all of his birthday presents, he stood before the group in the parlor and expressed his deep appreciation to everyone for their kindness.

"Tell us what it feels like to be sixteen years old, big brother!" Meggie said.

Paul grinned at her. "Well, I could say a lot of things about being sixteen, but the most exciting thing is that in just five years, I'll be old enough to wear a badge. Then I will become one of my papa's deputy United States marshals!"

There were cheers from the group, and the loudest cheers came from Paul's school friends, who were also his fellow athletes, and from his sisters.

Paul turned toward his father. "Papa, thank you so much for teaching me the fast draw with a Colt .45 revolver these past few years. I know that as a deputy U.S. marshal, I'll be facing outlaws who will try to outdraw me as you and Uncle Whip have when we've practiced."

John and Whip looked at each other; then Whip said, "Chief, the way your son is getting better and better at the fast draw and the accuracy with his new Colt. 45, soon he will be faster than me *or* you!"

Paul smiled at his father, then set his gaze on Whip. "I only wish those words were true, Uncle Whip. But there is only one John Brockman, and no man can outdraw or outshoot him."

At her son's words, a chill penetrated Breanna's heart. *In just five years, there will be two lawmen in this family. Lord, will I be up to this?*

Immediately, in the depths of her heart, she sensed a still, small voice in reply. *Breanna, by My grace, all things are possible.*

A sweet peace settled over her heart. Her mind then went to two of her favorite verses of Scripture . . . 2 Thessalonians 2:16–17: *"Now our Lord Jesus Christ himself, and God, even our Father, which hath loved us, and hath given us everlasting consolation and good hope through grace, comfort your hearts, and stablish you in every good word and work."*

Breanna casually covered her mouth with a hand. A small, secret smile curved her lips. *Yes, Lord.* She looked heavenward. *You will help me to handle it by Your grace.*

Whip Langford was chuckling at Paul's comment. "Paul, I agree with you on what you said about your father, but I have no doubt you will soon be faster on the draw than your uncle Whip!"

There was laughter in the group as Paul looked at Whip and grinned. "Well, you're safe, Uncle Whip. We'll never draw against each other."

Laughing, Breanna spoke up. "Hey, everybody, it's time for some birthday cake!"

A few minutes later, when everyone sat in a circle in the parlor with a small plate of chocolate cake in each one's hands, Breanna's sister, Dottie, said, "Well, Breanna, have Pastor Robert and Mary been told that in a few weeks you're scheduled to go back to your job at the hospital?"

The Baylesses looked at each other, eyes wide. Then the pastor looked at Dottie. "We sure haven't been told."

Breanna smiled and nodded. "John and I were planning to tell you and Mary quite soon, Pastor." She then looked at Matt, her brother-in-law. "My boss and I have agreed that I will be back on the job, mainly as a surgical nurse, the first full week of November."

Matt swung his gaze to Annabeth. "Annabeth and I, as well as all the other Mile High

Hospital staff, are very much looking forward to having Breanna back."

Annabeth clapped three times. "We sure are!"

Breanna's eyes filled with tears. "I am so grateful to our dear Lord for making it possible. I'm walking much better each day. It is truly a miracle, and I will never forget how God has blessed me. I pray I can share this miracle with other Christians in the future who need their Lord's help and give them hope."

Much joy was in the room as the guests showed their delight at Breanna's news. It was even on the faces of Paul's high school pals.

Annabeth laid her cake plate on a small table beside her chair, rose to her feet, and went to where Breanna was sitting. Bending down, she wrapped her arms around Breanna and hugged her tightly. "Oh, praise the Lord! I have very much missed working with you."

Breanna's arms wound around Annabeth's neck, and she choked up a bit. "And I have very much missed working with *you* too."

Annabeth kissed Breanna's cheek. "It's going to be wonderful having you back at the hospital."

"It's going to be so wonderful to *be* back

at the hospital!"

When the party was over and the Brockmans stood on the front porch watching their guests riding away in the moonlight, John ran his gaze over his wife and children. "Before we go upstairs for the night, I want us to pray together."

"Amen, Papa," Paul said. "You want to sit down and pray right here on the porch?"

"Sure." John took Breanna by the hand and led her to the most comfortable chair. When she was seated, John eased onto the chair next to her and took hold of her hand. Paul, Ginny, and Meggie quickly chose their chairs close by.

Still holding Breanna's hand, John said, "Let's bow our heads. I will lead in prayer." As heads were bowed and eyes closed, John said, "Thank You, dear Lord, for this celebration today and this evening of our son's sixteenth birthday. Breanna and I thank You for this wonderful son You have given us and for his desire to serve You and mankind. When Paul becomes one of my deputy marshals, his desire is to help make this area a safe and peaceful place for all who live here."

"Yes!" Paul said in a loud whisper.

"Also, dear Lord, Paul, Ginny, Meggie, and I want to thank You that in answer to prayer, our precious one will indeed go back to work at the hospital on November fifth."

"Yes, thank You, Lord!" Paul, Ginny, and Meggie all spoke the same words together.

John said, "Bless this precious family of mine, Lord. You know I trust You to keep them in Your loving care. In Jesus' blessed name I pray, amen."

A chorus of "amens" followed from John's family as they gathered around him, and Breanna tenderly squeezed his hand.

On Monday, November 5, just before dawn, John Brockman was awakened when he felt movement next to him. It was Breanna rising from the bed. He opened his eyes and stared at her shadowed form. "Sweetheart, are you all right?"

"Sure am!" Breanna slipped into her robe. "I'm just so excited about getting to go back to my job at the hospital." She took a deep breath. "You stay right here and rest, my darling husband. I've got to get ready now so I can eat breakfast with you and the children and we can be ready when Annabeth arrives to take the children to school on our way to the hospital."

John yawned and sat up. "I'll go ahead and get up too. You can get dressed and fixed up here in the bedroom while I shave and comb my hair in the bathroom."

Breanna smiled. "Whatever you say, honey."

As John left the bedroom, Breanna moved to the large mirror on the wall, took a hairbrush from the dresser, and brushed her long blond hair. She bound it in a bun at the nape of her neck, then went to the closet and took one of her white nurse's dresses off a hanger. She inspected it closely and said to the empty room, "Looks like it's in order."

She removed the robe, slipped on the dress, and fastened the row of buttons on the bodice. Then opening a dresser drawer, she took out one of her nursing caps and inspected it as she had the dress. She placed the cap on her head and turned about in front of the mirror. "Well, it looks like nurse Breanna Brockman is ready to go to work."

Leaving the bedroom, Breanna moved down the hall. Unaware that John had already awakened the children and gotten the girls cooking breakfast, she descended the stairs, carefully holding onto the banister. When she entered the kitchen, John and Paul were sitting at the table while Ginny was placing a platter of hot pancakes on the table and Meggie was pouring hot coffee into cups for her parents.

"Oh, Mama!" Ginny exclaimed. "It's so good to see you in your nurse's clothes again!" A small frown lined her brow. "Are you sure you feel up to going back to work?"

Breanna smiled at her. "At this moment, I feel perfectly capable of going back to work, sweetie. A few hours from now, I may not be so sure, but I need to get started sometime, so today is the day."

"Just don't forget to rest a little bit between jobs," John said.

"Oh, I'll do that, honey." She smiled at him.

When breakfast was over, John kissed Breanna and the girls and hugged Paul. Then he quickly went out, hopped on Blackie, and rode away, heading toward Denver to begin a busy day at work.

Annabeth Langford arrived some twenty minutes later. Paul helped his mother into the buggy, and when he and his sisters were aboard, Annabeth put the horse into motion.

Paul and his sisters were delivered to their schools; then Annabeth happily drove to the hospital, thrilled to be taking Breanna with her for the first day of work since her injury.

As they pulled up into the parking lot of Mile High Hospital, Annabeth looked at Breanna. "Hear me now. At the first sign of fatigue, you speak up loud and clear, and someone will relieve you."

"Yes ma'am," Breanna replied with a smile gracing her face.

When Breanna entered the office of her boss and brother-in-law, Dr. Matthew Carroll, he welcomed her back. "I have you scheduled to work with a surgeon you know well, Dr. Duane Gifford. His first surgery of the day is on the left kidney of a fifty-five-year-old woman."

"I've assisted doctors in that kind of surgery many a time," Breanna said.

As Dr. Carroll walked Breanna to the surgical unit on the second floor, hospital staff warmly welcomed her back. They entered the surgical unit, and Dr. Gifford approached them. "Welcome back, Nurse Brockman! I'm happy to have you assist me during the surgery."

Dr. Carroll left to return to his office, and Dr. Gifford and Breanna prepared for surgery. "Our surgery scheduled after this one is an appendectomy on a seventeen-year-old boy," Dr. Gifford said.

Breanna looked confident. "I'm ready, Doctor."

The fifty-five-year-old woman was brought in on a cart, placed on the surgical table, and the surgery began.

During the operation, Breanna felt the excitement of being back, doing the medical work she so dearly loved, but she soon found that being on her feet at the side of the surgical table caused some pain in her spinal column. Not wanting to say anything to Dr. Gifford, she stayed right there and aided him competently, using all of her skills to do her best for the patient.

By the time the operation finished, Breanna's pain caused her some weakness, and she was a bit dizzy. Again, she didn't let on to Dr. Gifford. She got a brief rest before the second surgery began, but during the appendectomy, pain hit her spinal column once more.

After a while, as the pain was getting worse, a sheen of perspiration formed on Breanna's brow. The dizziness became stronger. She struggled to do her job in assisting the surgeon but did not let on. However, as Dr. Gifford finished the operation and began stitching up the teenage boy's incision and knowing her part of helping during the surgery was over, Breanna took a step back from the table, blinking.

Dr. Gifford looked up, noting the sheen of perspiration on her forehead and paleness of her face. "Breanna, are you all right?"

She looked him in the eye. "I — I'm all right, Doctor. J-just a bit weary and a little dizzy."

Pointing to a nearby chair with his chin, Dr. Gifford said, "Go sit down over there, and I'll be with you shortly."

Breanna staggered dizzily to the chair and sat down.

Six

Nurse Brockman stayed on the chair, silently asking the Lord to give her strength and to stop her head from spinning. Within a few minutes, Dr. Gifford finished his work on the teenage boy, then smiled at Breanna as he headed for a nearby wooden counter where there was a large glass pitcher. "I'm going to get you a cup of water, Breanna."

She returned the smile. "I appreciate that, Doctor."

Seconds later, the doctor handed her a cup full of water. "I'm going out in the hall right now to see if I can get one of the orderlies to take that boy to his hospital room. I'll be back shortly."

Breanna swallowed a drink of water and nodded. "All right, Doctor."

Dr. Gifford hurried out the door into the hall, letting the door close behind him.

While drinking more water, Breanna looked at the boy on the operating table.

He was still under the anesthetic.

Less than five minutes had passed when Dr. Gifford came back through the door, glanced at the teenager who was still unconscious, and went to Breanna. "The water helping?"

"Yes, it is."

Frowning, the doctor looked down at her. "It's obvious that standing this long on your feet at the surgical table has been too much for you. You'd best not try it again for at least a few months."

Breanna nodded. "I — I agree, Doctor."

He smiled at her. "Good. The orderly will be coming to take our patient to his room in a few minutes. Right now I'll take you to Dr. Carroll and let him know how you were affected by assisting me with these two surgeries."

Dr. Gifford held on to Breanna as he walked her down the hall to the stairs, then carefully helped her descend them. They moved down the hall of the first floor to the office of the hospital's chief administrator, and when they entered, Dr. Carroll was at his desk. He looked up, smiled at both of them, and rose to his feet. "Well, how did it go, Breanna?"

The surgeon explained the effect that assisting him with the two surgeries had on

Breanna.

When Dr. Carroll heard it, his face resembled an ashen mask. "Breanna, I'm so sorry I let you come back to work before you were ready."

Dr. Gifford said, "I believe that Nurse Brockman shouldn't try to work as a surgical nurse for quite some time — at least a few months." He looked at Breanna. "I know you love being a nurse, but you've got to take care of yourself."

Breanna's lower lip was quivering, and her eyes showed her disappointment. "Matt," she said softly, "it's not your fault that I went back to work so soon. It's mine. I told you I thought I could do it. I'm sorry. You were only trying to make me happy. Looks like I proved to myself and to both of you that I'm not up to it yet."

Dr. Carroll moved around the desk. "Breanna, let me examine your back. I want to see if any damage has been done." He carefully pressed his fingers across her back, moving them slowly so he could examine her effectively. After a few minutes, he said, "I'm satisfied that no damage has been done."

His sister-in-law smiled at him. "Oh, that is so good! I don't think I could stand to give up nursing, at least not until I get too old to do it."

Dr. Gifford looked at the chief administrator. "Could you possibly give her an easier job until she's ready to go back to nursing so she could still be in the medical field?"

Dr. Carroll's face assumed a gracious look, and he gestured toward two wooden chairs that faced his desk. "Please, both of you, sit down."

As Dr. Carroll returned to his desk chair, Breanna and Dr. Gifford eased onto the chairs.

"Breanna, what I'm about to tell you struck my mind while I was examining your back. I was about to tell you of it."

Her eyes widened a bit. "Something good?"

"For *you,* yes. You know my secretary, Maybelle Nelson."

Breanna nodded. "Of course."

"Well, just this morning Maybelle told me that she and her husband are moving to St. Louis, Missouri, immediately because of his job. His company's head office is in St. Louis, and her husband has been given a promotion that will demand he begin working in the St. Louis office as soon as possible."

Breanna's eyes were fixed on the chief

administrator as she waited for his next words.

"Since the secretarial job in my office is now open, if you'll take the job, Breanna, I know you can handle doing paperwork for the hospital. And this way, you'll be able to do most of your work sitting down."

With a touch of sadness in her heart because of her body's reaction to working that day as a surgical nurse, Breanna smiled. "Yes, Matt, I will take the secretarial job. As Dr. Gifford said, at least I'll still be in the medical field."

Dr. Carroll could read the touch of sadness in Breanna's blue eyes. "Tell you what. Even though you will be my secretary, I'll still use you at times as a nurse, even to help with brief, simple surgeries and emergencies."

This brought a genuine smile to Breanna's lips. "Oh yes! Thank you, Matt! Thank you!"

Dr. Carroll rubbed his chin with a forefinger. "Because at times you will be doing nurse's work, I want you to wear your white nurse's uniform to work every day and keep a white cap here in the office too."

Breanna's face lit up. "Yes sir!"

Late that afternoon, Annabeth went by Dr. Carroll's office to tell Breanna she was ready to take her home. They walked outside to the parking lot. "How was your first day back?" Annabeth asked.

When Annabeth heard what had happened to Breanna while she was working with Dr. Gifford on the two surgeries, she told her friend how sorry she was. Then Breanna told her of the chief administrator's job offer to her as his secretary, yet with the promise to also allow her to do some occasional nursing work. Annabeth expressed the joy she felt for Breanna.

The same joy was shared later at suppertime when John and the children heard the story. As the Brockman family was eating, Breanna smiled bravely at her husband and children. "I can't say that I'm not disappointed with the secretary job, because surgical work is my first love. But in His wisdom, the Lord does not want me in heavy surgical duty right now, and He has given me peace that one day He will allow me to return to it. But for now, He has another place in the medical field for me. As it says in Hebrews 13:5, I must be content with such things as I have."

A proud smile flitted across John's handsome face as he looked at his wife. "I know you can handle it, sweetheart. You'll do great as Matt's secretary and part-time nurse."

"You sure will, Mama!" said Meggie.

Paul and Ginny quickly spoke their happy agreement.

On Wednesday morning, November 14, the Bank of the Rockies was robbed by four men. As they left the bank carrying bags of cash, they were suddenly faced with chief U.S. marshal John Brockman and five of his deputies, including deputy U.S. marshal Whip Langford.

One of Denver's male citizens had seen the robbers enter the bank and whip out their guns, and he had run to the federal building a block away to alert Chief Brockman.

Stunned to be facing six stern-faced lawmen whose guns were drawn, the four robbers dropped their weapons and the moneybags as commanded by Chief Brockman and put their hands above their heads.

Chief Brockman knew that the robbers were on the Wanted list in other parts of the West, and three days later they were sentenced in court by Judge Ralph Dexter to forty years at the Colorado State Penitentiary in Cañon City.

The next week, on Tuesday afternoon, a Wells Fargo stagecoach was held up by two men on its way to Denver from Cheyenne, Wyoming. The holdup took place just ten miles from Denver. The stage driver and his assistant found a telegraph office in a small town nearby and telegraphed the chief U.S. marshal's office to report the robbery, giving a description of the robbers and their horses and saying that they were headed south at an angle toward the mountains.

By this time, it was snowing in the area, but Chief Brockman and Deputy Langford went after the robbers, taking Whip's pet wolf, Timber, with them. They caught up to the robbers in the foothills of the Rocky Mountains, northwest of Denver, and as had happened many times in the past, Timber was a great help in capturing the outlaws the chief and his deputy were chasing.

The outlaws were taken to Denver and stood trial, with the Wells Fargo stage driver and his assistant in attendance. Presiding over the trial was Judge Dexter, who sentenced the robbers to fifty years at Cañon City's prison, keeping in mind their six-year record of bank and stagecoach robberies in the West.

Denver's newspaper, the *Rocky Mountain News,* wrote up the story, and Whip Langford's big gray timber wolf was named as a hero, as had been done many times before.

As the days and weeks continued to pass, Chief Brockman and his deputies, including Whip Langford, were kept busy dealing with outlaws, as were Sheriff Carter and his deputies. As the population of the West grew, there was more crime to deal with.

January 1889 soon came, and Paul Brockman enjoyed being on the boxing team at school, even more than he had enjoyed being on the rugby team. Already six feet one inch in height and weighing a muscular one-hundred-and-eighty-five pounds, he was one of the team's heavyweights.

Because Paul had been expertly taught by his father how to box, he quickly showed Denver High School's boxing coach, Shad Yarbrough, his strength, speed, and accuracy with his fists and his ability to punch very hard. Within two weeks of boxing practice with the other heavyweights on the school team, Paul had won every three-round boxing match with the other sophomores, as well as the juniors and seniors.

On Friday night, January 18, the first set of boxing matches took place at Denver High School against Fletcher High School, which was from an eastern suburb of Denver.

Paul's parents and sisters, Uncle Matthew and Aunt Dottie, as well as friends Whip and Annabeth Langford, were in attendance in the gymnasium. All eight of them were sitting in a row close to the ring. Paul had gone ahead of them about half an hour earlier in order to meet with Coach Yarbrough, along with the other boxers from his school.

When the Denver High School boxers came into the gymnasium through a side door and headed in the direction of the ring, Meggie pointed at her brother. "Papa! Mama! Ginny! There's Paul!"

All eight of them rose to their feet, waving at Paul and calling out his name. He smiled and waved back. Then he and the other Denver High School boxers along with their coach sat on benches on one side of the ring.

All of the matches in the high school league were three rounds each. The first two fights scheduled that night were light-weights, the next two were welterweights, the next two were middleweights, and the last two were heavyweights.

Everyone in the crowd enjoyed the fights, and boys from both schools were winning the matches. Paul's fight was the very last one, as he took on a heavyweight who was a senior and outweighed him by over thirty pounds. He was introduced to the audience by the ring announcer as Fletcher High School's heavyweight champion from last year, Woodruff Olson.

Paul's family and friends cheered him when the bell rang for the first round. Both boys immediately slugged each other with powerful blows, and as the round progressed, it looked like Woody Olson would put Paul down because of his greater weight. However, in the second round, Paul caught on to his opponent's style.

The crowd was entranced with Paul's change in round two as he suddenly began to dodge both fists in a surprising way, causing Olson to get off balance. Paul quickly jabbed a left to Olson's right cheek, making him stagger, then launched a terrific right cross to his left jaw. The blow exploded on Olson's jaw like a cannonball, and the big heavyweight crashed to the canvas. The bell rang in time to keep the referee from counting Olson out.

By the time the bell rang for the third round, Olson's mind was clear, and he left his stool, fists clenched in his leather boxing gloves, and began doing his best to take his opponent out.

He tried to use his weight to crowd Paul into a corner of the ring, where he could hit him repeatedly and put him down and out. However, John Brockman's son was not about to let him have his way. Each time Olson attempted to crowd him into a corner, Paul sidestepped him, drove a potent punch into his midsection, and moved to the center of the ring. The Denver High School fans cheered Paul on, especially his family and friends.

Seconds later, Olson tried again to back Paul into a corner, and Paul surprised him by sending a powerful left hook into his midsection, making him double over, then crossed a mighty right blow to his left jaw. Olson hit the canvas flat on his face.

As the referee began his count, Paul went to a neutral corner and waited.

Woody Olson staggered to his feet in time, looking at Paul Brockman with fire-filled eyes, and rushed toward him, pumping both fists. Paul dodged the fists and smashed him with a right cross that knocked him back on his heels. Before Olson could get set, Paul was on him with two powerful blows to the jaw, and Olson hit the canvas flat on his back.

The referee began his count again. This time, he made the count to ten, then stepped to Paul, took hold of his right wrist, and raised his hand in the air, pronouncing him the winner by a knockout.

Paul's family and friends, along with all the Denver High School fans, were elated. Paul's sisters hugged and congratulated him when he left the ring. Close behind them were his parents, his aunt and uncle, and the Langfords.

Week after week, Paul's family and friends enjoyed watching him box and be declared the winner each time — especially his muscular six-feet-five-inch, two-hundred-and-fifteen-pound father.

SEVEN

One morning in late February, Breanna was working on some official papers at her desk in the small office next to Dr. Carroll's office when the doctor stepped through the open door. "Good news, my dear sister-in-law."

Breanna looked up at him, an inquisitive look in her eyes. "I'm all ears."

Matthew smiled. "I know you like to work with our proficient surgeon Dr. Edgar Bates."

"I sure do!"

"Well, I need you to assist him this morning as he is working on a male patient in his seventies with cardiovascular disease."

"Do you know what caused the disease in this patient?" Breanna asked.

"Yes. A thorough examination showed us that rheumatic fever the patient had some seven years ago caused it."

She rose from her desk and put the official papers in one of the desk drawers. "I'll head for the surgical ward right now. This problem is extremely dangerous. We wouldn't want it to lead to congestive heart failure."

Dr. Carroll nodded. "This was the main reason I wanted to have you work with Dr. Bates on this case. I'm aware that you know much about cardiovascular disease and congestive heart failure. I hope it won't be too much for you."

"I'm sure the Lord will see me through it."

Less than ten minutes later, Breanna arrived at the room in the surgical ward where Dr. Bates was preparing to perform surgery on the man's heart. When the doctor saw her enter the room, he smiled. "Wonderful! Dr. Carroll said he was going to have you assist me with this surgery if you felt up to it."

"Well, Doctor, here I am!" she said with a giggle.

After over four hours of assisting Dr. Bates, Breanna entered her brother-in-law's office. He was at his desk and looked up as she moved toward him.

"Well, Matt, the cardiovascular surgery was a total success. Dr. Bates says the patient came through it exceptionally well, and he is going to live!"

"Wonderful! And I know part of the success was due to your being there to assist him."

Breanna blushed. "Thank you, Matt."

He shook his head. "No. Thank *you!*" Then he glanced at his pocket watch. "I see that this was a long surgery. How is your back feeling? Any pain?"

Breanna shook her head. "I'm a little stiff, and I feel in need of a rest at the moment. But I was very pleased to not be distracted during the surgery by back pain. God is clearly answering our prayers!"

"Amen to that," said Matt heartily, and gave his sister-in-law a hug.

Paul Brockman was doing well in his high school boxing, and as March came, he was undefeated with heavyweights in other schools within fifty miles of Denver. His parents and his sisters had attended all of Paul's boxing matches at Denver High School. Ginny and Meggie let it be known to Paul and their parents that they had bragged on their brother's boxing skills and victories all over the school. Paul was touched by his sisters' loyalty and adoration, though he did gently ask them not to brag about him but rather to thank the Lord for the joy they have in appreciating each other's talents.

One day in mid-March, Chief Brockman was walking along the boardwalk of one of Denver's downtown streets and came upon two husky men in their late twenties who were verbally giving a man in his sixties a hard time. John knew the silver-haired man. Truman Richardson was a carpenter who worked for one of Denver's construction companies.

As John was drawing near, one of the husky men punched Truman on the jaw, knocking him down. The man then began kicking him, and his friend encouraged him to kick even harder.

Anger flared inside John, and he dashed to the spot. People on the street gathered around as John skidded to a halt. "Hey! Stop that right now!"

The kicker's partner had not noticed the badge on John's chest. Speaking in a British accent, he growled at John, "Mind your own business, mate!" He swung a punch at John, who dodged the fist and countered with a cracking left-handed punch, followed swiftly with a powerful right-handed blow, knocking him down and out.

With fury written on his face, the man

who had been kicking Truman stomped up to John and noticed the badge on his chest. Snarling wickedly, he bellowed in his British accent, "Since you're a lawman, you had no business pounding on my friend with your fists!"

The chief U.S. marshal snapped, "I was given no choice!"

The kicker looked at John with blazing eyes. "My name is George Clive, mister lawman! Do you know who I am?"

"No, I don't."

The Briton moved a half step closer to John. "At the moment I am one of the contenders in England for the heavyweight boxing championship!"

Some of the people in the crowd gasped and began whispering to each other.

"If you weren't so old," George said, "I'd take you on bare-fisted right now!"

John squared his jaw. "I'm forty-three. That may be old for a boxer, but I'm telling you right now, Clive, to shut your mouth. Pick up your unconscious pal. You're both under arrest for beating up Truman Richardson. You can carry your pal to the county jail, which is only a few blocks away. You're both going to be locked up."

The eyes of the people in the crowd bulged as George Clive made a swift move toward the chief U.S. marshal. "I'm gonna put you down, bloke!" He swung a big fist at the marshal.

John adeptly dodged the fist and countered with a jarring punch, catching the big professional boxer with his mouth open. His teeth clicked like a steel trap. He cried out in pain, blood spurting from his mouth. Staggering toward the chief, he swung both fists.

John ducked them and swiftly caught him with a sledgehammer blow that whipped his head back and dropped him to the ground, out cold.

Both Brits lay unconscious on the ground.

John looked around at a couple of burly men standing together close by in the crowd. "Hector . . . Eldon . . . would you fellas mind helping me carry these two guys to the jail?"

"Be glad to," said Eldon.

"Sure will." Hector nodded.

Eldon noted that the first man John had put down was beginning to regain consciousness and pointed to him. "Guess he can walk to the jail, Chief."

John nodded.

Suddenly, people in the crowd began calling out, commending the chief U.S. marshal for taking out the two bullies — especially the one who was a professional boxer.

One man said, "Chief Brockman, the way you handled these guys, especially the professional boxer, I figure your son, Paul, must have taught you how to fight!"

John chuckled. "Paul indeed has taught me well."

The crowd laughed.

By this time, Truman Richardson was on his feet, rubbing his ribs that had been kicked by George Clive. He stepped up to John. "Chief Brockman, thank you for coming to my aid."

As John was telling him he was glad to do it, two other husky men stepped up, and one of them said, "Chief, the two of us will help Eldon and Hector get these two British bullies to the jail."

John nodded. "I appreciate that." He then looked back at Truman and frowned. "Are you hurt bad?"

Truman shook his head. "No sir. A bit bruised, but I'm okay."

John saw the reporter from the *Rocky Mountain News* as he was stepping up to him from the crowd and said, "Hello, Bart."

"Howdy, Chief," Bart Gilmore said. "I happened to be coming along the street when this trouble started. I saw the whole thing. There will be an article about it on the front page in tomorrow's edition of the *News* telling exactly what happened here."

Two county deputy sheriffs arrived to help get the two British men to the jail. George Clive, now conscious, struggled to stand. The crowd watched as the two Britons were taken toward the county jail at gunpoint by the two deputy sheriffs and the four husky volunteers.

March in Colorado could be one of its snowiest months, and that was proving true in 1889. That next evening the Brockman family gathered around the supper table as the wind howled outside and fiercely blowing snow fell from the sky.

After John led the family in prayer, they passed the food around the table. A powerful gust of wind slapped the side of the house and set the kitchen windows to rattling.

Paul glanced at the snow beating against the kitchen window. "Boy, this is one bad storm." Before taking his first bite of food, he continued. "Mama . . . Ginny . . . Meggie . . . I guess none of you have looked at today's edition of the *Rocky Mountain News*."

"Guess we haven't, son," Breanna replied. "None of us have had time. Why? Something special in the paper?"

Paul nodded, glanced at his father, then looked back at his mother. He could feel his sisters' eyes on him as he said, "Before my teacher started math class this morning, he said to me in front of the whole class, 'Paul, you must be very proud of your father for what he did yesterday.' I didn't know what he meant, but he was holding today's issue of the *Rocky Mountain News* in his hand."

Everyone at the table noticed that John was blushing.

Paul gave his mother and sisters the whole story that was in the article. Breanna and the girls were astonished.

"Honey, why haven't you told us about it?" Breanna asked.

John's face was still flushed with embarrassment as he replied, "Well, I was sure that you and the children would hear about the incident, but if I had been the one to tell you, it would appear that I was bragging, since one of them is a contender for the heavyweight championship of England. So I refrained from telling any of you."

A smile spread over Breanna's lovely face. "Darling, you are something else. Most men would have been bragging all over town of the notable deed you accomplished. But you take it all in stride and give God the glory for the great strength and outstanding ability you have with your fists."

"That's right, Papa!" said Paul. "Mama's got it right!" Both girls verbally agreed.

Smiling shyly, John ran his gaze over the faces of his dear ones. "It is by God's grace that I'm even still alive after the life I have lived and the characters I've met and had to deal with. He alone is my Protector, my wisdom, and my strength."

"You always know exactly what to say, my love." Breanna squeezed his hand. "Thank you for letting the Lord lead in your life, as you then lead our lives as husband and father."

After a few seconds of silence, Paul said, "Papa, I commend you for knocking out both of those British bullies. I sure hope that by the time I become one of your deputy U.S. marshals, I'll be as tough and as good with my fists as *you* are."

"I hope so too, big brother." Ginny smiled at Paul.

"Me too!" Meggie squealed.

John chuckled. "Oh, you'll be *tougher* and *better* with your fists than I am, Paul."

The next day, Judge Dexter sentenced the two British bullies to six months in the county jail for what they had done to Truman Richardson.

■ ■ ■ ■

Two weeks later, the area high school boxing championship matches took place in the Denver High School gymnasium.

In his final fight of the season, Paul Brockman's opponent was Bret Watson, a senior from Golden High School in Golden, Colorado. The rugged-looking Bret outweighed Paul by almost thirty pounds.

Paul's parents and sisters were there, as well as Pastor and Mary Bayless and Whip and Annabeth Langford.

The heavyweight fight was the last to take place that evening. When the bell rang for the first round in Paul's fight with Bret, both fighters went at it, swinging fast and hard.

It seemed pretty much an even match during rounds one and two, but in the third round, Paul got in an extra powerful left cross to Bret's jaw, staggering him. As Paul came after him, Bret tried to clinch to give himself time to clear his head, but Paul speedily evaded the clinch and hooked a mighty right hook to the jaw and jarred his bigger opponent to his heels.

Bursting with rage, Bret rushed back, swinging both fists as hard as he could. Paul dodged the fists and popped him hard on the nose, sending him into another stagger. Bret attempted to retaliate but could get no power into his blows.

Paul squared his jaw, drawing every ounce of strength he could into his shoulders and, transferring the strength into his arms, pounded his opponent with four exploding blows, knocking him against the ropes.

Bret hit the ropes hard, bounced back, stumbling over his own feet, and fell face-down on the canvas floor of the ring. He was out cold.

The referee counted him out. Cheers from all over the gymnasium rang out as the referee raised Paul's right hand into the air, stating emphatically that he was the winner by a knockout. The cheers grew even louder when he also declared Paul Brockman the heavyweight champion of the Central Colorado High School League.

While conversations took place all over the gymnasium, the boxers went to the locker rooms to change their clothes. When Paul reentered the gymnasium in his regular clothes, he saw that Bret Watson was still in the ring. He was now on his feet, but a doctor from Mile High Hospital was examining him to make sure he was all right.

Paul's parents and sisters stood nearby

talking to the Baylesses and the Langfords. Paul headed toward them, but he was quickly stopped by some of his schoolmates who were full of admiration for him.

The boys were congratulating Paul on winning the heavyweight championship when Paul noticed a husky man stomping toward him, anger blazing in his eyes and on his reddened face. Bret Watson looked like him. He had to Bret's father, who was the owner of Watson Feed and Grain Company in Golden.

Gus Watson drew up, glaring at Paul, the hostility in his eyes like the flare of a lightning bolt. Baring his teeth, the big man roared, "You didn't have to hit my son so hard, you thug!"

Paul felt his nerves twitching all over his body but kept a level tone in his voice. "Mr. Watson, in order to win a fight, it takes hard punches."

Gus, who was much heavier than Paul, angrily swung at him.

Paul dodged the punch and stepped back. "Sir, I don't want to fight you. Boxing is a sport and should be treated as such. I only did what I had to do in order to win the match against your son. Anyone who saw the fight would agree it was a fair and honest match."

"Bah! You didn't have to hit Bret so hard!"

Not far away, John Brockman was talking to a small group of people, but he quickly picked up on the fury of the man speaking to his son and the consternation on Paul's face. John excused himself and hurried toward his son, while a small group of high school boys looked on.

The big angry man charged at Paul, fists clenched. "I'm gonna beat you to a pulp for what you did to my boy!"

Paul dodged the first fist that came toward his face, then evaded the second one adeptly. He smashed Gus's right jaw with a powerful left hook, which stopped the big man in his tracks. Paul closed in on him, whipping a powerful right hook into Watson's midsection, causing him to double over, then followed with a dynamite left to the jaw. Watson went down hard on the gymnasium floor, out cold.

John moved in and laid a firm hand on Paul's shoulder. "Don't feel bad, son. You had to put him down. He gave you no choice."

Paul looked at his father and nodded. "He sure didn't, Papa."

By this time, a crowd had gathered, including Breanna and her daughters, the Baylesses, and the Langfords. They had watched the whole brawl take place. Some of the school officials had heard and seen it too, and as Gus was regaining consciousness, they scolded him for what he had tried to do to Paul Brockman.

Gus did not even reply to them. He staggered to his feet, gave Paul a hateful glare, and then in a wobbly fashion, walked in the direction of the locker room to find his son.

The Brockmans, Baylesses, and Langfords left the gymnasium and moved outside. As they drew up to their horse-drawn vehicles, Pastor Bayless patted Paul on the back, "I'm proud of you, Paul. It's really something for a sophomore to win the championship in his weight division."

Paul smiled at him. "Thank you, Pastor."

The Baylesses and the Langfords drove away in their buggies. When the Brockmans were about to climb into their wagon, Paul moved between his parents. "Mama, I really didn't want to hit Mr. Watson, but he wouldn't listen to me when I tried to explain."

Breanna patted his cheek. "Paul, my sweet boy, I understand. You had to defend yourself."

"You did fine, son," said John. "In fact, you could have beaten Bret's father more severely if you wanted to, but you didn't.

I'm proud of you." John laid a hand on Paul's shoulder. "Life on this earth isn't always easy. Sometimes quick and wise decisions must be made in the blink of an eye. Experience will be your teacher as you grow older. Most of all, let the Lord be your source of wisdom, son."

"I'll try to remember to practice your advice, Papa."

"Since you're going to be a lawman, you still have much to learn. As long as God allows it, I'll be here to help you as much as I can."

Breanna smiled proudly at her son. "Okay, family, let's head for home. I'm sure a nice hot bath will feel good to Paul's aching body."

Paul flashed his mother a smile. "Indeed it will, Mama." He gingerly moved his arms and shoulders. "Indeed it will."

The Brockmans boarded their wagon and headed for home with John at the reins. Breanna sat beside him on the driver's seat, and Paul sat on a bench in the bed of the wagon beside his sisters.

As the wagon rolled out of town toward the west, Ginny and Meggie told their brother that they thought he was already as tough and as good with his fists as Papa was.

John laughed heartily when he heard it.

Breanna giggled and said, "Girls, all those outlaws who are going to face your brother when he becomes one of Papa's deputy marshals had better stay clear of deputy U.S. marshal Paul Brockman!"

All the Brockmans had a good laugh together.

EIGHT

Quite often, John Brockman was invited to preach in churches in many parts of the West, even as he'd done during the years he was known as the Stranger.

On Sunday morning, April 14, 1889, Pastor Bayless had John scheduled to preach at Denver's First Baptist Church. When a ladies' trio finished a heart-touching gospel song just before the sermon, Pastor Bayless went to the pulpit and introduced John for the sake of the visitors in the audience.

John preached a powerful sermon on salvation, giving Scripture after Scripture on the wonder and beauty of heaven, where everyone goes when they die if, in repentence of their sins, they've received the crucified, buried, and risen Lord Jesus Christ into their hearts as their Saviour. He also gave them Scriptures on the horrors of the everlasting, burning hell, where everyone else goes when they die.

He pointed out that there are only two ways to die — in Christ or in their sins. To die in Christ is to go to heaven, and to die in their sins is to go to hell, which in its final state is called the lake of fire in Scripture.

During the sermon, John noticed two church members, a husband and wife named Wally and Linda Higgins, having a problem with a man sitting with them. During announcement time, Wally had introduced the man as his uncle Wayne Shelby, who lived in the Rocky Mountains in Central City. Wally explained that his uncle Wayne had been working in the gold mine at Central City for some five years. He had come to Denver that weekend to visit them at their request.

Though there were only whispers between the upset Mr. Shelby and the Higginses while John was preaching, he could tell that Wally's uncle did not like what he was hearing from the pulpit.

When John finished his sermon, several adults and young people walked the aisle at the invitation to receive the Lord Jesus Christ as their Saviour. Saved people also came to the altar, just to thank the Lord afresh and anew for their wonderful salvation.

Later, while the new converts were being baptized by Pastor Bayless, John Brockman noticed from the platform that Wayne Shelby moved to the aisle from his pew and stomped up the aisle toward the double doors that led into the vestibule and outside. Wally and Linda hurried after him.

Moments later, when Pastor Bayless had dismissed the service, John, Breanna, and their children moved outside. As they neared their wagon, they saw an angry Wayne Shelby standing with Wally and Linda, who seemed perplexed.

When Shelby saw the chief U.S. marshal, he headed toward him. John and his family halted as the gold miner drew up, looking at John with fierce eyes. Before John could say a word, Shelby hissed through gritted teeth, "I want you to know, Brockman, that I absolutely disagree with you, as well as with my nephew and his wife, who talked me into coming to church this morning!"

John kept his voice low as his family and the Higginses looked on. "What is it you disagree with, sir?"

"Well, just let me put it real plain. I'm an atheist. There is no God. There is no heaven, and there is no hell."

As John started to speak, Shelby interrupted him. "I'll have you know, Brockman, that I have studied all phases of those three subjects — God, heaven, and hell — and before I moved to Central City from Chicago, I used to deliver lectures against Christianity. I know for sure there is nothing to it!"

Controlling his temper, John said, "Please tell me if a man who will lecture against *nothing* is anything more than a fool." While Wayne was attempting to come up with a possible reply, John said, "In the Scripture, in Psalm 14:1, it says, 'The fool hath said in his heart, There is no God.' "

Shelby's features went dark red. Before he could utter a word, John said, "Let me remind you that I just preached from God's Word, warning lost sinners that if they die without repenting of their sins and receiving the Lord Jesus Christ as their Saviour, they will go to an everlasting, burning hell. Only those sinners who have repented of their sins and unbelief and received the Christ of Calvary as their Saviour will go to heaven."

Shelby frowned and curled his upper lip. "So you're telling me that as an atheist and an unbelieving sinner, I will go to hell when I die, right?"

"That's right." John lifted up his Bible. "But when you hit the flames of hell, you will no longer be an atheist. You will know God exists then! There are no atheists in hell. While screaming in the flames of hell now, they all know that there indeed *is* a God and that He means every word He says in His Bible. Like sinners here on earth who believe God does exist but try to add religious deeds to gain salvation instead of receiving Jesus into their hearts as their Saviour, you will burn in hell forever."

By this time, a number of people entering the parking lot to go to their buggies and wagons began to gather close by and observe the scene.

John went on. "A few years ago, there was a man here in Denver who was an atheist. His name was Chester Percival. When he became very, very ill, and the doctors told him he was dying, he wrote on a piece of paper the things he wanted said at his funeral. He died shortly thereafter, and the man who conducted the funeral read Mr. Percival's comments to those in attendance. They were an attack on the Bible and Christianity, saying they were nonsense and that Christians used the Bible to spread ignorance and to impede the progress of the human race. He closed his statements with the simple words, 'That's all.' "

Shelby frowned but did not comment.

"But that wasn't all," John went on. "The book of Hebrews in the Bible, chapter 9 and verse 27, says, 'It is appointed unto men once to die, but after this the judgment.' "

He looked Shelby straight in the eyes. "Are you going to tell me you will never die?"

"W-well, I w-will d-die, yes."

"Now, listen closely," John said. "The Bible verse I just quoted says you *will* die. It also says you *will* face the judgment. The second statement is as true as the first statement. After you die, Mr. Shelby, the Bible says you *will* face the God you say doesn't exist, and then you will be cast into the lake of fire, which is hell in its final and everlasting state. God says you will burn there forever."

Shelby gave the chief U.S. marshal a blank stare, then pivoted and stomped away, muttering angrily to himself.

As the people watched Mr. Shelby stomp away, Wally and Linda Higgins stepped up to John and thanked him for telling their uncle Wayne exactly what he needed to hear.

John said, "I will be praying for Wayne, that the Lord will use the Scripture he heard in the sermon, and just now, to convince him that He exists, to convict him of his lost condition, and to bring him to salvation."

"We will be praying the same way, Chief Brockman," said Wally.

That night, just before bedtime in their ranch house, John and Breanna gathered their children together in the parlor. John said, "I want us to pray together that the Lord will make Wayne Shelby so fearful of burning in hell that he will get saved."

"Papa . . . ," Meggie said with a perplexed frown on her little face.

"Yes, sweetie?"

"I don't understand at all how some people, like Mr. Shelby, don't believe that God exists. Is there something wrong in their brains?"

"Well, Meggie," John said, "the problem is in their cold, hard hearts. However, a cold, hard heart does affect the brain, which affects people's thinking. Some people don't want to admit that there is a holy God, a Supreme Being, because they don't want Him interfering with their lives. Nor do they want to have to answer to Him for the way they live. But they *will* have to answer to Him, like it or not. All a person has to do is look around at God's magnificent creation. It took the master Craftsman to design and create the universe, including this earth. Everything is wonderfully made by the hand of almighty God. And His masterpiece is the human body. Only a fool could deny that there is a God!"

With a thoughtful look in her eyes, Meggie said quietly, "Then let's pray, pray, pray that Mr. Shelby will see the light. It would be so awful to go through life saying there is no God, then to die and wake up in the hell he said didn't exist! How can anyone be that dumb?"

A smile crept across Breanna's face as she hugged Meggie. "They aren't dumb, sweetheart. Satan has blinded them to the truth of God's existence."

Meggie nodded. "Mm-hmm. I see what you're saying, Mama. Let's pray for Mr. Shelby, 'cause I know that God is much stronger than Satan, and He can open Mr. Shelby's eyes to the truth."

"Indeed He can, little lady," John said, "and we will all claim God's faithful promises and pray together earnestly that this is exactly what the Lord will cause to happen."

During the days and weeks that passed, as Wayne Shelby worked in the gold mine at Central City, many of the Scriptures he had heard in John Brockman's sermon and those Scriptures John had quoted when talking to him in the church parking lot kept coming into his thoughts.

He fought against them fiercely, trying with all his might to shake them out of his mind. The horrible thought of burning in hell forever tormented him, but he just shook his head and put his thoughts on other things. Then at night when he was in bed trying to sleep, those same Scriptures invaded his thoughts again.

On Tuesday, May 14, Chief Brockman rode into the mountains to meet with the town marshal in Central City, Mike Gunther. Gunther needed to talk to him about becoming a deputy U.S. marshal in Colorado Springs. Gunther's letter had explained his need to live there because of family ties, and John had fully understood the importance of Mike's need to move there.

As John was riding toward Central City through the towering Rockies, he thought of Wayne Shelby. "Lord, it was exactly a month ago today that I talked to Shelby about his atheism and his need of salvation. Our family and the Higginses have been praying hard that You would do whatever it takes to bring Shelby to Yourself and save him. Since I'm going to be in Central City, where he lives and works, I am going to find

Shelby and try to talk to him again about Your existence and about salvation. Please help me."

It was late in the afternoon when John left the office of town marshal Mike Gunther, after assuring him that he would make it possible for him to become a deputy U.S. marshal at the Colorado Springs federal marshal's office very soon.

Swinging into his saddle, John rode the short distance out of Central City to the town's gold mine. As he drew up, several miners came out of the mine shaft, and John heard them talking about how glad they were that their work was done for the day.

John whispered, "Please, Lord, help me to be able to have my talk with Wayne Shelby. He's so heavy on my heart."

Finally John saw Shelby coming out of the mine with other miners. Shelby saw the chief U.S. marshal instantly. His features stiffened, and he looked apprehensive as John rode toward him, but Shelby stopped, allowing the other miners to pass him, and waited for John to ride up and draw rein.

John swung down from the saddle and stepped up to Wayne. "Mr. Shelby, I've to come to Central City on business. Since I was already here, I thought I would come to the mine and see you."

Shelby's heart was beating rapidly. "See me about *what?*"

"I'm still very concerned about you. I wanted to talk to you once more about your need to make the Lord Jesus Christ your Saviour."

Shelby was shaken by John's presence. Suddenly hearing about salvation again had his stomach quivering. He did his best to hide his nervousness, saying, "Chief Brockman, I mean no offense toward you as a law officer, but — but —"

"But what?"

Wayne's next words were flung at John like bullets. "I'm just not interested in your gospel stuff!"

With that, Shelby turned and walked away, hurrying from the mine.

John's heart was heavy as he swung atop Blackie and rode toward home. As he put Blackie to a gallop, he said, "Lord, I just can't give up on that man. My family and I will keep praying for his salvation."

On Wednesday night at the midweek church service, John told Wally and Linda Higgins about seeing Wally's uncle at the mine the previous day and how Wayne had flat-out said he was not interested in John's "gospel stuff."

"I'm sorry Uncle Wayne spoke to you in that manner, Chief, but Linda and I will keep praying for his salvation."

"We sure will." Linda nodded.

"Well, the Brockman family is going to do the same. We don't want him to go to hell."

"Thank you," Wayne said. "Let's just claim God's prayer promises and trust Him to do whatever it takes to bring Uncle Wayne to Himself."

NINE

On Friday evening, June 7, John sat down to the supper table following a busy day at the office. After prayer, they all started eating, and he looked at Breanna. "Honey, have you read today's edition of the *Rocky Mountain News*?"

Breanna shook her head. "I haven't had time. Why?"

"Well, when it was delivered to my office this morning, I saw on the front page that a new commander had been assigned to Fort Logan by the United States Army. He arrived just yesterday to take charge of the fort. When I saw his name, I realized that it was familiar to me."

"Oh?"

"Mm-hmm. Ryan Alden. Nearly twenty-two years ago, when he was a lieutenant stationed at an army camp near Emporia, Kansas, I had the joy of leading him to the Lord. He is now a major general. The article said that he is a widower. His wife died just over three years ago."

"Oh," Breanna said, "I'm sorry to hear that."

"Papa," asked Meggie, "where is Fort Logan?"

"It's just west of Denver, honey, a few miles north of here at the edge of the foothills."

Meggie nodded. "I've heard people talk about it, but I just didn't know where it was. I sure am glad you got to lead the man who is its new commander to the Lord. Are you gonna go see him?"

John smiled at her. "Yes. I've already planned to go to the fort tomorrow and see him."

"Papa," said Paul, "I would like to meet Major General Alden. Since tomorrow is Saturday and there's no school, could I ride along with you to the fort?"

"Of course, son. I will be glad to have you go with me."

At midmorning the next day, John saddled up Blackie, and Paul saddled up Blackie's father, Chance. Chance was solid black just like his son and was getting old. He could not gallop anymore, but John had said they would only walk the horses to the fort, so

Paul could ride him.

John and Paul rode side by side beneath a sunny blue sky. "Papa, how did you get to lead Lieutenant Alden to the Lord?"

"Well, son, one day in August of 1867, when I was known as the Stranger, I delivered four outlaws to the Lyon County sheriff in Emporia, Kansas. After leaving Emporia toward the west, I came upon three soldiers from a nearby army post who were shooting it out with a band of six Potawatomi Indians. I rushed in to join the soldiers, and when I quickly shot two of the Indians off their horses, the other four decided to ride away. Two more were shot off their horses by the soldiers as they were riding away, and the other two were soon out of sight. Then I found that all three soldiers had received bullet wounds from the Indians before I arrived, but they'd fought back as best as they could."

Paul looked at his father. "Brave guys, I'd say."

"That they were, son. The four Potawatomis who had been shot off their horses were all dead. And sadly, when I was trying to help the wounded soldiers, two of them died."

Paul frowned. "Oh. That's too bad."

"Yes. The one who was still alive was

Lieutenant Ryan Alden. I rushed the lieutenant to a clinic in Emporia, and the doctor was able to remove the slug from his shoulder."

"Good! Now tell me the rest of the story."

"Well, I stayed with the lieutenant for two days at the clinic. My main reason was to try to talk to him about salvation when he got to feeling a bit better. Finally, on the evening of the second day, Lieutenant Alden was able to sit up and talk to me, so that's when I shared the gospel with him. I had him read several salvation verses to me from my Bible. I had the joy of leading him to the Lord then and there. The next day, I took him to the army post. The post's medic told me he would take good care of the lieutenant."

"Uh-huh. That makes sense."

John smiled. "Sure does. The day after that, before leaving to head for Nebraska where I had some business to handle, I encouraged the lieutenant to go to the First Baptist Church in Emporia, where I had preached about a year before, and to present himself for baptism because he had received the Lord Jesus Christ as his Saviour. Lieutenant Alden assured me that he would do so."

"Praise the Lord!"

"Amen!" John nodded. "I have not seen Lieutenant — now Major General — Ryan Alden since."

"What a story, Papa. I can hardly wait to meet Major General Alden."

When John and Paul arrived at Fort Logan, they drew rein at the entrance gate. A young corporal standing guard in the twelve-foot-high tower noted John's badge and leaned over the railing. "Hello, sir. Lawmen are always welcome here. What can I do for you?"

Noting the two stripes on the young soldier's shirt sleeve, John said, "Corporal, I am Chief United States Marshal John Brockman from Denver."

The corporal smiled. "Oh! I've heard much about you, sir. It's good to meet you. My name is Gary Skelding. What can I do for you?"

"Corporal Skelding, I am an old friend of Major General Alden's. I learned just yesterday that he is now commander of Fort Logan. I would like to see him."

"Certainly, sir!"

"And, Corporal . . ."

"Yes sir?"

"I would like to introduce you to this young man with me. He is my son, Paul."

Corporal Skelding chuckled. "He looks so much like you, Chief Brockman, I figured he had to be your son." He then looked at Paul. "Welcome to Fort Logan, Mr. Paul Brockman!"

Paul smiled. "Thank you, Corporal."

Corporal Skelding turned and looked down at a young army private standing on the ground just inside the gate, who was listening to the conversation. "Private Smith, as you have heard, Chief Brockman and his son have come to see Major General Alden."

Private Smith quickly opened the gate. "Chief Brockman, you and your son may dismount and lead your horses into the fort right now."

John and Paul swung down from their horses, then led them inside the fort. As the private took them over to the general's office, he said, "Since Major General Alden knows you, Chief Brockman, you can go ahead and knock on his door." With that, he walked back toward the fort's front gate.

John thanked him as he and Paul tied Chance and Blackie to the hitching post near the door of the building. Then father and son walked up to the door. John knocked and, seconds later, Major General Ryan Alden opened it.

Alden had matured a great deal, but John still would have known him if they had simply met on a street somewhere. Even though nearly twenty-two years had passed since they had last seen each other, the general smiled. "Well, I'll be! It's the Stranger! The man who led me to the Lord!"

Paul looked on with a smile as he watched his father and the general embrace each other in a manly but affectionate way. Indeed, there was a glad reunion between the two men.

John quickly gave Alden a short version of why he was no longer called the Stranger and explained that he was John Brockman, the chief U.S. marshal of the Western District of the country, with his office in Denver. He then introduced the general to his son, Paul.

General Alden smiled and embraced Paul in the same manner as he had embraced John, and running his eyes between them, he said, "Mr. Stranger, I — I mean, Chief Brockman, this boy really looks like you."

John smiled. "I'm proud to agree that he does. I'm also proud to tell you that Paul plans to become one of my deputy U.S. marshals when he turns twenty-one. He's sixteen now, so he's got a few years to go, but I really believe he will stick with his plan."

General Alden smiled at Paul. "Well, my boy, I sure hope your plan works out."

"With the Lord's help, it will, sir."

Major General Ryan Alden's eyes widened. "Why are we standing out here? Come on into my office so we can sit and talk."

John and Paul followed the general into his office and were offered comfortable padded chairs while the general sat on another, facing them.

John told the general how he had read in the *Rocky Mountain News* that Ryan had been made commander of Fort Logan. He then added in a soft tone that the *News* also pointed out that Ryan was a widower.

Alden's eyes misted. "Yes. Lila went home to be with the Lord in March of 1886, Chief."

"Well, she's waiting up there for you, General. You will have all eternity together."

"Sure will." The general nodded. "Lila's being saved goes back to *you*, Mr. Stranger."

John's eyebrows arched. "Me?"

"Yes. Let me tell you the story." Ryan Alden began by telling John that he had been baptized at Emporia's First Baptist Church some two weeks after John had led him to the Lord. Then he told him how he met a lovely young lady in Emporia about a year after he had become a Christian. Her name was Lila Shields. He had the joy of leading her to the Lord, and she was baptized at his church the next Sunday.

Tears filled his eyes as he told John of marrying Lila a short time later, what a wonderful marriage they had, and how she had become quite ill and died.

The tears now spilled down Alden's cheeks. "Chief Brockman, if you had not led me to the Lord, I would not have led Lila to Jesus, and she would not have gone to heaven."

The general rose from the chair, bent over John, and hugged him once more, saying with joy, "My sweetheart is indeed in heaven, and I will certainly join her there someday!"

There was rejoicing in the Lord among Alden and the Brockmans because of this.

"General, do you have any children?" John asked.

A wistful expression filled Alden's eyes. "No sir. Lila was not able to have children. And with Lila's passing, that leaves me alone, family-wise. But the army has sort of become my family, and I'm grateful for that."

"I'm sure you are." John smiled. "We all need someone to call family. My family and I are members of Denver's First Baptist Church, and I invite you to come to the services tomorrow. Our pastor's name is Robert Bayless, and he is really a great preacher. You will like him and his preaching, I guarantee it. And, of course, I want you to meet my wife, Breanna, and our daughters, Ginny and Meggie."

"Chief, I really want to meet them. I will be there tomorrow."

"Great!" Paul popped his hands together.

"Amen!" John told the general how to find the church in Denver and gave him the times of the services.

Having done this, John said, "You were talking about family, General. Because you are saved, you know you are in the family of God, which takes in every born-again child of God in heaven and on earth, and there's a good crowd of us at First Baptist Church. So you do have family outside of the military. We have such a friendly church. You'll feel very welcome there."

The general grinned. "Well, as I said, I'll be there tomorrow, and no doubt, I will present myself for membership."

"You might as well plan to stay for the whole day, General. Knowing my wife, she will want you to come to our house for Sunday dinner, and Breanna and our two daughters are tremendous cooks. Believe me, you wouldn't want to miss out on dinner at our house!"

A look of glee passed over Ryan Alden's face. "Well, after eating all those army meals for so long, that sounds like a little bit of heaven to me. Now tell me about Breanna, Ginny, and Meggie."

Cheerfully, John told the story of how, as the Stranger, he met Breanna, fell in love, and married her at Denver's First Baptist Church on Sunday afternoon, June 4, 1871. He went on to tell the general about his three fine children and how the Lord had blessed them with sweet spirits, intelligent minds, and fine characters.

Alden said, "Wow! What a story! God sure has blessed you, Chief Brockman."

"Indeed, God has blessed me beyond measure in giving me such a beautiful and wonderful wife, such a wonderful son, and such wonderful daughters!" John then noticed Paul smiling broadly. "What are you smiling about, son?"

"I was just thinking how the Lord has blessed Mama with such a wonderful husband and my sisters and me with such a wonderful papa!"

After spending over an hour with Major General Alden, John looked at his pocket watch. "Well, General, Paul and I had better head back to Denver. We've taken up quite a bit of your time."

Smiling, Fort Logan's commander said, "I've loved every minute of it. But I realize you have things to take care of at home."

General Alden rose to his feet. John and Paul did the same. When the general stepped outside with them, Paul's attention was drawn to a shiny wagon standing a few yards away. Two soldiers had drawn up in it and had just finished unhitching the horse team that had pulled it, and now were leading the harnessed horses toward the corral several yards away.

"Wow!" Paul eyed the wagon as it glistened in the bright sunlight. "I have never seen a wagon made completely of metal before. And I've never seen a wagon with a big cage built into the wagon bed either. What is it used for?"

"Well, Paul," replied the general, "the wagon is made of iron. The army has iron wagons just like this one all over the West. You know there are wild, angry Indians all over the West making war against the white people because they have been or are being forced onto reservations."

Paul nodded. "Yes sir."

"When the army has to battle the fierce Indians and capture some of them during a battle, the soldiers take them in these iron wagons to places where the warriors are imprisoned for their acts of violence."

"I understand, sir. I just never knew these iron wagons existed."

Chief Brockman interjected. "General, I know about the iron wagons, but I have never seen one up close."

"Well, come on, Chief. I'll let you get a close look at this one." General Alden led father and son to the wagon that was shining in the sun. "The wagon bed is eight feet wide and twelve feet long. As you can see, the cage fits the bed exactly. The iron straps that form the cage are four inches wide, and the straps run vertically and horizontally."

Father and son nodded.

"Each opening between the straps is only two inches square. This is to make it so no captive can reach between the straps and grab a soldier. The cage is six feet high."

Looking again at the top of the cage, then down to its floor where it sat on the bed of the wagon, John said, "That's what I guessed. Six feet."

The general showed them the hinged iron gate at the rear of the cage, which was held shut by a heavy-duty padlock. "In using these iron-caged iron wagons, soldiers have been known to cram more than a dozen Indian warriors into them."

Paul sighed. "I hope that one day soon, the Indians will decide to make peace with the white people and make no more war against them."

The general and Paul's father agreed. Then John and Paul swung into their saddles.

John took the reins in hand. "Thanks for showing us the iron wagon, General. It's quite interesting."

"Sure is, General Alden," Paul agreed.

Then John said, "We'll look forward to seeing you at church tomorrow."

With a wide smile adorning his face, Alden said, "I definitely plan to be there."

Looking down from his mount at Fort Logan's new commander, Paul said, "General Alden, I am very glad that I got to meet you."

As John and his son rode away, they looked back toward the fort a few times and talked about how much they liked Major General Ryan Alden.

"It won't hurt Chance if I put him to a mild trot before we head for home," Paul said.

"Sure. Chance can't gallop anymore, but a mild trot won't bother him. Let's go!"

TEN

At Central City's gold mine, Wayne Shelby was forty feet down into the earth, using a steel-headed pick to chip gold from a solid wall of it by the light provided from a flaming kerosene lantern. He was working alone, but he could hear miners in other areas at his level using their picks.

As Shelby swung the pick, his mind went back to his conversation with the chief U.S. marshal in the parking lot at Denver's First Baptist Church.

John Brockman's words echoed in his brain: "*Please tell me if a man who will lecture against nothing is anything more than a fool.*"

As Shelby thought of those ice-edged words, wrath welled up inside him. He stopped swinging the pick and dropped it on the dirt floor of the cave. His face was set in a harsh and furious mold as he shook his fists and growled, "You think because I don't believe your nonsense about God, heaven, and hell, that you're smarter than I am, Brockman! Ha!" He leaned down, grabbed the pick handle with both hands, and swung the sharp point of the steel head against the cave wall. When chips of gold splattered from the solid wall, Shelby hissed, "I wish I could whack your head with this pick, Brockman!"

He viciously hit the wall again, breathing hard. "You and your quote from the Bible that the fool has said in his heart that there is no God! *You* are the fool, Brockman! You're a fool for believing that Bible and quoting stupidity from it! It's the *wise* man who says there is no God!"

Gritting his teeth, Shelby kept swinging the pick against the wall of gold while trying to get John Brockman's words out of his thoughts.

But the words kept coming into his mind. He could hear Brockman reminding him that he had just preached from God's Word, warning lost sinners that if they died without repenting of their sins and receiving the Lord Jesus Christ as their Saviour, they would go to an everlasting, burning hell.

While breathing even harder, Shelby's own words that he had spoken to John Brockman then came back to him: *"So *you're telling me that as an atheist and an unbelieving sinner, I will go to hell when I die, right?"*

Brockman's pointed reply as he lifted up his Bible echoed in Wayne's mind: *"That's right, but when you hit the flames of hell, you will no longer be an atheist. You will know God exists then! There are no atheists in hell. While screaming in the flames of hell now, they all know that there indeed is a God and that He means every word He says in His Bible."*

Gasping for air in his anger, Shelby stopped swinging his pick, set the top of it on the dirt floor of the cave beside him, took a deep, quivering breath, and let the handle of the pick fall to the floor. He took a few steps to where his canteen was sitting on a rock shelf, and picked it up, unscrewed the lid, and drank several gulps of water. When he'd had his fill, he replaced the lid, then set the canteen back on the rock shelf. Returning to his spot, he bent down and grasped the pick handle with both hands again, and began chipping away at the wall of gold. While doing so, he was thinking evil thoughts about John Brockman while trying to put his mind on some other subject.

When John and Paul arrived at their ranch,

the sun was just beginning to lower over the jagged Rocky Mountains to the west. The glaring steel blue sky directly above them was beginning to lose its brightness as the golden sun descended.

Paul was scanning the sky, and out of the endless space came slow-changing colored shadows from the few white clouds riding the wind. The setting sun was turning the valley where the Brockman ranch was located into a soft, red sweep of beauty, and the golden blaze on the rugged mountain peaks seemed to lift them higher toward the sky.

Taking it all in as he and his father rode their horses past the ranch house toward the barn and corral, Paul said, "Wow, Papa! Isn't that a beautiful sunset?"

"Sure is. Our great God sure knows how to create indescribable beauty, doesn't He?"

Paul chuckled. "Oh, yes. Like He created Mama."

John smiled as they drew up to the corral gate. He swung down from his saddle. "I agree wholeheartedly with that, son. There aren't enough words in the English language to fully describe her awesome beauty!"

As Paul dismounted, he smiled at his father over Chance's back. "I sure hope when it's time for me to fall in love and get married that the Lord will give me a young lady with Mama's kind of beauty."

John opened the corral gate with one hand while holding onto the reins with the other. "I've got a feeling He will do just that, son. Of course, there is no other woman as beautiful as your mother, but I'm sure the one God has for you will be close."

Paul grinned. "Well, as beautiful as Mama is, close will be good enough."

When the two stallions had been un-saddled and unbridled and given hay and grain for their supper inside the barn, John and Paul headed for the house. At that moment, the Langford buggy pulled up to the front porch, then passed from view as Whip was drawing rein.

John chuckled. "Looks like your uncle Whip and aunt Annabeth may be having supper with us."

Paul also chuckled. "What's new? We all love having them, don't we? And they love being here."

"You're right on both counts, my boy."

As they drew up close to the back porch and saw that the kitchen windows were wide open, John sniffed the air and sighed. "Mmm-mmm. Smells like your mother and sisters are cooking pork chops."

Paul sniffed in a breath filled with delicious aromas. "I think you're right, Papa, and boy, am I hungry! Something about being outdoors in the fresh air and sunshine makes me just ravenous."

"Yeah," John said as they moved up the back porch steps. "Me too."

John opened the door, and when father and son stepped into the kitchen, Breanna was leading Whip and Annabeth into the kitchen from the hallway. Ginny and Meggie were both busy at the stove.

"Well, howdy, Whip and Annabeth!" John said.

The Langfords returned the greeting; then John hugged Breanna. "Are they having supper with us?"

"They sure are," Breanna replied, smiling. "They just stopped by to spend a few minutes with the girls and me, so I asked them to stay for supper. There will be enough food for all of us."

John chuckled. "I don't doubt that for a minute."

"So how did it go at Fort Logan?" Breanna asked.

"I'll tell you all about it during supper," John said, then gave Annabeth a brotherly hug and Whip a pat on the back. He then went to his daughters at the stove and hugged them both at the same time.

"Time to sit at the table, everybody." Ginny carried a steaming coffeepot to the table.

The Brockmans and the Langfords sat around the large kitchen table. Heads were bowed, and John led in prayer, thanking the Lord for His great love and wonderful ways and for the food before them.

As soon as he had closed his prayer in Jesus' name, John started passing the platter heaped with golden-brown fried pork chops, fluffy mashed potatoes, and smooth, creamy white gravy. Followed by the platter were bowls of green beans with chopped onions, pickled beets, homemade applesauce, and a basket of biscuits.

As they began to eat, John looked warmly at Breanna and his daughters and said, "This meal is fit for a king."

Mother and daughters beamed happily back at him.

"Save room for spice cake!" Breanna admonished John, Paul, and their guests.

"No problem there, Mama!" Paul replied, and John, with his mouth full, nodded, as did Whip and Annabeth.

While everyone was enjoying the well-prepared meal, John and Paul told Breanna, the girls, and the Langfords of their visit with Major General Ryan Alden at Fort Logan.

Everyone was thrilled with the story.

Paul then ran his gaze around the table and said, "I'd like to tell you about the iron wagon Papa and I saw at Fort Logan. I mean, it was really something to see!"

"Well, tell us about it," said Meggie. "It's an army wagon of some kind, huh?"

"Yeah, little sis. It's really fascinating how it is built and what the army uses the iron wagons for."

"Well, tell us!" Ginny chimed in.

While still eating, Breanna, the girls, and Whip and Annabeth listened closely as Paul told them all the things General Alden had told him and his father about the iron wagons used by the army in the western part of the United States.

Everyone found the description of the iron wagon very interesting. And they were deeply impressed when Paul told them that the iron wagons were used by the army to transport captured Indian warriors to places where they would be held as prisoners by the army.

As supper came to a close, Paul was still talking about the iron wagon. "You know what? That iron wagon so enthralled me that I wish I could ride in one sometime."

John chuckled. "Well, son, maybe someday you'll get to ride in one."

"I sure hope so, Papa."

On the following morning, when Major General Ryan Alden rode his horse onto the parking lot of Denver's First Baptist Church, he saw a few people standing beside a wagon and a buggy. He quickly recognized the Stranger and his son, Paul, among them.

John and Paul headed toward him, radiant. The general dismounted at the hitching post where he had stopped and quickly tied the reins to the post.

As John and Paul drew up, they both shook hands with Alden, saying how good it was to see him again. Then John pointed toward the small group of people by the wagon and the buggy. "General, come with us. Paul and I want to introduce you to the rest of our family and to some very special friends."

Alden smiled as they guided him to Breanna, Ginny, Meggie, deputy U.S. marshal Whip Langford, and his wife, Annabeth. Breanna and the girls as well as Whip and Annabeth warmly welcomed Fort Logan's new commander to First Baptist Church.

Then the group entered the auditorium.

Just inside the door stood Pastor Robert Bayless and his lovely wife, Mary.

Since John and Paul had ridden back into town to visit with the Baylesses on Saturday evening and told them all about Fort Logan's new commander, both pastor and wife welcomed the general warmly. Paul and his sisters excused themselves and headed for their Sunday school classes.

Pastor Bayless turned to the general. "My wife and I have been told a great deal about you, General Alden. Could I have a few minutes alone with you right now?"

Alden smiled. "Certainly."

John looked at the general. "Breanna and I, along with the Langfords, will be here in the auditorium for the adult Sunday school class. We'll save you a seat."

Alden nodded. "See you shortly."

The pastor led General Alden to his office, and as they sat on a comfortable sofa together, Pastor Bayless explained that Chief Brockman had told him the whole story of how he had led him to the Lord in Emporia, Kansas, in August of 1867 and that he had been baptized some two weeks later in the First Baptist Church there.

Alden beamed. "That's correct."

"Chief Brockman told me that you would present yourself for membership here."

Alden leaned forward. "That is the plan, Pastor. I assure you that my pastor at First Baptist Church in Emporia will grant a letter from that church to this one recommending me for membership."

"Well, from all that Chief Brockman told me about you, I will be glad to have you as a member of the church. You just come forward this morning when I give the invitation after the sermon to present yourself for membership. I will ask you to give testimony of your salvation before the church, being led to the Lord by John 'the Stranger' Brockman, and you can tell them that you were baptized shortly thereafter at the First Baptist Church of Emporia, Kansas."

"I will be glad to do so, Pastor Bayless. I know I will be happy as a member of this church."

After the service, General Alden was welcomed into the church by the members as they passed by him in the vestibule. He was surprised to find four soldiers from Fort Logan along with all the others. Those four told the general that they were very glad to learn he was a Christian and that they were happy he was now a member of their church too.

With a broad smile on his lips, Alden told the soldiers that it was a blessing for him to learn that they were his Christian brothers.

The Brockmans were standing close by, and Breanna said, "General Alden, you are still planning to have Sunday dinner with us, aren't you?"

"Sure am!"

"Good!" John said. "We'll all be in our wagon, so you can just follow us on your horse. All right?"

"Sure enough." The general nodded. "Let's go."

Alden followed the Brockman wagon as they drove away from the church, and soon they were in the country, heading west toward the Rocky Mountains.

Letting his horse follow close behind the wagon, the general allowed his mind to drift back in time. The image of his lovely wife floated before him. "Oh, Lila, my love," he whispered, "how I miss you. Honey, you would love this part of the country, with its majestic mountains, azure blue sky, and tall pine trees. It truly is a beautiful place, and if you were still with me, we could so enjoy life here.

"Of course, where you are now, sweetheart, has to be the most beautiful place of all . . . *heaven!* I — I just keep clinging to our life together from the time we met until the Lord took you home."

Sharply bringing himself back to the present, Alden squared his shoulders and sat up straight in the saddle. "Thank You, Lord, for letting me get back together with the man who led me to You and for bringing me to this warm and friendly church. I am indeed grateful."

The ride to the Brockman ranch was spectacular on that bright day. There was just a slight breeze, and the air was filled with the perfume of springtime flowers. The magnificent surroundings, including the ranches, the forests, the gurgling streams, and the lakes on both sides of the road occupied the general's attention as he followed the Brockman wagon, staying back far enough so he didn't have to breathe the dust stirred up by the spinning wheels.

When they arrived at the ranch, John guided the wagon to a halt in front of the house. "You can tie your horse to one of the hitching posts there at the end of the porch, General."

Alden smiled. "Will do, Chief."

As the general dismounted and tied his horse to a hitching post, he was impressed with the neat and trim, two-story house. He noticed the multicolored tulips and crocuses in bloom around the front steps of the porch. "What a grand place, Lila, my dear," he said in a slight whisper. "You would indeed love it here."

After John helped Breanna down from the driver's seat of the wagon and Paul helped his sisters down from the wagon bed where he had been sitting with them, mother and daughters entered the house while Paul and John invited their guest to sit with them on the front porch. They had only been seated for a couple of minutes when Meggie came through the front door carrying a platter bearing three glasses of cool lemonade.

"Gentlemen," Meggie said with a cute grin that emphasized her dimples, "maybe this lemonade will tide you over until dinner is ready. Won't be much longer!"

John grinned back at her. "Thank you, Meggie, sweet." Then taking a sip of the cool drink, he looked at the general. "While we're waiting for dinner, I'd like to tell you the story of our Meggie and how she came to be part of our family."

Ryan's eyes widened. "You mean Meggie wasn't *born* into the Brockman family?"

"No, but you'll enjoy hearing how she became a Brockman."

"Well," said Meggie, "I've got to get back to the kitchen. I hope you like the story, General Alden. I sure do!"

ELEVEN

On the next day, Monday, June 10, in the gold mine at Central City, Wayne Shelby was working alone deep in the mine while Ed Stubler and Charles Fawley were working together by lantern light on the other side of a rock wall nearby.

At one point, when Wayne sat on the floor of the cave beside his burning kerosene lantern to rest for a few minutes, he noted that there were no sounds of Stubler's and Fawley's picks striking gold on the other side of the rock wall.

Then he heard Charles talking to Ed about his need to turn to the Lord Jesus Christ in repentance of his sins and ask Him to save him.

Shelby heard Stubler say, "Charlie, I've thought a lot about it since you started talking to me on the subject a few weeks ago, but I'm not sure I want to do that."

"Why not?" came Charles's voice.

Wayne heard a pause followed by a frustrated sigh. "Charlie, it all seems like fanaticism to me. I don't want to get involved in it."

Knowing what a kind man Charles was, Wayne could picture the genuine concern on his face as he heard Charles say, "I've already shown you that God's Word says if you die without being saved by the Lord Jesus, you will burn in the flames of hell forever. That's not fanaticism. That's the wise thing to do. If you don't, then when you're screaming in the flames of hell for all eternity, you'll wish you had been saved."

Hearing Charles Fawley's words clearly in his private cave, Wayne felt a shiver slither down his spine at the thought of burning in hell forever. He muttered, "The idea of a burning place called hell is nonsense." He rose to his feet, grabbed his pick, and went back to work, struggling to get the idea of a burning hell, where John Brockman told him he was going, out of his thoughts.

Between swings of his pick against the gold in the mine, Wayne overheard Charles say, "Ed, will you do something for me?"

"What's that?"

"Will you come to First Baptist Church next Sunday and just listen to my pastor preach?"

There was a brief pause, then Ed's voice carried from the other side of the wall. "Tell you what, Charlie. I'll give it some thought, and I'll let you know later in the week."

Wayne shook his head at what he was hearing and went back to swinging his pick rapidly and striking the gold so loudly that he couldn't hear any more that the two men were saying to each other.

Nearly two weeks passed. On Saturday, June 22, the Brockmans had Whip and Annabeth Langford for supper at their home in order to help them observe their first wedding anniversary, which was actually the next day.

When everyone was seated in the dining room, Breanna looked across the table at Whip and Annabeth. "Are you two going somewhere tomorrow to celebrate your anniversary?"

The Langfords gazed at each other joyfully; then Whip said, "Yes, we are, Breanna. We're going to church to hear our dear pastor preach as usual."

Meggie giggled. "Hey, that's neat!"

"It sure is!" agreed Ginny. "I think it's wonderful that you are going to church to celebrate your anniversary."

"Yes!" Breanna exclaimed. "What better way to celebrate the fact that you have been husband and wife for a whole year now."

Whip and Annabeth looked deeply into each other's eyes. Whip reached out with his left hand, and with his forefinger, tipped up Annabeth's chin. With his right hand, he lifted his plate off the table, which was yet empty, and used it to cover their faces as they enjoyed a sweet kiss.

Paul began clapping, and the rest of the Brockman family joined in the applause.

When the kiss was complete, Whip lowered the plate, grinning, and said to his wife, "Darlin', each time we kiss, it just gets sweeter!"

Annabeth looked around the table at the Brockmans, then gazed at her husband. "It sure does, sweetheart! It sure does!"

"Well," John said, "let's pray so we can get started on this anniversary supper."

Heads were bowed, eyes were closed, and John led in prayer, thanking the Lord for the food. He also thanked Him for bringing Whip and Annabeth together as husband and wife on June twenty-third of last year. When he closed the prayer in Jesus' name and said, "amen," everyone else at the table echoed his "amen."

During the meal, the discussion at the table was about Whip and Annabeth's year of marriage.

John smiled. "I'll tell all of you this much. Whip has been even better as a deputy U.S. marshal since he married Annabeth."

Annabeth giggled and looked at John. "I've taught my husband a lot about being a deputy since we've been married."

Everybody laughed. Paul, Ginny, and Meggie each spoke of how much Uncle Whip and Aunt Annabeth meant to them. Breanna did the same.

When the meal was over, Breanna pushed her chair back, rose to her feet, and started stacking the dishes. Running her gaze to John and Whip, she said, "Paul has to go do his chores at the barn and the corral, but I think you men ought to take your coffee and sit together on the front porch. It is such a lovely evening."

John stood. "Sounds like a good plan to me."

"Yep. Me too." Whip also rose.

Paul got to his feet. "Well, I'll go take care of my evening chores. See you later, Uncle Whip and Aunt Annabeth." They both nodded genially at him, and Paul hurried out the back door.

Breanna, Annabeth, Ginny, and Meggie quickly tended to washing and drying the dishes and cleaning up the kitchen. When they were finished, Ginny hugged her mother. "Mama, I think you need some rest now. You and Aunt Annabeth ought to just sit here at the table, have some tea, and spend time together. Meggie and I need to go upstairs, take our baths, wash our hair, and get our clothes ready for church tomorrow." She turned to Annabeth. "You will stay for a while and visit with Mama, won't you?"

Annabeth smiled. "Of course I will. You girls run along and do what you need to do. Your mama and I will spend some time together."

Both girls hugged Annabeth, then their mother, and hurried from the kitchen into the hall, giggling.

Breanna went to the cupboard, poured two glasses of cool tea, and placed them on the table. The women sat facing each other across one corner of the table.

Breanna relaxed her painful back against the chair. She noticed that Annabeth was staring out the kitchen window and silently asked the Lord for guidance. Then she reached across the corner of the table and laid her hand on top of her best friend's hand. "Honey, I — I've noticed a bit of tension in you and Whip this evening. Because you and Whip love each other so much, I can't believe there is a problem between

160

you." She stroked Annabeth's hand. "Is there something you would like to share with me?"

Annabeth's lips pinched and quivered as she fought back the tears starting to fill her eyes.

"Sweetie, I'm your friend, and your sister in Christ. You can tell me anything, and it will go no further than this kitchen, if that's the way you want it."

With the tears now trickling down her cheeks, Annabeth took both of Breanna's hands in hers and squeezed them. She sat immobile for several seconds. Then, heaving a huge sigh, she let go of Breanna's hands, pulled a handkerchief from her dress pocket, and dabbed the tears from her face.

Breanna, with a loving and caring expression in her eyes, waited patiently for Annabeth to gain control of her emotions.

Stumbling over the words that were so hard to utter, Annabeth said just above a whisper, "B-Breanna, Whip and I h-have been married a year t-tomorrow as you kn-know." Once again, she had to stop and blink back tears.

"Yes, my dear. I was there on that happy occasion."

A small smile formed on Annabeth's lips. She took a deep breath. "Whip and I want to have children. We had hoped that one would be on the way by now, but it's not going to happen."

Breanna's eyebrows arched. "What do you mean?"

More tears surfaced, and Annabeth dabbed at them with the handkerchief. "This morning, while working at the hospital, I finally got up enough nerve to talk to Dr. Carroll about our desire to have a baby. He was so kind and immediately, with the help of two nurses, examined me. The — the —" Fresh tears welled up in her red-rimmed eyes. "The results of the examination are devastating. The sad news is that I will never be able to have children. Oh, Breanna, this is so hard for both of us to accept." Annabeth broke into sobs.

Breanna was taken aback by the news, but her love for her hurting friend overrode the shock. Leaving her chair, she bent over Annabeth and wrapped her arms around her, trying to soothe her friend as she sobbed out her grief.

After a few minutes, when Annabeth's tears were spent, she dried her face with the handkerchief and looked into Breanna's sympathetic eyes.

Breanna squeezed her tightly. "Oh, my dear Annabeth, I'm so very, very sorry. I know this is something no married woman ever wants to hear. You and Whip are both relatively new Christians. Even people like John and me, who have been saved for many years, don't always understand God's ways. He doesn't ask us to understand, but He tells us to trust in Him and His judgment because He has a divine plan for our lives. In His own precious Word, He says in Isaiah 55:8, 'For my thoughts are not your thoughts, neither are your ways my ways, saith the LORD.' But He promises to always make a way for us, and He is always the same 'yesterday, and to day, and for ever,' as the Bible says in Hebrews 13:8."

Breanna kissed her friend's forehead. "Honey, I know you are grieving now and that this has been a terrible blow, but God, in His wisdom, has a plan for you and Whip, and as you learn to accept His will, He will reveal that plan to you. In Psalm 18:28, David wrote under the inspiration of the Holy Spirit, 'For thou wilt light my candle: the LORD my God will enlighten my darkness.' Then it says in verse 30, 'As for God, his way is perfect: the word of the LORD is tried: he is a buckler to all those that trust in him.' "

Annabeth was nodding while wiping more tears. Tenderly hugging her friend, Breanna said, "So you see, my dear one, the same Lord Jesus that has saved your soul from hell, and forgiven all of your sins, and dwells within your heart, has a special plan just for you and Whip!"

A light beamed in Annabeth's eyes. "Oh, thank you, Breanna. I wish I knew God's Word as well as you do. No, I don't understand why I can never have children, but I do trust my wonderful Lord, and I know that He will give Whip and me what is best. We just must remain faithful and not be afraid, for we are in God's hands and under His control."

Breanna nodded. "Exactly, my dear friend. Exactly."

The two women shared a long hug. As they let go of each other, Breanna said, "I'm here for you, Annabeth. Always remember that."

Annabeth smiled. "I could never forget that, my special friend."

Breanna smiled back. "Well, I guess we'd better go check on our husbands. I hope what I've told you will be a help to Whip."

"I'm sure it will. Now that I've talked with you about it, I think I can help him too."

"I'm sure you can, sweetie," said Breanna, "but if I know John, he's already noted the tension in you and Whip and has already asked Whip about it. I'm sure that John already knows and, in his wisdom, has already been a help to Whip."

"I have no doubt that you're right on this, Breanna. Let's go see our husbands."

Arm in arm, the ladies left the kitchen, moved up the hall, and stepped out onto the front porch in the early moonlight. Both men stood, and Whip said, "I told the chief, honey. Have you told Breanna?"

"Yes, I have, and she has helped me in a tremendous way, quoting Scripture that has already given me peace in it all."

Whip grinned. "Well, these two are sure alike, aren't they? John has done the same for me." He opened his arms and folded Annabeth into his tender embrace.

Likewise, John opened his arms and did the same with Breanna.

TWELVE

The summer moved on. On Tuesday morning, August 20, at the Central City gold mine, seven miners were working deep in one section of the mine. The man leading the other seven was Lewis Johnston, one of the mine's assistant foremen. Included in those working under Lewis's authority were Wayne Shelby, Charles Fawley, and Ed Stubler.

While Wayne was digging gold just a short distance around a corner from where Charles and Ed were working, Wayne heard them talking about Ed's recent salvation in Jesus Christ and his baptism at Central City's First Baptist Church.

"Charlie, my friend, I can never thank you enough for caring enough about my eternal destiny to get me under your pastor's preaching." Ed chuckled and added, "He's also *my* pastor, now. Praise the Lord!"

"That's right, Eddie!" Fawley chuckled.

"It's such a joy to know that since you repented of your sins and took Jesus into your heart, instead of going to hell, you will go to heaven when your life here on earth is over."

"Boy, is it ever. I'm so glad I'm saved!"

When Wayne heard the joyous conversation, anger welled up in him. He gritted his teeth and thought, *I wish I didn't have to hear about heaven and hell!*

Hours passed, and early that afternoon, Wayne was doing his usual job in the depths of the mine, working some sixty feet from Charles Fawley and Ed Stubler, but in sight of them.

While Wayne was swinging the pick, Chief Brockman's piercing words about him heading for the flames of hell suddenly came through his mind. Anger gripped him stormily, and he swung the pick harder than he had ever swung it, hitting the gold violently. Doing so threw him off balance, and he stumbled backward, falling on top of the burning kerosene lantern. Instantly, the flames caught his right pant leg on fire, and the blaze moved quickly up his leg.

Twisting about frantically on the dirt floor, Wayne howled because of the horrible pain and threw dirt on the flames to extinguish them. Just as the flames on his pant leg were turning to smoke, Charles and Ed ran to him.

"Wayne!" gasped Charles. "What happened?"

Through clenched teeth and still tossing dirt on the smoking pant leg, Wayne gasped, "I — I stumbled and fell on the lantern!"

Quickly Fawley picked up Wayne's canteen and poured water on the burned leg.

Assistant foreman Lewis Johnston ran up, then skidded to a halt. The other four men working in that section of the mine were on Johnston's heels.

"I heard a loud cry," said Johnston. "Must have been you, Shelby. What happened?"

The other four men stared at the burned pant leg.

Speaking weakly, Wayne explained about the accident.

Johnston knelt down, tore the partially shredded wet pant leg open, and looked at the burned skin. "Wayne, I'll take you to the Central City Clinic. We've got to get that burn taken care of."

Wanting to appear to be tough, Wayne said, "It's not that bad, Lewis. I can walk to the clinic by myself."

"Well, okay," replied Johnston, "but I want you to head there right now."

Wayne scrambled to his feet with a nod.

"I'll do that, all right."

He thanked Charles and Ed for coming to his aid, then limped away and began climbing out of the mine. When he reached ground level, he headed into town. As he walked with the pain from the burns on his calf, shin, and ankle of his right leg, Wayne thought of what a horrible thing it would be if what Chief Brockman told him what the Bible said about hell was true.

He clenched his teeth. "I'm hurting bad enough now, but how horrible it would be to be completely engulfed in flames and burn in hell forever!"

Soon Wayne arrived at the Central City Clinic, which was run by one doctor, Nicholas Darrow, and his wife, Emily, who was his only nurse.

Upon entering the clinic, Wayne was welcomed by Mrs. Darrow, and she instantly ushered him to a back room, where her husband had just finished placing a cast on a local rancher's broken arm.

Moments later, Dr. Darrow gave Wayne some laudanum to ease his pain. Then he and his wife put salve on the burns and bandaged up his leg. When Wayne left the clinic, limping on the burned leg, his heart pounded from the thought of spending eternity burning in hell.

He drew up in front of Central City's general store on Main Street and sat on a bench on the boardwalk. "I've got to get this matter of salvation settled," he whispered to himself as people walked by. "What Chief Brockman preached on and what he told me when we talked after the service most certainly is true!"

Wayne didn't understand why, but he had no doubt now that God indeed did exist, that there was a beautiful heaven and a fiery hell, and that the crucified, risen Jesus Christ was the only way to salvation. He also knew that if he died that moment, he would go to hell.

Standing up at the bench, Wayne thought, *I must get help immediately. I don't know how to receive Jesus Christ as my Saviour, but I know where I can find out!*

Remembering that he had heard Charles invite Ed to First Baptist Church of Central City and knowing that the church was just a few blocks from where he stood, Wayne headed down Main Street, limping but moving as fast as he could. Wagons, buggies, and men on horseback moved both ways on the street as Wayne threaded his way among the people on the boardwalk.

Before long he saw the familiar white church building with the steeple that had a cross at the top of it. "I sure hope the pastor is at the church."

Just as he drew up to the church building, Wayne heard people shouting on the street behind him. They were saying that there had been a cave-in at the Central City gold mine. The cave-in hit one section, and six miners were dead. Several miners were digging for the bodies right now.

Wayne came to a limping halt and gulped, realizing that the six dead men were Charles Fawley, Ed Stubler, and the other four he was working with in that section before he left to go to the clinic.

Standing at the bottom of the steps that led up to the front door of the church, Wayne swallowed hard and clenched his teeth. *If I hadn't been burned by that kerosene lantern, I would have been with those six men! I would be dead now too . . . and I would be burning* in hell!

Struggling up the steps as he held on to the handrail, Wayne shuffled to the door and knocked on it as hard as he could. He waited to hear footsteps inside, but there were none. He knocked again, but still there was no response. *Oh, dear God. I want to be saved. I need to talk to the pastor. Please help me.*

At that precise instant, an elderly, white-haired man came around the corner of the church building, heading for the boardwalk, but he halted when he looked up on the porch and saw Wayne. He stepped up close and asked, "Were you wanting to see Pastor Duran, sir?"

When Wayne had seen the sign in front of the church, he noted that the pastor's name was Brent Duran. He nodded as he limped toward the steps. "Yes sir, I am."

The old gentleman pointed toward the rear of the building. "Pastor's office is back on this side. I know he's in his office because I was just in there talking to him."

Making his way back down the steps, Wayne said, "Thank you, sir." Then he rounded the corner of the building and headed in the direction of the pastor's office.

The next morning at Denver's First Baptist Church, Pastor Robert Bayless was in his office with his wife when there was a knock at the door.

Mary was on a wooden chair in front of the desk. The pastor had a copy of the day's issue of the *Rocky Mountain News* in his hand. Laying it on the top of the desk, he rose from his chair. "I'll see who this is, honey."

Mary turned on the chair to watch as her husband opened the door, and her expression brightened as she saw who it was. Brent Duran, one of Robert's "preacher boys." Brent had surrendered to preach under his ministry some seven years previously, and after graduating from Bible college, had been sent out by the First Baptist Church of Denver to start a new church, the First Baptist Church of Central City.

In the nearly four years of the church's existence, it had grown well under Pastor Duran's ministry. Pastor Bayless had performed the wedding for Brent and a lovely young lady of Denver's First Baptist Church named Marcia Jones immediately after Brent's graduation from Bible college.

By the first look at Brent's face when he opened the door, Robert could tell that he was upset. "Brent, it's good to see you! Come in."

Brent stepped in, his features pinched, and as they moved together to where Mary was now standing, Robert said, "Brent, you look troubled. Is something wrong?"

The young preacher ran his gaze to Mary, then back to Pastor Bayless. "Do you two know about the cave-in at the Central City gold mine?"

Pastor Bayless stepped around his desk

and picked up the day's issue of the *Rocky Mountain News*. "We just received today's newspaper from the delivery man. We had only seen the headlines about the cave-in."

"Please go ahead and read it aloud to Mrs. Bayless, Pastor. Then I'll fill you in on some things."

Robert nodded, then turned to Mary. "Honey, sit back down on the chair. Brent, have a seat on the one next to it."

When the two had eased onto the wooden chairs, Robert sat on his desk chair, opened the newspaper, turned to page three, and read the cave-in story aloud. He and Mary learned quickly what had happened at the mine and that all six of the miners who were working in the section that had collapsed were killed.

Pastor Bayless shook his head in sadness. "This is really a tragedy."

"It sure is." Mary nodded.

"Two of the miners who were killed were members of our church . . ." Brent faltered briefly. "Charles Fawley, whose wife's name is Grace, and a single man named Ed Stubler."

"Oh my!" Mary gasped, her eyes wide.

"Let me tell you about these two men," said Brent. "Charles Fawley had been witnessing to Ed Stubler on the job, and on

Sunday morning, June 16, brought him to church. Ed Stubler walked the aisle at the invitation, was led to the Lord by one of our counselors, and I had the privilege of baptizing him."

"Well, amen!" Pastor Bayless said with a wide smile.

"Yes, amen!" said Mary. "How wonderful it is that Charles had been instrumental in bringing Ed to the Lord and now they're together in heaven!"

"That's wonderful, all right," Pastor Brent Duran agreed. "I might add that both Charles and Grace Fawley were saved under my preaching, in the same service, just over a year ago. Grace is expecting their first child, which is due to be born in about a month. Of course, she is terribly torn up over her husband's death."

"Oh, bless her heart," said Mary. "I can understand that."

"Marcia has her at the parsonage right now. I know the Lord will use her to give Grace comfort, strength, and courage."

"I'm sure He will, Brent," Pastor Bayless said.

Brent looked at his mentor. "Do you remember when Wally and Linda Higgins brought Wally's uncle, Wayne Shelby, to church with them?"

Pastor Bayless nodded. "I sure do. Wally's atheist uncle works at the Central City gold mine. Chief Brockman was preaching for me that morning. The Brockmans, the Higginses, Mary and I, and the whole church have been praying for Wayne's salvation."

A smile spread over Brent's features. "I brought up Wayne Shelby just now because I have something wonderful to tell you."

Pastor Bayless's eyes widened. "Are you going to tell us that Wayne Shelby isn't an atheist anymore? That he is —"

"Your brother in Christ!" cut in Brent.

"Oh, glory!" gasped Pastor Bayless.

"*Double* 'oh, glory'!" shouted Mary. "Tell us about it. You're brightening our day."

"Well, late yesterday afternoon, Wayne came to my office at the church shortly after the cave-in at the mine. Of course, I didn't know who he was. We had never met. Wayne told me that he had been working in that precise section of the mine that collapsed and would have been killed along with those six men, except for something that happened to him earlier that day."

"What was it?" Mary asked, eager to hear how God's hand had been working on the atheist who had so many Christians praying for him.

Brent explained what happened to Wayne.

"Oh," Pastor Bayless said. "Sure sounds to me like the Lord was working in answer to a lot of people's prayers."

"For sure." Brent grinned. "From what Wayne told me when we began talking in my office, I saw clearly that the Scriptures on salvation, heaven, and hell that Shelby had heard Chief Brockman preach and the additional Scriptures that Chief Brockman had given him when they were talking after church had been driven deep into his heart and mind by the Holy Spirit. Without a doubt, the painful burn on his leg frightened him even more about burning in hell."

Pastor Bayless clapped. "Wow! Praise the Lord! He knows how to get to an atheist's heart and mind, doesn't He?"

"Wonderful!" exclaimed Mary. "Sounds like that man really and truly got saved."

"Amen, ma'am," said Brent. "And I'm going to baptize him during the midweek service this evening."

"Hallelujah!" Pastor Bayless said, his eyes sparkling with joy.

"I was just thinking," said Mary. "This is a wonderful illustration of how God uses some people to plant the seed of the Word and others to bring in the harvest."

"Right!" both men said in unison.

Mary smiled. "Luke 8:11 says, 'The seed

is the word of God.' Mark 4:14 says, 'The sower soweth the word.' First Peter 1:23 says, 'Being born again, not of corruptible seed, but of incorruptible, by the word of God, which liveth and abideth for ever.' Chief Brockman planted the seed of the Word in Wayne Shelby's heart, and you brought in the harvest, Brent."

Pastor Duran blinked at the tears filling his eyes. "How wonderful it is, the way almighty God produced the seed of the Word and allows His born-again people to use it to bring lost souls to salvation and to bring glory to the wonderful Saviour, our dear Lord Jesus Christ, both by the power of the Holy Spirit."

Brent pulled a handkerchief from his hip pocket and wiped away the tears from his eyes and cheeks. "My mind has gone to the widowed Grace Fawley again. It's going to be so hard for her when the baby is born, with its father dead. She needs lots of prayer."

"That's for sure," said Pastor Bayless. "Mary and I sure will be praying for her. And I will put her on the prayer list at our church too."

Mary's gentle eyes misted with tears. "Oh, the poor young lady. Whatever will she do with no husband to provide for her and her dear wee one?"

Pastor Robert shook his head and ran a palm over his face. "There certainly is very little work for a woman in the gold mining business. Just a few secretarial positions in their business office, and even less of an opportunity to do that for one carrying a baby. Maybe I'll suggest to her that she try to come to Denver to live. Her chances of finding some suitable employment and someone to care for her baby when she is working would be far greater in a city the size of Denver than in Central City."

"Makes sense, Pastor," said Brent.

"Tell you what, Brent," said Pastor Bayless. "Mrs. Fawley doesn't know me. Instead of my making the suggestion to her, how about you doing it?"

"I'll try."

Pastor Bayless nodded. "If you can persuade her to come to Denver, tell her that Mary and I would like to talk to her. Perhaps we can come up with some sort of plan that would be beneficial for her and the baby."

"We will sure try," Mary added.

"Thanks to both of you," said Brent. "As I told you, Grace is with Marcia at the parsonage right now. I'm sure Marcia will agree with your thoughts on this. We will do our best to see that Grace comes to Denver.

That's really the only answer for someone in her circumstances."

Brent rose to his feet. "I need to be going. I had actually come to Denver today to buy a new dress for Marcia for her birthday, which is coming up in a few days. But I did plan to stop and see the two of you while I was here."

The Baylesses also stood, and Robert said, "Before you go, Brent, I would like for us to pray for Grace Fawley."

Brent smiled. "Yes! Will you lead us, Pastor?"

The three of them bowed their heads and closed their eyes. With compassion in his voice, Pastor Bayless prayed for Grace, that the Lord would give the new young widow peace and comfort in her husband's death and would help her in a special way when it came time to give birth to her baby. He then asked the Lord to provide a way for Mrs. Fawley to have an income for her and the baby and to give them a place to live in Denver.

When the prayer was finished, Brent put his arms around Pastor Robert and Mary, hugged them, and told them he loved them. Then he hurried off on his shopping errand.

Mary sighed. "Oh, darling, my heart goes out to that dear Grace Fawley and her fatherless babe. I didn't think to ask Brent about any family she might have somewhere who could help her. But I'm sure if she did, Brent would know about them. We really must do something to help her."

"We will, my dear," said Robert. "The Lord will open the way for us to help her and supply whatever the need so we can do it. We only need to pray and believe, for we know that He is faithful."

THIRTEEN

At the federal building, chief U.S. marshal John Brockman was at his desk in his office, reading the *Rocky Mountain News* story of the cave-in that had happened at the Central City gold mine the day before, when his deputy on duty at the front desk, Darrell Dickson, knocked on the door.

The chief laid the newspaper on his desk. "Come in, Darrell!"

Dickson opened the door and stepped in a few inches. "Chief, there's a man here from Central City who would like to see you. His name is Wayne Shelby."

At the mention of that name, there was a thoughtful creasing of John's brow, followed by a thin smile. Though a bit stunned, the chief rose to his feet, wondering if the atheist's visit had something to do with the cave-in at the mine, where he was employed.

Darrell frowned. "By the look on your face, Chief, you must know him."

John nodded. "I do. Send Mr. Shelby in."

As Darrell stepped back into the hall to invite Shelby into the chief's office, John rounded his desk and took a few steps toward the door. He motioned for the miner to enter. After Shelby stepped into John's office, the deputy closed the door, leaving the two men alone.

Shelby's face was pale. "Chief Brockman, I have something to tell you."

John let a smile curve his lips. "All right."

The miner took a nervous, shaky breath. "I am no longer an atheist."

John's mouth fell open. "Wonderful!"

Before the chief could ask any questions, Wayne Shelby went on. "I am now a blood-washed, born-again Christian! I have the Lord Jesus living in my heart as my Saviour!"

Pleasantly stunned, John grabbed Wayne's right hand with his own, shook it vigorously and with his left hand, pointed at the small couch there in the office. "Sit down. I want to hear all about this."

When they were comfortably seated, Wayne began his story. Choking up and wiping tears every few seconds, the former atheist shared with John how the thought of burning in hell forever had plagued him day and night since he heard the chief preach at

Denver's First Baptist Church.

John smiled. "I'm glad it did plague you, Wayne. I sure prayed that it would."

Wayne smiled in return. "Thank you for praying for me." He then mentioned the cave-in at the Central City gold mine the previous day.

"I just now read the *Rocky Mountain News* article about it," John said, "including the names of the six men who were killed."

Wayne nodded sadly. "Chief Brockman, I had been working with all six of those men yesterday in the very section of the mine where the cave-in took place, and if I had been there when it happened, I would have been killed too."

"God's hand was on you, Wayne. If you had been killed at the mine, you would be in hell right now."

"You see, Chief, as soon as this leg was bandaged by the clinic doctor, I hurried as fast as I could to First Baptist Church to talk to the pastor about being saved."

John's eyes lit up. "So Pastor Brent Duran led you to the Lord."

A wide grin spread over Wayne's face. "Yes sir. I am going to be baptized by Pastor Brent Duran in the midweek service tonight!"

"Well, my whole family and also a great

number of the people in Denver's First Baptist Church have been praying for your salvation."

"Oh, bless their hearts. And thank you so very, very much, Chief Brockman."

John laid a steady hand on Wayne's arm. "I'm so glad the Lord drove the truth of His existence into your heart and mind and, in answer to our prayers, used His Word to draw you unto Himself."

"God's Word is really powerful. I know that now. Thank you, Chief Brockman, for caring enough about a lost, hell-bound atheist to tell him the truth from the pulpit and face to face."

"It was my pleasure. What a joy it is to watch God work through His powerful Word."

Wayne nodded. "I hope the day will come when I can help people see the truth about heaven, hell, and salvation through the Lord Jesus Christ and see them saved."

"You follow the teaching and preaching of the great preacher who will become your pastor when you get baptized tonight, and you'll see this fulfilled in your Christian life, Wayne. It's called soul-winning. The Lord wants every Christian to be a soul-winner."

"That's what I want to be!" Wayne slipped his pocket watch from the pocket of his trousers, then glanced at the time. "Chief Brockman, I need to head back to Central City."

John rose to his feet. "All right. I'll walk out with you."

As the two men made their way into the outer office, Deputy Dickson, who was seated at the desk, looked up. "Did you two have a good talk, Chief?"

"We sure did. I'm walking Mr. Shelby out to his buggy now."

"Oh." Darrell looked at Wayne. "Nice to have met you, Mr. Shelby."

"Same here." Wayne gave the deputy a warm smile.

John and Wayne headed for the front door of the federal building. At that instant, both men heard a gunshot. They saw that two gunslingers had apparently just drawn against each other in the middle of the street. People were gathered along the boardwalk looking on. Some of the women were showing a great deal of fear, including mothers attempting to get their children to a safe place.

One of the gunslingers buckled over, a slug obviously in his midsection, but his gun fired. A short distance up the street were a pair of horses hitched to a wagon with no one in the driver's seat. One of the horses had been nicked on the neck by the stray bullet.

Both horses let out wild whinnies and in terror bolted down the street in John and Wayne's direction, the wagon bouncing and swerving dangerously behind them.

"Boy, those horses are coming fast!" gasped Wayne.

John nodded, his eyes wide. "They sure are!" He caught sight of an elderly man using a cane as he walked slowly across the street. Spencer Lannan was stone deaf.

The wild-eyed, terrified horses galloping down the street were headed directly toward the old man. John and Wayne began to shout at Spencer, but he couldn't hear them and sensed no danger.

John dashed into the street and surprised Spencer by grabbing him from behind and moving him out of the horses' path. Spencer looked back at the man who had grabbed him and shouted, "Chief Brockman! What are you doing?"

The horses raced by with the wagon bouncing and swerving behind them, and Spencer gasped. Gripping the chief's upper arms, the silver-haired man said, "Oh, Chief Brockman, thank you! Thank you! If those horses and that wagon had hit me, I would be dead right now."

Moving his lips carefully, so Spencer could read them, John said, "I am just so glad I could get to you before they collided with you."

The old man smiled. "I'm going to pray that the Lord will give you a great big reward for saving my life when we get to heaven!"

By this time, Wayne Shelby was beside John. His eyes sparkled. "Chief Brockman, you not only know how to get souls saved, but you are also good at saving lives! You kept this elderly gentlemen from being killed."

John smiled. "Wayne, this dear man's name is Spencer Lannan. He is a fine Christian and is a member of First Baptist Church."

Spencer was smiling at Wayne; then John leaned especially close to the elderly man, once again moving his lips carefully, and said, "Wayne won't mind if I tell you, Spencer, that he used to be an atheist, but he's now a Christian. He's getting baptized this evening at the church Brent Duran pastors in Central City."

"Wonderful!" Spencer extended his hand to Wayne, and as they grasped each other, Spencer said, "Welcome to the family of God! You and I are now brothers in Christ!"

Tears filled Wayne's eyes. "Thank you, and God bless you!"

A local man named Omar Cammit stepped up. "Chief Brockman, the gunslinger who was just shot by the other gunslinger in their shootout is dead. But he didn't die from the bullet in his body. When the other gunslinger saw that the crowd's attention was drawn to where you saved Mr. Lannan, a few of us saw him pull a knife and stab the wounded gunslinger in the heart."

John's jaw clenched. "Omar, is the killer still around?"

"No sir. After he stabbed his opponent, he jumped on his white stallion and galloped away to the north. I've seen his photograph in the newspapers several times. He's that well-known gunslinger from Wyoming, Chet Hayden."

The chief nodded solemnly. "I know about him and what he looks like. You say he's riding a white stallion?"

"Yes sir."

"Totally white?"

Omar nodded firmly. "Yes sir. Body, legs, mane, and tail."

John's face was a bit flushed as he spoke to Omar and the people standing around listening. "As you all know, the law here in the West will not arrest a gunslinger who kills another gunslinger in a fair fast draw. However, since the man who just outdrew the other gunslinger wounded him without killing him but then stabbed him to death, he is guilty of murder. I've got to go after him."

Wayne said, "Chief Brockman, I really have to head for Central City."

"Of course," John said. "You go right ahead."

"See you later," Wayne said warmly, then pivoted and headed for his buggy.

John waved and called out, "Happy baptism, Wayne!"

Omar Cammit said, "Chief, I know you're in a hurry to go after Hayden, but I thought I should tell you that a couple of other men said they knew who the murdered gunslinger was. I've heard of him but never saw a picture of him. They said his name is Nave Kitchin, and he's from Nebraska."

"Oh," said John. "I know a lot about him. He was pretty fast with his gun until he turned sixty. He should have quit then, but he still felt he could handle any gunslinger who challenged him."

Omar shrugged. "Guess there has to come a day when a fella just slows down on the draw."

John nodded. "Right. Omar, would you do me a favor?"

"Sure."

"So I can get on the trail of Chet Hayden, will you go to my office and tell Deputy Darrell Dickson at the front desk what I'm doing?"

"Of course."

"And if I'm not back here at the office to head home at my normal time, would you ask him to send one of the deputies to my ranch to tell Breanna what I'm doing? It could take me a while to catch up to Hayden."

"Sure will, Chief," Omar replied with a smile. "Are you gonna take at least one deputy with you?"

"No time. I've got to run back to get Blackie and head north. Hayden is from Laramie, Wyoming, and I figure since he rode north out of Denver, he's heading back there."

The chief U.S. marshal ran to the corral at the rear of the federal building, swung into Blackie's saddle, and put his big black stallion to a gallop.

Chet Hayden had been riding fast for almost an hour, looking back over his shoulder to see if anyone was following him, when he neared a small village known as Platteville, Colorado. Chet knew this town had a general store and a small café with a water pump for travelers to use to give their horses a drink.

He drew rein to slow his white stallion, looked over his shoulder again, noting that there was no one following him, and hauled up at the water pump. After dismounting, he pumped the trough better than half full with water. He took reins in hand and led the stallion up to the trough. The sweaty horse took several gulps of cool water, then bobbed its head.

Hayden smiled. "Okay, boy, I'm rather hungry, so I'm goin' into the café to get somethin' to eat."

He led the horse to the hitching rail in front of the store and went inside.

A half hour later, Chief Brockman, who had kept Blackie at a hard gallop, caught sight of a white horse tied to the hitching rail in front of the Platteville General Store. As he drew up, he saw that the white stallion was sweating and figured this could well be Chet Hayden's horse.

Two other horses, both brown in color, were tied to the rail, and a farm wagon was parked nearby.

Slipping up to the edge of one of the

store's front windows, John peered inside and saw a man and woman at a small table, eating. And at the table next to them, Chet Hayden was also eating. Other customers moved about the store.

John took a deep breath. He would have to wait till Hayden came out before arresting him. It could be too dangerous for the store clerks and the other customers to confront him inside.

Just then, Hayden rose from the table, wiping his mouth with a napkin.

John backed away from the window and hurried behind one of the wagons parked right next to where Hayden's horse was tied. He ducked down beside the wagon so the gunslinger couldn't see him and fixed his eyes on the general store's front door.

Seconds later, Hayden came out and headed for his stallion. As he untied the reins from the hitching rail, the chief U.S. marshal stood, Colt .45 in hand, and as he cocked the hammer, he said, "Hold it right there, Hayden! You're under arrest! Get your hands in the air!"

In total surprise, Hayden twisted around and saw the black barrel of the cocked Colt .45 aimed straight at his face and the badge on the lawman's chest. He recognized chief U.S. marshal John Brockman. Hayden had seen his picture in newspapers many times. Hayden's flesh went cold as he raised his hands over his head.

Brockman rounded the wagon at the rear, keeping his gun pointed at the gunslinger's face. "I'm arresting you for the murder of Nave Kitchin."

Hayden swallowed hard. "Whattya talkin' about? He and I squared off in a fast draw. You can't arrest me for that!"

"No, but I *can* arrest you for murder. Kitchin was still alive when you stabbed him in the heart. You thought nobody would see you, since the crowd was watching me save the elderly gentleman about to be run down by those galloping horses. However, a few people saw what you did, and they will testify of it in court, I guarantee you."

Chet Hayden's heart was pounding. It pounded even harder when Brockman moved up real close with the gun's muzzle still aimed at his face.

"Reach down real slowlike, Hayden, and pull that hunting knife on your waist out of its scabbard."

Hayden obeyed the command, and it was clear that the blade was covered with blood.

"Drop it!" said Brockman. The knife hit the ground. "Now lift your gun out of its holster with the tips of your fingers and drop it also!"

When this was done, the chief told Hayden to turn around. Once Hayden had done so, John holstered his own gun and cuffed the gunslinger's hands behind him. He then picked up Hayden's knife and gun and placed them in his own saddlebag.

John hoisted him into the saddle of the white stallion, then mounted Blackie, took the reins of the white horse in hand, and led Hayden toward Denver.

There was a cold, heavy sinking in Chet Hayden's stomach.

He was locked up in the county jail that evening and stood trial before Judge Dexter on Monday, August 26. Eight Denver citizens testified under oath at the trial, telling judge and jury that they had seen Hayden stab the wounded gunslinger, Nave Kitchin, in the heart while he was still breathing.

The attorney Hayden had hired was unable to do a thing to get him off. The jury came forth with a guilty verdict, and Judge Dexter sentenced him to be hanged at sunrise on Thursday, August 29, under the authority of the county sheriff.

On Wednesday, August 28, Chief Brockman visited Hayden in the jail and tried to give him Scripture on the subject of heaven, hell, and salvation in the Lord Jesus Christ, but flaming in anger, Hayden told Brockman he did not want to hear it. Heavy at heart, John left the jail.

At sunrise the next day, Chet Hayden was hanged.

FOURTEEN

As the days and weeks passed, Annabeth Langford continued with her nursing career, still feeling the weight in her heart that she would never be able to conceive nor bear a child. She had often prayed privately that the Lord would give her the strength she needed to face the fact that she could never be a mother.

On Thursday afternoon, September 12, Annabeth finished helping one of Mile High Hospital's surgeons with an appendectomy on a twelve-year-old girl, then headed for the washroom to cleanse the girl's blood from her hands.

As she was passing the delivery rooms, even though the doors were closed, she heard the cries of two newborn babies. Her throat clogged for a few seconds, simply from knowing that two mothers had just brought their babies into the world.

Tears were in Annabeth's eyes as she

reached the washroom, opened the door, and went in. No one else was there at the moment. Annabeth dabbed at the tears in her eyes with a towel, then began washing her hands at one of the sinks.

Even though it had been nearly three months since Dr. Carroll had given his heart-wrenching diagnosis, the desire to be a mother was still within her heart.

When she was drying her hands, Annabeth said, "Dear Lord, I still haven't adjusted to the fact that I will never give birth to a child. The yearning is still strong within me."

She took a deep, shuddering breath, then placed the towel in a basket for washing. "Lord, Whip is carrying this difficult situation in his heart too. He is trying so hard to be brave, but I've watched him look at babies at church, in stores, and on Denver's streets with longing in his eyes. Of course, he's not aware I have seen this. He's trying to be so strong for my sake, and oh, how I love him for it. But Lord, there is such emptiness within me. Ever since I entered my teenage years, I've wanted to be a wife and mother. Now the mother part of that dream will never be fulfilled."

Annabeth thumbed tears from her eyes. "Please, dear God, help me to accept Your will and be content with such things as I have. I am indeed so blessed with my precious husband, with such dear and caring friends, and such a loving church family. I'm the nurse I always wanted to be, and caring for the sick was Your calling for my life. Help me, Lord, to be as grateful as I should be for Your glorious gift of salvation and to accomplish and carry out Your will for this life that You have given me."

By this time, more tears were streaming down Annabeth's cheeks. She heard the voices of two surgical nurses outside the washroom door. Annabeth hurried to the basket where she had placed the towel, picked it up, quickly dried her cheeks, and closed off her prayer in Jesus' name just as the door opened.

That Saturday, both Whip and Annabeth both had the day off from their jobs. At mid-morning, Whip was doing yard work around the house, and Annabeth was sweeping floors inside and dusting furniture.

Whip took in the beauty of the towering Rocky Mountains a few miles to the west and the foothills in between. He also ran his appreciative gaze around the level area to the east of his home. There was green grass bright with late summer flowers, and the area was dotted with groves of graceful fir trees and pines and spruces, lifting their branches that shone brightly in the golden sunlight beneath the clear blue sky.

Soon Whip finished the yard work and placed his tools in the small toolshed near the barn. Closing the door, he pivoted, and his attention was drawn to the small fenced-in area nearby where his big, gray pet wolf, Timber, was kept. The area also included a small wooden shed, which was Timber's living quarters. Timber entered and exited the shed through a low, hinged door at the bottom of the shed on the front, next to a normal-size door.

Whip's attention had been drawn to the spot because Timber was standing on his hind legs at the fence, wagging his tail and looking at his master. As Whip drew nearer, Timber went to all fours and hurried to the gate, whining a warm welcome to his master. Whip opened the gate and grinned. "Howdy, boy!"

As Whip entered the fenced-in area, Timber was quickly on his hind legs again, but this time he placed his paws on his master's chest, panting happily as he was being petted.

While Timber and Whip shared their affection for each other, Whip marveled that this once-wild wolf had become like a tame German shepherd or any other big, loving dog. However, the times when Timber traveled with him as he was pursuing outlaws, Timber attacked them when commanded to do so by his master and was every bit a fearsome, snarling, growling, wild wolf.

Ruffling the fur on top of Timber's head, Whip said, "What a tremendous help you've been to me, boy, in capturing outlaws so many times."

Timber let out a yip as if he understood what his master had said.

Whip chuckled. "I wish you could wear a marshal's badge. You sure deserve it!"

Timber ejected another yip and wagged his tail.

After spending a few more minutes with his pet wolf, Whip left the fenced-in area and headed toward the house. As he walked, Timber gave off a soft yip.

Whip turned and looked back at his wolf, who was standing at the gate and wagging his tail. "I know, boy. You want to chase outlaws with me again. Probably won't be too long."

Timber yipped again as his master neared the back porch.

While Annabeth was dusting furniture in the parlor, she was unaware that her husband was about to come in the house. Since she was alone, she began praying out loud, saying, "Dear Lord, please help me to control this deep desire within me to be a mother. It just won't go away." As she prayed on, Annabeth did not hear the back door open, nor did she hear her husband's footsteps as he drew up to the parlor.

When Whip saw that his dear wife was praying, he remained silent and let her proceed.

Annabeth's eyes were closed as she leaned against the back side of the sofa. "Lord, I know You are fully aware of my dilemma. I come to You often with it because I need peace about it, which only You can give me. I love You, dear Lord, and I'm looking to You for help in this heartrending situation. I know You are going to help me. Please help me like David asked You to help him with a burden he was carrying in Psalm 141:1, 'Lord, I cry unto thee: make haste unto me; give ear unto my voice, when I cry unto thee.' Please, dear Lord, make haste unto me in this heavy burden I am carrying. Please give me release from the burden, and give me peace real soon. In Jesus' precious name I pray, amen."

When Annabeth opened her eyes, she saw her husband standing in the open doorway of the parlor. He quickly walked toward her, opening his arms. With tears filling her eyes, she smiled at him.

Whip folded her into his arms and tenderly kissed Annabeth. "Sweetheart, though you cannot give birth to a child of your own, I have an idea."

Easing back in his arms, Annabeth wiped the tears from her eyes. "What is your idea, honey?"

Looking at the sofa, Whip said, "Let's sit down here, and I'll tell you."

Whip let his wife sit first, then eased down beside her, putting an arm around her shoulders. He looked into her eyes. "Since we know you can never bear a child, how about we adopt a child when one comes available?"

Tears welled up in her eyes again as a smile graced her beautiful face, erasing the lines of despair. "Oh, Whip, my darling, do you honestly feel that this is our solution?"

Smiling himself, Whip replied with a lilt in his voice, "Yes, sweetheart, I do!"

"Oh, Whip, I've thought about it too, but I haven't brought it up to you because I didn't think you'd want to adopt a child."

Whip helped her wipe the tears from her cheeks with his free hand. "Honey, I think it is the most wonderful and gratifying thing we could do."

"There's no way for us to know how long it might be before a child is available, but the Lord knows our hearts and our desires, and His Word says in Psalm 37:4, 'Delight thyself also in the LORD: and he shall give thee the desires of thine heart.' "

"Yes, it does," said Whip. "Let's pray about it together right now."

With his arm still around his wife's shoulders, Whip led in prayer, asking the Lord that whenever some little child in the Denver area was put up for adoption, He would make it so they knew about it and would allow them to adopt the child.

When Whip finished praying, Annabeth was crying and sniffling. Gripping her husband's free hand, she looked at him through her tears. "Oh, darling, I just know our Lord is going to make it possible for us to adopt a little child. And — and when He does, I'll resign from my nurse's position at the hospital and be a full-time mother. I'm sure Dr. Carroll will understand."

Whip kissed her lips softly. "Sweetheart, that'll be fine. I have no doubt that Dr. Carroll will thoroughly understand why you want to be a full-time mother. And as for us, we can make it financially on my deputy marshal's salary."

Annabeth smiled. "Thank you for talking to me about our adopting a child. It's just the perfect solution for filling this strong desire in my heart. I know that in His time, God will give us a child to love, raise, and teach of His love and the salvation that He provides through the blood of our Saviour."

Thrilled at his wife's response to his idea, Whip kissed her again, then folded her into his arms and held her tight. A deep sense of peace filled both of their hearts.

On the following Friday, Annabeth was working at Mile High Hospital. Just as she finished helping one of the surgeons repair a broken kneecap on a young man in his early twenties, Nurse Edna Colter entered the room. She smiled when she saw that the doctor was covering the patient with a sheet on the surgical table and that Annabeth was just putting away the surgical instruments after sterilizing them.

Edna greeted the doctor, then stepped up to Annabeth. "Honey, Dr. Carroll wants to see you as soon as possible. It appears that you're about finished here."

Annabeth nodded. "Yes, I am. Do you know what Dr. Carroll wants to see me about?"

"He has an emergency assignment for you."

"You'd better hurry, then, Annabeth," said the surgeon.

With a gracious expression, she said, "I will."

With that, Annabeth hurried out the door with Nurse Colter behind her. Moments later, when Annabeth entered the office of the hospital's chief administrator, she found Dr. Carroll in conversation with Breanna. Dr. Carroll's back was toward Annabeth, but Breanna was facing her.

Annabeth smiled at her friend. Then the doctor finished what he was saying, and Annabeth said, "Hello, Breanna."

Breanna smiled back. "Hello, Annabeth." She hurried to her best friend. The two women hugged each other. Then Breanna said, "I know about your emergency assignment, but I'll let the boss tell you."

Dr. Carroll stepped closer to Annabeth. "I want you to help Dr. Bates deliver a baby. The young woman who is about to give birth to her first child is Grace Fawley, the widow of Charles Fawley, one of the miners killed in the cave-in at the Central City gold mine."

"Oh, I see," Annabeth said. "I remember hearing that Charles and his wife were

Christians and members of Central City's First Baptist Church."

"That's right," said the doctor. "Mrs. Fawley will be in delivery room number four in just a few minutes. She's having some serious difficulties. Two hospital attendants are taking Mrs. Fawley to the delivery room, and Dr. Bates is waiting there for her and for you too, Annabeth. I just sent word to him that you will be assisting him."

"I'll go right now, Doctor." Annabeth hugged Breanna, then hurried out the office door.

Just as she entered the appointed delivery room, she saw two hospital attendants lifting the expectant mother off a padded cart onto the bed. Dr. Bates greeted Annabeth warmly. "I was very pleased when Dr. Carroll sent word that you would be assisting me. You have helped me deliver babies many, many times."

"I'm glad he chose me, Doctor." She turned her attention to Grace Fawley, who was obviously in a great deal of pain. The baby would be born quite soon.

As soon as the attendants had helped Grace get settled on the bed, they nodded at Dr. Bates and hurried out of the room with the cart.

Both doctor and nurse began preparations

to deliver the baby. Though Grace was in much pain, she said with strained voice, "M-my husband, Charles, was one of the miners who was killed in the cave-in at the Central City gold mine in August. Th-that's why he is not here. B-but I will see my husband again in heaven because he was born again, and so am I."

"I'm so glad to hear that, ma'am," said Dr. Bates. "I'm a born-again child of God and so is nurse Annabeth Langford."

Grimacing in pain, Grace said, "Oh, I am so glad to know I have people working on me who know the Lord Jesus as their Saviour."

"And we are glad to know that *you* are saved, ma'am," said the doctor. "Isn't it wonderful to have the Lord Jesus in your heart?"

Grace managed to say, "It certainly is," before gritting her teeth in pain.

As they worked to deliver the baby, Grace began to hemorrhage. Doctor and nurse worked hastily, doing all they could to stem the bleeding, but it swiftly grew worse.

Biting down hard to keep from screaming, Grace reached toward Annabeth and grasped both of her hands in her own. Then gasping and pushing down, Grace worked hard to push the little one out into the world.

"You're doing fine, Mrs. Fawley." Dr. Bates tried to calm the nearly hysterical woman but sent a glance to Annabeth with deep concern in his eyes.

In her extreme pain, Grace's mind ceased to function properly. "Charles! Charles! Where are you? I need you now! Please come and help me!" Then she moaned, looking agitatedly around the room. "Charles! Help me!"

Annabeth sponged her head with cool water. "It's going to be okay, Mrs. Fawley. Your husband is in heaven, remember? You're in God's hands."

Dr. Bates sought Annabeth's eyes, his own filled with horror as he did everything possible to stem the red tide of blood.

In her agony, Grace pushed again with all her might, and suddenly the baby slid into the doctor's waiting hands. After quickly cutting the cord, Dr. Bates handed the baby to Annabeth and put his attention back on the struggling mother. Her face was ashen, and her eyes were closed as she continued to hemorrhage in spite of all of his efforts.

As the baby began to cry, Dr. Bates told Grace that it was a beautiful little girl. Grace showed her joy from the sweet news, but the bleeding steadily grew worse.

He worked on the young mother with great care and deep concern while Annabeth lovingly bathed the crying wee one at a nearby table, talking softly to her. "What a precious little girl you are." She kissed the top of the baby's downy head. "Your lungs are good, that's for sure."

Annabeth put a diaper on the baby, then wrapped her in a small blanket. She glanced at the doctor. He met her eyes and slowly shook his head.

Annabeth gasped softly as she looked at Grace's pale face. Holding the precious bundle close to her own heart, she made her way toward the bed. Grace lay motionless, her eyes closed. Annabeth stepped closer to the bed. She thought Grace had already passed from this fragile life into heaven. As she looked closer at the woman, however, she saw that Grace was breathing shallowly. Her chest was barely moving.

Praying in her heart for help and holding the baby tightly, Annabeth leaned over the bed and whispered, "Grace. Grace, can you hear me?" She watched the patient closely, but there was no response.

The baby ceased her crying, and Annabeth cradled her close and looked lovingly at her. The baby opened her eyes and looked straight up at Annabeth. Tears misted Annabeth's eyes, and again she prayed, *Dear Lord, it appears You are going to take Grace home today. But — but would You please just give her a little more time so she can see and hold this precious child?*

Suddenly awed but ever so thankful, Annabeth saw Grace blink her eyes, then slowly open them.

"Grace, dear," Annabeth said quietly, "can you hear me?"

Watching closely, the doctor fixed his eyes on the new mother.

Barely perceptible, the ashen-faced woman nodded her head, and her cloudy eyes moved from Annabeth's face to the bundle she was holding.

Grace moved her arms, trying valiantly to reach for her baby. Her strength, however, was gone, and her arms dropped back onto her body. She sent a silent plea from her eyes to Annabeth, who understood the heartfelt message.

Ever so gently, Annabeth placed the now-sleeping child onto her mother's frail chest and wrapped both her arms around the babe.

Dr. Bates looked on in amazement at the nurse's handling of the situation.

A small, serene smile curved Grace's lips

as she lovingly marveled at this precious miracle. Finally, after taking her eyes off the baby girl, she gazed at Annabeth and tried to form words.

"What is it, Grace?" Annabeth prayed that the Lord would help her to know what Grace was trying to say.

Grace's lips were barely moving as she tried to speak.

Annabeth leaned down closer, hoping to hear the words Grace was trying so desperately to convey.

Barely even a whisper came from the dying mother, but Annabeth could make out the words as she said, "You . . . take . . . baby . . . your own."

In her heart of hearts, Annabeth knew the meaning of those five words. It was almost as though the Lord Himself had spoken them.

Dr. Bates stood in stunned silence.

With tears raining down Annabeth's cheeks, she wrapped her hands over one of Grace's hands as it was holding the baby close to her heart. "Yes, Grace, I will love and care for your baby. You have my most solemn promise."

Grace lifted her cloudy eyes to Annabeth and slowly gave a brief nod. Then after looking at her dear little one again, she closed her eyes. A vestige of peaceful serenity encompassed her. Annabeth left the slumbering babe in her mother's arms and stepped away from the bed, giving mother and daughter time alone together. Annabeth felt the miracle God was performing.

Suddenly, the young mother gasped, glanced upward, then stared at Annabeth and Dr. Bates with wide eyes, and said in a nearly breathless voice, "It's Jesus! It's Jesus!" And with a peaceful smile on her lips, she breathed her last breath.

With tears streaming down her cheeks, Annabeth looked at the doctor, who was silently staring at the smile on the dead woman's lips. He then met Annabeth's gaze but remained silent.

Blinking back her tears, Annabeth gently lifted the slumbering baby from her mother's lifeless arms. Gazing tenderly at the baby girl, Annabeth kissed her little cheek, snuggled her close in her arms for a few seconds, then placed her in a nearby cradle.

"This was really something, Annabeth," Dr. Bates said. "I've heard of a few Christians dying and being given a glimpse of their Saviour's face just as He was about to take them to be with Him. I have never seen it happen until just now."

Annabeth nodded. "I have also heard of it

happening, Doctor. But like you, I've never seen it happen before." She paused. "Bless Grace's heart. She has now joined her husband in heaven."

"Yes. She sure has." He paused. "Annabeth, I know that you learned in June that you will never be able to give birth to a child."

Annabeth nodded.

"I plainly heard the dying mother tell you to take the baby as your own, didn't I?"

Annabeth choked up slightly, stepped away from the cradle, then lowered herself onto a stool. "Yes. And my husband and I recently agreed to adopt a child. We have prayed much, asking the Lord to give us the child He wanted us to adopt when it was His time to make it happen."

"Well, from what I saw and heard, I would say the Lord wants you and Whip to take this baby as your own. If there would be any question about it when you apply for adoption, I will most certainly testify that just before she died, Mrs. Fawley told you to take the baby and make her your own. I saw something almost miraculous between the two of you." The doctor's gentle expression lent credence to his words.

"Thank you, Doctor. With all my heart, I will carry out Grace's wishes. I will go right now to the federal building, and if Whip isn't out on an assignment somewhere, I'll tell him the story and bring him to the hospital immediately to see this sweet baby."

The doctor glanced at the sleeping baby. "Annabeth, is Dr. Carroll aware that you and Whip are planning to adopt a baby?"

She shook her head. "No. We haven't told anyone but the Lord."

"All right. While you're going after Whip, I'll go to Dr. Carroll's office to tell him what happened here and that I heard the dying Mrs. Fawley ask you to take her baby and make her your own. Is that okay?"

Annabeth's eyes filled with tears. "Oh yes! Thank you, Dr. Bates. That will help us with the whole situation."

At that moment, the baby awoke and rolled her little head back and forth and made soft cooing sounds.

Annabeth slipped off the stool and moved toward the cradle, a smile spreading on her face. As she stepped up to the small table where the cradle was, she looked down at the tiny girl. Her skin was a healthy pink, and her breathing was even and normal. The baby made another cooing sound; then a wee little fist found its way to her rosebud mouth.

The baby was holding Annabeth in fascination as she stared down at her. Dr. Bates stepped up beside her. "I would suggest you head for the federal building now so you can make contact with Whip right away."

She smiled. "Yes, Doctor. I just have trouble taking my eyes off this little doll. I'll be going now. Would you please take the baby with you when you go to Dr. Carroll's office? I'm sure Breanna will watch over her."

"I will do that, Annabeth. Now, you go find that husband of yours who is about to become a daddy!"

FIFTEEN

Whip Langford was coming out of Denver's gun and ammunition store, carrying a box of .45-caliber cartridges that he had just purchased to replenish his supply.

As Whip moved down the boardwalk on Broadway in the direction of the federal building, his mind went once again to the big subject in Annabeth's life and his. "Lord," he said in a soft whisper, "it will mean so much to Annabeth and to me when You bring about the adoption that we want to see happen. I can tell that my precious wife thinks about it a great deal, though she tries to keep it to herself so as not to put me on edge. She knows I want that child in our home as much as she does. Please, Lord, help us both to keep calm about it until it's Your time to bring it to pass. Help us to be patient."

Whip was crossing the street toward the next block when a young mother came toward him pushing a baby carriage. As they drew abreast of each other, he stopped, looked down at the baby boy in the carriage, then smiled at his mother. "He sure is a cute little guy."

The mother drew the carriage to a halt and smiled back, noting the badge on Whip's chest. "Thank you, Deputy. He looks very much like his father."

"I'm sure, little fella, that your papa is very proud that you look like him."

"That he is," said the mother.

Whip touched the brim of his hat in a gentlemanly manner. "Take care of the little guy." And he moved on.

Whip was midway down the next block when he approached a five-story brick apartment building. He heard the shrill voice of a young boy cry out from the balcony of the fourth floor. "No, Becky! No! Get down from there!"

Whip looked up to see a little girl about three years old clinging to the railing that ran along the balcony. She had light brown hair and was clad in a red and white plaid dress.

Whip figured that the boy, who looked to be about six or seven years of age and probably was her brother, had just noticed her up on the railing from inside the apartment and was running toward her as he was calling out for her to get down.

Suddenly the little girl lost her hold and peeled over the edge of the rail.

Whip dropped the box of cartridges on the boardwalk, and with lightning speed, dashed up to the building and stopped directly below the falling girl. Watching the screaming child descend toward him, Whip braced himself and opened his arms to catch her. By this time, people on the street were looking on with horror in their eyes.

When the little girl fell into Whip's arms, he cushioned the impact as much as possible, then held her close to his chest. "It's all right now, honey."

She began sobbing, simply from the fear that gripped her, and as people drew up, he was speaking to her in a soothing tone, and her sobs eased.

Most of the men and women in the crowd knew who Whip was, and they spoke their commendation to the deputy U.S. marshal for the way he had saved the little girl from death, or at least from being seriously crippled from the fall.

As Whip held the trembling girl in his arms, the boy who had been on the balcony ran over, followed by a woman with hair that was turning silver. She seemed familiar to him.

"Deputy Langford." She ran her gaze between Whip and the little girl in his arms. "I'm Martha Wilson. I've seen you and your wife at First Baptist Church on several occasions since I moved here to Denver some three months ago and joined the church."

"Oh, yes ma'am," said Whip. "I knew you looked familiar."

"Thank you! Oh, thank you for saving my little granddaughter's life!"

Whip smiled. "I'm just glad I was close enough to get here so I could catch her, ma'am. I heard this boy here call out to her when she was up there on the balcony. Her name is Becky, right?"

"Yes. Becky Wilson. She's three years old. And her brother's name is Ronnie. He's six years old. Their parents — my son, Bill, and his wife, Eunice — are from Santa Fe, New Mexico. They came through Denver on their way to Cheyenne, Wyoming, to visit some friends and left my grandchildren with me. They'll be back in a couple of days."

The grandmother stroked the little girl's pallid face and spoke words of comfort, telling her that everything was all right now. Becky gave Whip a gracious smile, thanked him for catching her, then reached for her grandmother.

After talking to Martha Wilson and her grandchildren for a few minutes, Whip picked up the box of cartridges he had dropped and told them he had to get back to the federal building.

As Whip walked away, he thought about holding Becky in his arms. He thought of how he would like to have a little girl. A few minutes later, when her brother had come toward him with the grandmother behind him, Whip thought, *Well, it could be a boy. I just want the child that the Lord will choose for us.*

In the chief U.S. marshal's office at the federal building, Deputy Darrell Dickson looked up from the desk where he was seated in the front office and saw Mrs. Langford come through the door.

Dickson rose to his feet and smiled. "Hello, Annabeth."

She smiled in return. "Hello, Darrell. Is Whip here?"

Dickson shook his head. "No ma'am. But he should be back soon. He had some free time, so he went to the gun and ammunition shop to buy some more cartridges for his Colt .45. I expect him back any —"

Darrell's words were cut off as the door

opened again and Whip came through the door, holding a box of cartridges in one hand. A grin spread over Whip's face when he saw his wife. He hurried to her. "Honey, I've got something to tell you! I just had the joy of saving a little girl's life!"

"Well, I'd love to hear about it, sweetheart," Annabeth replied, looking delighted. "Then I have something about a little girl to tell *you!* I need you go to the hospital with me right now. You can tell me about saving that little girl's life while we're walking over there."

"Okay, but I need to get Chief Brockman's permission. He may have something he wants me to do immediately."

"No way to know," said Darrell. "The chief happens to be at the hospital right now. He had something he needed to talk to Mrs. Brockman about, so he went over there to see her. After that he has some other stops before he returns to the office."

Whip looked at his wife. "Well, sweet stuff, looks like we can head for the hospital." He looked at Dickson. "Will you put this box of cartridges on my desk, Darrell?"

Taking the box in hand, Darrell said, "Sure will."

As the Langfords headed for Mile High Hospital, Whip told Annabeth about how he had caught little three-year-old Becky Wilson when she fell from the balcony. "Whip, that's a wonderful story! Now, let me tell you *my* story."

Whip listened intently as Annabeth told him of assisting Dr. Bates at the hospital as he delivered Grace Fawley's little daughter. Then she explained that as Grace was dying, she asked Annabeth to take the baby for her own.

Whip's eyes widened, and his mouth hung open. "Annabeth! Are you going to do it?"

She took hold of her husband's hand and pulled him to a stop. "Honey, I am certain in my heart that the sweet little newborn girl is the one the Lord wants you and me to adopt. Grace has gone home to heaven to be with her husband, Charles. The Lord already had this planned, and I have no doubt that He also planned for us to adopt their baby girl."

Whip's eyes filled with tears. "Oh yes! No question in my mind about it! Where is the baby now?"

"She is in Dr. Carroll's office at the hospital. Dr. Bates took her there at my request when I left to go to the federal building. Breanna is taking care of the baby until you and I get there."

Whip grinned. "So Breanna and Dr.

Carroll both already know about the up-coming adoption."

"They sure do! Dr. Bates has already told them the whole story by now."

Whip gripped her hand tightly. "Well, sweet stuff, what are we waiting for? Let's get to the hospital. I want to see my new little 'almost' daughter!"

A few minutes later, when Whip and Annabeth arrived at Dr. Carroll's office, they found Breanna sitting on the small sofa, holding the newborn baby.

Instantly Breanna rose to her feet and rushed the little blond baby to Whip, who took her into his arms with happy tears in his eyes.

"I'm so glad you are going to adopt the Fawley baby," Dr. Carroll said. "Do you plan to go to county judge Ralph Dexter and apply for the adoption?"

Whip nodded. "Tomorrow morning. Can the baby stay at the hospital tonight, Dr. Carroll?"

"Certainly. And Dr. Bates will go with you tomorrow when you apply for the adoption, just so there won't be any problems. He can testify to what Grace Fawley said."

"We'll talk to Dr. Bates before we leave the hospital," Whip said, "and set a time that will be convenient for him."

The next day, Whip and Annabeth went to Judge Dexter's office in downtown Denver in their buggy, accompanied by Dr. Bates, who drove his own buggy. When the doctor saw there would be no problem for Whip and Annabeth to adopt the baby, he excused himself, saying he needed to get back to the hospital.

The Langfords told the judge that they wanted to name the baby Elisabeth Grace. The name Grace, of course, was in honor of her real mother. A few minutes later, when the adoption papers had been signed by the judge, Whip and Annabeth overflowed with joy from their hearts that beautiful little blond six-and-half-pound Elisabeth Grace Langford was now officially their daughter.

When they left the judge's office and stepped outside, the couple's feet seemed to barely touch the ground as they thanked the Lord for giving them little Elisabeth Grace.

As they headed toward a nearby hitching post where the horse and buggy stood, Annabeth looked up at her husband. "Honey, can you spare a couple of hours from the office? We need to buy some baby bottles and milk. We also need to buy little Elisabeth some diapers and clothes, as well as a crib and blankets."

"Of course, sweetheart." Whip gave her a big smile. "This is a great event in our lives. Since Dr. Carroll and Breanna are expecting us to show up at the hospital to pick up the baby, we'll stop by there first, and I'll run in and let them know about the shopping we need to do. Then when we're done, we'll go back to the hospital, pick up our little daughter, and take her home."

"Yes!" Annabeth said, as they stepped up to the wagon. "That's how we'll do it!"

Whip helped Annabeth into the buggy, untied the horse from the hitching post, climbed in beside her, and put the horse to a trot.

Later, when the shopping was done and Whip and Annabeth entered Dr. Carroll's office, they found Breanna just finishing feeding the baby milk from a bottle.

When the new parents were ready to leave with their baby, Breanna invited them to come to the Brockman home for supper and to spend a little time with them so the family could get to know little Elisabeth Grace. The Langfords accepted the invitation, saying they would be there in time for supper.

At First Baptist Church the next morning, September 22, Pastor Bayless was beaming at announcement time. He stood and told the story of Grace Fawley's death in childbirth on Friday and of the adoption of the orphaned newborn by Whip and Annabeth. He had the adoptive parents stand with Annabeth holding little Elisabeth Grace in her arms.

The crowd applauded and cheered, congratulating the Langfords on becoming parents.

After the church service, Whip and Annabeth approached Dr. Carroll and his wife, Dottie, in the parking lot as they were about to climb in their buggy and head for home.

Holding little Elisabeth Grace in his arms, Whip stepped up and said, "Dr. Carroll, Annabeth needs to talk to you."

Annabeth was just a step behind her husband, standing close to his side.

Dr. Carroll smiled. "I'm quite sure what you want to talk to me about, Annabeth. Now that you have this baby, you are going to resign your position at Mile High Hospital in order to be a full-time mother. Right?"

Annabeth grinned sheepishly. "I should have brought this up to you the same day we adopted her, Dr. Carroll, but there was no time."

"Annabeth, I have a number of nurses employed at the hospital to choose from, one of whom I will put in your place." He paused a few seconds, then added, "Of course, nobody could really take your place, but you understand what I mean."

Tears moistened Annabeth's eyes. "I understand, Dr. Carroll. You're so kind. Thank you for being such a wonderful chief administrator to work for."

"You have my blessings, Annabeth, in your new life as a mother."

"And you have *my* blessings too," Dottie chimed in.

Annabeth brushed away the tears from her eyes. "Thank you both so very much."

"Yes," said Whip, "thank you both so very much."

The Brockman family was standing close by. John took a few steps closer to them and said, "We didn't mean to listen in on what was being said, folks, but with your wagon so near, we couldn't help but hear the conversation."

"No problem, Chief," said Whip.

Breanna moved up beside her husband and looked at the two couples. "Why don't you all come to the ranch and have Sunday dinner with us?"

The Carrolls and the Langfords exchanged glances, and Dottie said, "Let's do as my sister is asking, okay?"

"Sounds good to me," said Whip.

"Me too," replied Dr. Carroll. "Let's go!"

When they all arrived at the Brockman ranch and entered the house, Dr. Carroll set his soft gaze on his fourteen-year-old niece, Ginny, and smiling, put an arm around her shoulders. "I wish you were old enough to have had nurse's training. I would love to hire *you* in Annabeth's place. You would be perfect for the job."

Her uncle's words made Ginny very happy. Smiling up at him, she said, "Uncle Matt, when I *do* get old enough and after I *do* finish nurse's training, I will apply to you for a job."

Dr. Carroll squeezed her tenderly. "You'll get the job too, sweet girl!"

Meggie, who was standing close by, spoke up. "Uncle Matt, will you want me to work for you when I get old enough to take nurse's training and graduate from nursing school?"

Letting go of Ginny, Dr. Carroll hugged Meggie. "I sure will, sweetheart! You and your sister will have jobs at Mile High Hospital, I promise."

The women and the girls went to the kitchen while the men and Paul sat down in the parlor, with Whip holding little Elisabeth. Breanna had learned to always be prepared for Sunday dinner company, and this day was no exception. Before leaving for church, she had placed two large chickens seasoned with sage dressing into the oven. The girls had peeled a large amount of potatoes and cut them into wedges, and they were ready in cold water, waiting to be put on the stove and boiled. The garden salad was also ready, as were apple pies for dessert.

During dinner, little Elisabeth Grace Langford was sleeping soundly on Ginny's bed. Most of the talk at the table was about Whip and Annabeth's new little daughter.

SIXTEEN

Time moved on. Paul Brockman still had his heart set on becoming one of his father's deputy U.S. marshals when he turned twenty-one. John Brockman continued to work with his son, doing all he could to prepare him in every way to be a topnotch lawman.

Paul Brockman graduated from high school in May of 1891 and turned nineteen on October third of that year.

When Paul entered the kitchen for breakfast the morning of his birthday, he was surprised to find the rest of the family already there. Ginny and Meggie were standing between their parents near the table, and when Paul looked at them questioningly and moved toward them, they began singing "Happy Birthday" to him.

Paul stood there grinning until they had finished singing to him. Then he hugged his mother first. Ginny and Meggie were hugged next. Then Paul planted a manly hug on his father.

When all were seated at the table for breakfast, John led in prayer, thanking the Lord for Paul, then for the food. As they began to eat, Breanna told her son that his big birthday party scheduled for that evening was still on.

Paul smiled, knowing that the Carrolls would be there as well as the Langfords, Pastor and Mrs. Bayless, and some of the boys he had graduated from high school with. "I'm looking forward to it, Mama." He reached across the table to pat her hand.

John drained his coffee cup and placed it back on the table. "Son, I have something very important I want to talk to you about right after breakfast, before I head for my office."

Paul nodded genially. "Yes sir."

"What's it about, Papa?" asked Meggie.

"Mama knows what it is," replied John. "I'll let her and Paul tell you and Ginny after I head for Denver."

"All right," said Meggie.

When breakfast was over, John took Paul into the parlor while the girls helped their mother clean up the kitchen and do the dishes. They sat on overstuffed chairs facing each other. "Son, I want to hire you to do paperwork in my office right away. Ordinarily, no one can be on the payroll of the U.S. marshal's staff until he is twenty years old, but I obtained permission from the federal authorities in Washington, D.C., to hire you at nineteen because you are my son. Interested?"

Paul's face had already brightened. "I sure am!"

"Good. You will not only do paperwork but anything else needed in relation to me and all the deputies."

"That's fine with me!"

"You see, son, this will very much help you to learn about how a federal law office is run and will aid in preparing you to become a deputy U.S. marshal when you turn twenty-one. I know this kind of work may sound a little tame compared to wearing a gun and going after outlaws, but it's all part of the job, and it's important that you learn all of the inner workings of the job."

"I understand, Papa." Paul smiled. "Sure, I'd like to put on a badge, strap on my Colt .45, and go after outlaws right now, but that will have to come all in good time."

"Right, son. You've grown up watching me function as the chief United States marshal here in the Western District, but until you put on the badge and the gun belt and actually have to handle the bad guys, you still won't know all that is involved in being a lawman. You are young yet, Paul, and I want you as well-trained as possible before that badge has a place on your chest."

"Thanks, Papa. I will be a good student and learn all I can about the job that's coming when I turn twenty-one. But mostly I will learn with you as my example. You're the best lawman there is."

John looked pleased. "You've got me somewhat overrated, son, but I'm glad you feel that way about me."

John and Paul were unaware that Breanna had been privy to most of this conversation as she stood in the hall beside the open parlor door. Walking away quietly down the hall, she said in a low voice, "Dear Lord, it's been one thing to have my husband in law enforcement all these years, but — but in a couple of years, my only son will be putting himself in harm's way. As I have prayed all these years for John, please give Paul wisdom in wearing the badge, and give him Your protection as he performs the task You are leading him to do. Help him to make a difference in people's lives, just as his father has, and please give me the grace and strength I need daily to stand by both of them."

As Breanna closed her prayer in Jesus' name, the "peace of God, which passeth all understanding," spoken of in Philippians 4:7, made its way into her heart and mind. "Thank You, Lord Jesus. Thank You."

On Friday, May 20, 1892, in the auditorium at Denver High School, Ginny Brockman graduated from high school at age seventeen and received her diploma with her proud family and many friends there to observe it.

On Monday, May 23, Breanna and Ginny drove the family buggy into town to the Colorado School of Nursing. There, Breanna registered Ginny to enter her freshman year and begin preparation to become a nurse. The school year would begin the first week of September.

Ginny was all smiles as she and her mother climbed into the buggy and sat on the driver's seat. Breanna hugged her. "Ginny dear, I am so proud of you! You graduated at the top of your class in high school, and now you are on your way to making your lifelong dream of becoming a nurse a reality."

Ginny kissed her mother's cheek. "It's all because of the example you've given me as a nurse, Mama."

Breanna radiated her pleasure at the compliment, but then turned gently solemn. "Being a nurse is not an easy road to travel. You will face many difficult problems, but overall, it is so rewarding. And even though you will often find that you cannot heal every patient you labor over, keep your eyes on the Lord and be thankful for those who pull through their ailments. When some do not get healed by your earnest efforts, and even die, you will know that you did your best for them. Be ever so thankful that at least you were able to help ease their suffering. Just remember, honey, that when it comes to life or death, God is in control, not you. Not even the doctors. Be loving and kind, because that is really what patients need most of all. Always take time to listen when they speak to you of their ailments, because the patient knows his or her body best."

Ginny nodded. "That makes sense, Mama."

Breanna went on. "There will be times when things will happen that will cause you to question your decision to become a nurse. When it seems that you have failed too often in your chosen profession, just remember that the Lord is always with you, and you will see that there are many more people ahead who are in need of your services and your help. Pray for guidance as you work to help every patient. He will lead you and give you wisdom."

Ginny nodded again. "Yes, Mama. I know He will."

"I can tell you this, Ginny. I have observed you through the years as you've helped me when Paul and Meggie and even your papa were sick or injured. And I know you will make a wonderful, caring nurse. I'm so thankful that you want to follow in my footsteps in the medical profession. God will bless and use you to help heal bodies, be a witness for Him, and heal sin-sick souls as well."

Ginny, who had led some of her schoolmates to the Lord over the years, smiled. "I will do my best, Mama."

Breanna hugged her again. "I love you, my precious daughter. May God go with you as you begin this path."

Ginny hugged her mother back. "And I love *you,* Mama. I pray I can be even half the nurse that you are. I'm so excited to get started, and my goal, with God's help, is to be the best nurse He enables me to be."

"You'll do just fine, my Ginny girl. You have the right heart attitude, and that's what matters."

Tears of joy streamed down the cheeks of both mother and daughter as they hugged each other again.

Paul Brockman turned twenty-one on Tuesday, October 3, 1893. At eleven o'clock on Wednesday morning and wearing an official uniform, he was sworn in at the federal building by his father before a group of deputy U.S. marshals. With tears filming his eyes, chief U.S. marshal John Brockman pinned a deputy marshal's badge on his son's chest. The deputies applauded, then went to Paul, telling him how glad they were that he was now one of them. Some also brought up that the older he became, the more he looked like his father. This pleased Paul very much.

At this time, Chief Brockman was forty-eight years of age, and his wife, Breanna, was forty-four.

Deputy U.S. marshal Whip Langford was thirty-seven, and his wife, Annabeth, was thirty-four. Little Elisabeth Grace Langford, now called Lizzie by her parents and friends, was four years old.

John assigned his son to carry out his deputy U.S. marshal's job by working with some of the much-experienced deputies, especially Whip, whom Paul greatly admired. Sometimes John even had Paul going after outlaws with him.

As the days passed, Paul proved himself to be excellent in handling himself with outlaws. His boldness, courage, and lightning speed on the quick draw, along with absolute accuracy with his gun, were spoken of in newspaper articles and by his fellow deputies.

Paul was praying daily that the Lord would bring the right Christian young lady into his life to become his wife. He had dated many Christian girls in high school, but nothing serious ever took place between him and any of them. Paul believed the Lord already had the right young lady picked out for him to one day be his wife, and he was eager to meet her.

On Sunday, November 5, during the invitation at the close of the sermon at Denver's First Baptist Church, a Christian couple named Nathan and Janet Bryson, along with their lovely, Christian nineteen-year-old daughter, Noreen, walked the aisle to present themselves for membership.

Nathan and Janet had moved to Denver from Chicago, Illinois, in mid-October and started visiting the church. Noreen, who had beautiful brunette hair like her mother, had remained in Chicago when her parents first moved to Denver because of a job obligation and had just arrived in Denver by railroad the day before.

Sitting with his parents and his sisters in their favorite pew, Paul's curiosity about the pretty young lady with the Brysons was cleared up by Pastor Bayless when he explained why Noreen had not been in the previous services with her parents.

Pastor Bayless had all three Brysons give their salvation testimonies before the congregation, and when the vote to accept them as members was a full one hundred percent, as explained to them by Pastor Bayless, the Brysons smiled happily.

When Paul Brockman saw Noreen Bryson's magnificent, captivating smile, it did something to him.

After the service, the members were passing by the Brysons in the vestibule to welcome them into the church. When the Brockmans introduced themselves, Paul, wearing his uniform and badge, felt a special warmth in his heart when he welcomed Noreen as a member of the church.

She smiled and extended her hand. "This is such a friendly church. Thank you, Deputy Paul Brockman, for your warm welcome."

With Noreen's hand in his own, Paul felt

a shiver of excitement make its way up his spine, and his heart quickened its pace. He shook her hand gently, wishing he could hold it longer but did the gentlemanly thing and released her. As her hand slipped from his, Paul immediately felt an emptiness fill his entire being.

He told her again how glad he was that she and her parents had joined the church. She smiled at him. Then more people were moving up to the Brysons, and she turned her attention to an elderly woman.

Paul swiveled and headed toward the front door, but before he went outside, he took a few seconds to look back over his shoulder at the lovely brunette, who was still in conversation with the older woman.

At home after Sunday dinner, Paul went to his room upstairs for some quiet time. He lay on his bed, looked up at the ceiling, and reminisced about his all-too-short encounter with Noreen Bryson. Paul found her exceptionally charming.

Having learned from his parents years ago to take everything he felt was important to his heavenly Father, Paul prayed, "Dear Lord, I realize I've only met this young lady one time, but my heart did some strange things when I shook her hand. If indeed Noreen Bryson is the one You've chosen for me, then show her real soon, and also give us both Your peace to proceed in a relationship. You know, Lord, I am not one to just date one girl after another and never want to get serious, so please help me to be content until You reveal Your own perfect will in this to me. Thank You, Father. In Jesus' precious name I pray, amen."

Paul lay in the darkness. He really liked that beautiful, sweet girl. It sure would be all right with him if Noreen was the one God had chosen for him.

The next day, Paul was moving along the boardwalk on Curtis Street in downtown Denver when he saw Noreen come out of a clothing store ahead of him. She was alone. Moving toward her as she stood looking around at the other stores on that block, Paul prepared himself to talk to her and get to know her better. He was within fifty feet of her when a man about his own age stepped up to Noreen and started talking to her with a flirtatious look in his eyes.

There were quite a number of people on the boardwalk between Noreen and himself, which slowed him down, but as Paul neared them, he could tell that Noreen did not like what the young man was saying.

"Leave me alone, mister!" Noreen

snapped.

As Paul was weaving his way among the crowd on the boardwalk, he could see that the man was obviously drawn to Noreen because of her good looks, and he kept talking to her. Drawing nearer, Paul saw Noreen turn to walk away from the annoying man, but he quickly grabbed her by the arm, stopping her. "Don't be afraid, young lady! I mean you no harm. I just want to get to know you!"

Noreen tried to free herself from the rude man's grasp. "Let go of me!"

Paul drew up and looked the man in the eye. "Let go of her, mister!"

The man snarled at Paul and, despite his badge and uniform, snapped angrily, "Mind your own business, lawman!" He let go of Noreen's arm and took a swing at Paul's jaw.

Paul dodged the fist and lanced a powerful left to the forehead that jarred the man to his heels, then swiftly crossed a whistling right that smashed his jaw with a hammer-like blow that knocked him down and out.

The people on the boardwalk stopped, marveling at the speed of Paul Brockman's fists and the power that went with it. The man he had punched lay absolutely still, definitely unconscious.

Noreen glanced down at the unconscious man who had given her trouble, then smiled at Paul. "Thank you, Deputy Brockman, for stopping that rude man from bothering me."

Paul smiled back. "It was my pleasure, Miss Bryson."

"You can call me Noreen."

Feeling a touch of joy, Paul replied, "Okay, Noreen. And you can call me Paul."

As Noreen watched Paul silently, the crowd began to move on, with the majority of them taking a good look at the unconscious man on the boardwalk.

Paul took a deep breath and said, "Could I take you out for supper some time soon at one of Denver's restaurants?"

Noreen's smile disappeared. "That would be a date, Paul, and people who date often get serious about each other."

Paul grinned. "Yes, that's true."

Noreen frowned at him.

"What's the matter?" Paul asked.

"Well, since you're a lawman, I could never get serious about you. So it's best that we do not date each other."

"Do you have something against lawmen?"

She shook her head. "No, but I would never marry one. I know that too many men here in the West who wear badges get killed in the line of duty, and I absolutely will not put myself in a position to so easily become a widow."

Quite stunned and disappointed, Paul said, "I'm sorry you feel that way."

The man on the floor of the boardwalk began to move, blinking his eyelids and letting out a groan.

Paul took the handcuffs from his belt, bent over, and rolled the man facedown. Then forcing his hands behind his back, Paul handcuffed him. The young deputy picked him up, stood him on his feet, and held on to him so he wouldn't fall. "I'm taking you to jail, mister, for attacking a federal deputy marshal."

As Paul walked away, holding onto his prisoner, who was stumbling somewhat, he looked back over his shoulder and in a friendly manner said, "I'll see you at church in the midweek service, Noreen." *Well, Lord, it's plain that You haven't chosen Noreen Bryson for me. I will keep on praying and waiting for You to bring that right Christian young lady into my life.*

SEVENTEEN

As time moved on and Paul Brockman continued his career as a deputy marshal, he proved himself to be exactly like his father in temperament and courage as well as being extremely fast on the draw with his Colt .45 revolver and the use of his fists when necessary.

One chilly day in late November, Paul was walking along the boardwalk on Broadway, heading back toward the federal building after having delivered a written message and some official papers to Judge Dexter from his father. He paused to talk for a few minutes with Willie Henderson, one of the young men who had graduated from Denver High School with him and now was employed at a lumber company in the town of Aurora, an eastern suburb of Denver.

After the two friends had exchanged some details about their careers, Willie patted Paul on the arm. "Well, I'd better be getting back to work, Paul. See you at church on Sunday."

"Sure enough," Paul said with a smile. "See you then."

As Willie was walking toward a nearby hitching post where his horse was tied, Paul's attention was drawn to a man in his early thirties who was standing in the street some fifty feet away, staring straight at him with a scowl on his face.

It was the infamous gunslinger Buck Steffan, whose photograph Paul had seen in newspapers several times in the last two years. Steffan had taken out several other gunslingers in Wyoming, Colorado, Nebraska, and Kansas.

Already people on the boardwalk and in the street recognized Steffan and stopped to look on as he headed alongside the boardwalk toward Paul, his evil eyes fixed on him.

Paul knew what was about to happen. Apparently because he was wearing a lawman's badge, he would have to face the blood-hungry gunslinger. Quickly he stepped onto the dusty street and made a beeline for the approaching Buck Steffan.

As Paul and the gunslinger drew within thirty feet of each other, both came to a sudden halt.

"Listen to me, Steffan. You get on your

horse and ride right now!"

Steffan chuckled. "Hey, deputy U.S. marshal Paul Brockman, have I broken some law that you would order me to get out of town?"

Paul was shocked to hear Steffan call him by name, and it showed in his eyes. "How do you know me?"

Steffan glared at him venomously. "I've heard that you became one of your pa's deputies. You sure do look a lot like him. I knew who you were the instant I saw your face. I've been here in Denver before and saw your pa. Do they call you Stranger too?"

"No, they don't. Now like I said, you get on your horse and ride. Right now! We don't want gunslingers in this town."

Malice glimmered in Steffan's dark eyes. In a gritty voice, he said, "I asked you if I'd broken some law that you would order me to get out of town. Well?"

"Not that I know of, but like I said, we don't want gunslingers in this town. Get out!"

The people in the crowd that surrounded the two men exchanged glances, knowing that Deputy Paul Brockman was exactly like his father. When he gave an order, he meant it.

Steffan's back arched, and he spread his

feet a bit, taking the gunfighter's stance as his right hand lowered over the gun in his holster. "I ain't leavin'! Go for your gun! It'll please me to take out the Stranger's kid!"

Paul's face suddenly looked like chiseled stone. Slowly lowering his own hand over the gun on his hip, he said stiffly, "I want you out of town immediately. Wherever your horse is, get on it and go!"

Steffan shook his head. "I ain't goin' till you and I have it out!"

Paul squared his jaw and narrowed his eyes. "I can outdraw you, Steffan. I don't want to kill you, but if you force this quick draw, I'll have to keep the bullet from hitting someone in this crowd. Now get going!"

The well-known gunfighter laughed. "How do you know you can outdraw me?"

"I just know it. It's time for you to leave!"

Suddenly Buck Steffan's hand flashed down for his gun.

The crowd saw Paul's lightning-fast draw in action as he drew his Colt .45 and fired it. Even before Steffan could cock the gun in his hand, the slug plowed through his heart, killing him instantly; the gun dropped into the dust of the street as he fell backward and hit the ground hard.

Bart Gilmore from the *Rocky Mountain News* happened to be on the street when the confrontation began. He made his way through the crowd as they were commending Paul for the way he had handled the situation.

As he drew up to John Brockman's son, he said, "Paul, it was plain to see that you didn't want to kill Buck Steffan. You tried so hard to get him to leave town so no one else here would get killed. I'm going to write this up in my column so everybody will know the truth."

Paul smiled at him. "Thank you, Bart. I appreciate your attitude about the incident."

As time progressed, Paul was gaining confidence as a lawman. By the time he turned twenty-two, Paul had arrested many outlaws who were now in jail or prison and had sent some to their graves after shooting it out with them. Other outlaws, whom Paul had chased down and arrested, had been hanged as murderers. Among those outlaws were some Paul had led to Christ after they had been imprisoned, before they were executed.

On Monday, February 4, 1895, Paul walked into the First National Bank of Denver to make a deposit. As he approached the window of teller David Barrett, who was also in his early twenties, Paul smiled. "Howdy, David. I'm always glad when no one is at your window so I can do my banking business with you."

The handsome young teller smiled back as Paul handed him the check and deposit slip. "Howdy, yourself, Paul. It's always good to see you."

Paul had witnessed to David of his need to receive the Lord Jesus Christ as his Saviour on several occasions since David had come to work at the bank. David had always kindly told him that he didn't believe what the Bible said about a burning hell.

As David handed Paul his deposit receipt, Paul took it with a word of thanks, then said, "David, I sure wish you would come to church and hear my pastor preach. I'm very concerned about your eternal destiny. As I've told you several times, without being born again by repenting of your sins and receiving the Christ of Calvary as your Saviour, you're going to a never-ending, burning hell when you die."

David licked his lips nervously, then met Paul's gaze. "Paul, I — I've been thinking about all the times you've asked me to come to church. Maybe I really ought to come and hear your pastor preach. If there really is a burning hell, I sure don't want to go there."

Encouraged, Paul replied, "There *is,* and according to God's Word, if you die without being saved, that's where you're going."

David nodded solemnly. "I will come to your church next Sunday morning."

Paul smiled. "Promise?"

David smiled back. "I promise."

The bank's silver-haired president, Randall Kaylor, stepped out of his office, which was close to the tellers' cages, and seeing the young deputy U.S. marshal, he called out, "Hey, Paul!"

Paul looked his way. "Hello, Mr. Kaylor."

"Would you come into my office before you leave?"

"Of course," Paul said. "I'm through here. I can come right now."

"Good! Come on."

Paul told David he would see him Sunday, then hurried into the bank president's office.

Standing in front of his desk, Randall Kaylor said, "I read in the *Rocky Mountain News* last week of how you had single-handedly pursued and captured that well-known outlaw Lou Ambers and that after his trial, he will be going to the Cañon City Prison for a long stretch."

Paul nodded. "Yes sir."

"I won't hold you here, Paul, but I just had to compliment you on being such a good lawman, just like your father."

"Thank you, sir. Papa taught me everything I know about being a lawman."

A moment later, as Paul stepped out of the bank president's office, he saw a foul-looking man behind the tellers' cages, holding a revolver to David Barrett's head. He was commanding the other tellers to fill one of their canvas moneybags with cash and bring it to him. If they refused, he said, he would blow David's head off.

Paul noted that the hammer on the robber's gun was not cocked.

While the other terrified tellers were placing cash in the moneybag as frightened customers were looking on, Paul slipped up behind the robber, who was unaware of his presence. Quickly Paul placed the muzzle of his Colt .45 revolver against the robber's head, knocking his hat off, and loudly cocked his gun.

"Take your gun away from the teller's head, mister! Right now, or I'll blow your head off!"

The robber was shocked and frightened. He hastily lowered his weapon.

Paul snatched the gun from the robber's

hand, and while the bank president looked on, Paul cuffed the robber's hands behind his back. Paul grabbed the back of the robber's shirt collar. "Okay, mister. I'm taking you to jail."

"Paul," said Randall Kaylor, "thank you for what you just did."

Paul smiled at him. "You're welcome, sir. His hammer wasn't cocked, so it gave me an edge on him."

The robber licked his lips nervously but said nothing.

David Barrett said with a shaky voice, "I — I want to thank you too, Paul, for saving my life."

"My pleasure, David. Tell you what. I'll be back here at the bank at closing time this afternoon. I want to talk to you."

David nodded. "Fine. I'll look forward to it."

Paul guided the handcuffed robber out the door, holding his gun barrel against his side, and steered him toward the county jail.

At three o'clock that afternoon, Bible in hand, Paul returned to the bank, which was in the process of closing for the day, and found David Barrett balancing his financial work in his teller's cage. When David saw the Bible in Paul's hand, he said, "Looks like I'm going to get a sermon."

Paul smiled. "Well, you might call it that, but after what happened to you today, I don't want to wait until Sunday for you to come to church to hear God's plan of salvation. I want to give it to you right now. Okay?"

David nodded. "As close as I came to getting killed today, I'm ready to listen. I'll be finished here in just a few minutes."

Four minutes later, David led Paul to an empty room to give them some privacy. Paul could plainly see that David was still shaken up.

The two men sat at a table, side by side, and Paul laid his Bible in front of him. As he opened it and began flipping pages, he said, "David, I want to show you about hell first so that you'll see where you are headed at this moment."

David licked his lips nervously and nodded.

Arriving at the passage he wanted, Paul said, "The Bible says over and over that hell is a place of real, literal fire. People who die without Jesus Christ as their Saviour go instantly to hell. Here in Luke chapter 16, the Lord Jesus tells the story of two men who died. One man was saved. The other was lost. Verse 20 here tells us about a beggar named Lazarus. Now look at verses 22–24 and read them to me."

Paul slid the Bible a few inches toward David so he could see it well. David focused on the stated passage. " 'And it came to pass, that the beggar died, and was carried by the angels into Abraham's bosom: the rich man also died, and was buried; and in hell he lift up his eyes, being in torments, and seeth Abraham afar off, and Lazarus in his bosom. And he cried and said, Father Abraham, have mercy on me, and send Lazarus, that he may dip the tip of his finger in water, and cool my tongue; for I am tormented in this flame.' " David looked at Paul. "Jesus did say the rich man was tormented in flame."

"Right," said Paul. "The term 'Abraham's bosom' represents *blessedness after death,* David. What we know as heaven. Understand?"

"Makes sense, since it is the opposite of hell here, and Jesus quoted the man in hell as saying he was tormented in flame."

Paul smiled. "I'm glad you see that. Now, let me show you some more verses on hell." He flipped back to the Old Testament and stopped at Psalm 9. "Now read verse 17 to me."

David set his eyes on the verse. " 'The

wicked shall be turned into hell, and all the nations that forget God.' "

"The 'wicked,' David, is anyone who dies in their sins who has never been forgiven."

David nodded solemnly.

Paul flipped to the book of Revelation and turned to chapter 20. "I could show you plenty more on hell in this Bible, but after I show you one more passage, I want to move on. Here in Revelation we have the horrible scene at the Great White Throne of Judgment, where all the people are brought out of hell to stand before God and have all their sins totally exposed. The saved people will be there to observe it. Read me what it says in verses 14 and 15 about when the judgment is over."

David focused on the verses. " 'And death and hell were cast into the lake of fire. This is the second death. And whosoever was not found written in the book of life was cast into the lake of fire.' "

"So, hell in its final state is called the lake of *what?*"

David grimaced. "Fire."

"Right, and since the saved people — whose names are written in the book of life — are there to look on, it says that those whose names are not in the book of life will be cast into hell in its final state . . . the lake of fire. They will burn there forever. No hope of it ever ending."

David palmed perspiration from his brow. "I — don't want to go there, Paul."

"Good! Now let me show you how to go to heaven instead." While flipping pages in his Bible, he said, "God's only begotten Son died on the cross of Calvary to provide a way for all sinners to be saved, forgiven of their sins, and go to heaven when they die. You *are* a sinner, aren't you?"

David's face flushed. "Yes. I've done plenty of wrong in my life."

"I'm glad you're willing to admit it. Lots of people I've talked to about being saved won't admit any wrongdoing." Paul came to the page he wanted, then placed the Bible in front of David. "This is Romans chapter 3. Read me verse 23, will you?"

" 'For all have sinned, and come short of the glory of God.' "

"Notice it says *all,* David. So all humans — except babies and little children — are guilty sinners before a holy, righteous God."

He nodded. "Yes."

"That includes me, and that includes you."

David nodded again. "I see that."

"But there is a difference between you and me," Paul said. "I am a sinner who has had all of his sins washed away in the blood of Jesus Christ and forgiven. Therefore, when I die, I will go to heaven. If you died this very instant, where would *you* go?"

David's features crimsoned. "I — I would go to hell."

"Right. And you already told me that you don't want to go there."

"That's right!"

Paul turned a couple of pages. "Now read me this verse." He was pointing to Romans 6:23.

David took a deep breath. " 'For the wages of sin is death; but the gift of God is eternal life through Jesus Christ our Lord.' "

"Now, think about it, David. If you get what you earn by sinning against God, it's death, isn't it?"

"Yes."

"That's more than physical death. Even saved people die physically. So if you die without being saved, the wages you receive for a lifetime of sin is to burn forever in the lake of fire."

David nodded. "I understand."

"Now look at Romans 6:23 again. There is not only death mentioned, but *eternal life.* That has to mean forever with God in heaven, doesn't it?"

"It has to."

"All right, now notice the word *gift*. Eternal life can't be earned by good works and religious deeds. It is a gift. If you earn something, it is a wage, right?"

"Uh-huh."

"But if you receive it as a gift, is it earned?"

"Absolutely not."

"Correct. It is by grace. In Ephesians 2:8–9, God says, 'For by grace are ye saved through faith; and that not of yourselves: it is the gift of God: not of works, lest any man should boast.' Salvation, forgiveness of your sins, and a place in heaven forever do not come from human works but by God's grace, which is a gift. Understand?"

"Like never before in my life."

"Good," said Paul. "Now, let me ask you, do you believe that Jesus is the virgin-born Son of God?"

"Yes, I do," David responded without hesitation. "I have never doubted it, since it is such a strong part of the Christmas story I have heard all of my life."

"I'm glad. Now look at Romans 6:23 again. 'But the gift of God is eternal life through Jesus Christ our Lord.' See that? Salvation — eternal life — does not come through anything we can accomplish, like being baptized, taking communion, or saying prayers. When a person does get saved, he or she is commanded in the Word of God to get Scripturally baptized *after* getting saved, but baptism does not save anyone. Salvation only comes through the Lord Jesus Christ. He came into the world by the miraculous virgin birth, lived a perfectly sinless life, and purposely died on the cross of Calvary, shedding His sinless blood for our sins. Do you understand that?"

"Yes. It's making sense to me, Paul."

Paul smiled. "Now let me ask you, did Jesus stay dead after He was crucified and buried?"

"Oh no. He came back to life."

"Right. Now that's the gospel, David. Christ's death, burial, and resurrection. In Mark 1:15, Jesus said, 'Repent ye, and believe the gospel.' Repentance is acknowledging to Him that we are guilty sinners and results in a change of direction. When we repent of our sins, we turn from them unto the living Christ and call on Him to forgive us and to come into our heart and save us because we believe the gospel."

David nodded. "I see."

"Now, let's go back to Romans chapter 3," Paul said, flipping pages. "Look what it says in verse 24. 'Being justified freely by his grace through the redemption that is in

Christ Jesus.' To be justified, David, is to stand before God just as if you had never sinned. Redemption is the same thing as salvation. Please notice that the saved person is justified *freely.* We cannot earn it. It is by grace."

"Yes. I now understand."

"And our redemption — our salvation — is where, David?"

"In Christ Jesus."

"Right. Not in our good works. Not in baptismal water, not in communion elements, nor some mortal religious leader. Just in Jesus Christ. Understand?"

"I sure do."

"Good." Paul flipped some pages. "Now, I want to show you something else." Laying the Bible before David again, he said, "Read me John 1:12. It speaks of receiving Jesus."

David nodded. " 'But as many as received him, to them gave he power to become the sons of God, even to them that believe on his name.' "

"To believe on His name means to believe that Jesus is who the Bible says He is — the Saviour. The name *Jesus* means 'Saviour.' Do you believe on His name? That He is the one and only Saviour?"

David smiled. "Yes."

"All right, then God's Word says right here

262

that if you will receive Jesus, you will become a son of God. Right now you are not a child of God, and only God's children go to heaven when they die. Ephesians 3:17 says, 'That Christ may dwell in your hearts by faith.' You must repent of your sins and receive Jesus into your *heart* to be saved, David. When the Bible speaks of your heart in this context, it's not talking about that muscle that pumps the blood through your body. It's talking about the center of your soul — the very *heart* of your soul."

"That makes sense," said David. "I understand."

Paul looked him in the eye. "Do you want to be saved?"

"I sure do!"

"Okay. Let me show you how." Paul flipped pages again, stopped at Romans chapter 10, and said, "Here. Read me verses 10 and 13."

David set his eyes on verse 10. " 'For with the heart man believeth unto righteousness; and with the mouth confession is made unto salvation.' " Then he looked at verse 13. " 'For whosoever shall call upon the name of the Lord shall be saved.' "

Paul looked at David and saw that his eyes were misty. "When do you want to be saved, David?"

Tears began to spill. "Right now, Paul!"

Paul closed the Bible and put his arm around David's shoulders. "Let's bow our heads, and you call on Jesus. Tell Him you are repenting of your sins, that you want to be forgiven of them, and that you want to be saved, and ask Him to come into your heart and be your Saviour."

When David had finished calling on the Lord for salvation, tears flowing, Paul prayed, thanking the Lord Jesus for saving David, and asked Him to help David to be a good, strong Christian and to use him for His glory.

The following Sunday, David Barrett went to Denver's First Baptist Church and sat in the morning service with Paul Brockman and his family. David walked the aisle at the invitation, testified to the pastor how Paul had led him to the Lord, and was baptized.

The Brockmans invited David for Sunday dinner at their home that afternoon, and while he was there, the rest of the family noticed that David seemed quite attracted to Ginny and that Ginny seemed quite attracted to him also.

Eighteen

John Brockman continued to be invited to churches in many parts of the West to preach. On Monday, April 1, 1895, the chief U.S. marshal received a telegram from Pastor Alex Duffy of the First Baptist Church in Phoenix, Arizona, where he had preached many times over the years. Pastor Duffy asked if Chief Brockman would come and preach for him in the Sunday morning and evening services on the fourteenth of that month.

After going to Denver's Union Station and purchasing train tickets to and from Phoenix, John went to the telegraph office and sent a message to Pastor Duffy, saying he would be glad to come and preach for him and that he would arrive by train on Saturday afternoon so he could spend the evening with Marshal Danford Pierce.

On April 14, John arrived in Phoenix at three o'clock and found both Pastor Duffy and Marshal Pierce there to meet him. After chatting with both men for a while, Pastor Duffy excused himself, saying he would see Chief Brockman at church in the morning.

Marshal Pierce took the chief to his buggy in the railroad station parking lot. As they headed across town in the direction of the Pierce home, Danford asked about John's family.

John told him about Breanna's accident in the hospital and that she was seriously injured but how the Lord had answered prayer and healed her. John then told Pierce the story of how he and Breanna had adopted Meggie and what a blessing she had been to the family ever since.

The marshal turned the buggy onto his property and said, "She sounds like a real sweet girl."

As the buggy pulled to a halt next to a small barn, John replied, "That she is, my friend. That she is."

Danford Pierce stepped out of the buggy, and as John was doing the same, Pierce said, "I want to hear about Ginny and Paul."

John smiled. "I'll tell you about them inside."

Later that evening, after the marshal had prepared supper and the two men had eaten together while talking about work, they went into the parlor. As they sat on overstuffed chairs facing each other, Marshal Pierce said, "All right, Chief, tell me about Ginny and Paul now."

John told him that Ginny was now twenty years old and would graduate from the Denver School of Nursing next month. He added that Ginny would then go to work at Denver's Mile High Hospital.

Pierce smiled. "That's great! Is there a young man in Ginny's life?"

"Ah . . . yes. Ginny recently fell in love with a fine Christian young man who is twenty-two and a member of our church. His name is David Barrett. He's a teller at Denver's First National Bank. He came to Denver from Cheyenne, Wyoming, just over a year ago to take the job in the bank."

Pierce smiled again. "I'm glad to know that Ginny has a fine Christian young man in her life."

John nodded happily. "There's no question that Ginny and David's relationship is getting serious. Breanna and I love David, and so do Paul and Meggie."

"Sounds good."

"It will be a blessing if the Lord has chosen Ginny and David for each other. He and Paul are especially close."

John then told him about Paul being one

of his deputy U.S. marshals, of Paul's protecting David's life during a bank robbery in February, how Paul had led David to the Lord later that very day, and that David had been baptized at First Baptist Church the following Sunday.

"I can see why Paul and David are close."

"They're real buddies, for sure," John said.

"I want to know about Paul becoming one of your deputies. This is great!"

John gave him the details about Paul having worked in his office from the time he turned nineteen and that he had made Paul one of his deputies when he turned twenty-one.

Marshal Pierce grinned. "I have a feeling that Paul is already a topnotch deputy U.S. marshal."

"You're right about that, my friend. Paul has already put a lot of outlaws behind bars. He has also been forced by some gunslingers to draw against them. Paul is really fast and accurate with his gun. And I'll say this. With Paul's office experience and the kind of lawman he is now, he could be heading up a U.S. marshal's office just like you do."

"Wow!" said Pierce. "As young as he is and the relatively brief experience he has under his belt — but because he is your son,

I have no doubt that he could handle the job."

John smiled. "Thanks for the compliment, but even if he wasn't my son, believe me, he could still do it."

"It's good that you have such confidence in your son. I'm sure he deserves it."

"He sure does." John paused and rubbed the back of his neck. "From what I can pick up in the newspapers, the Apaches are giving a lot of trouble to the people of Arizona and to travelers who pass through here on horseback and in wagons."

"They sure are."

John and Danford discussed the fact that the U.S. Army had a great number of soldiers out of Fort Huachuca in Arizona, located a bit south of Tucson, who were setting up in camps along the main east-west road in southern Arizona Territory. They were there to do what they could to protect settlers and travelers from the Apaches.

John and Danford both expressed gladness that at least some of the Apaches who had been placed on reservations by the United States government were no longer going after white people. They would be glad when *all* of the Apaches went off the warpath.

■ ■ ■ ■

The next day, when John Brockman preached a powerful sermon on salvation in the morning service at Phoenix's First Baptist Church, Pastor Alex Duffy and the church members were thrilled to see a good number of visiting adults and young people walk the aisle at the invitation to receive the Lord Jesus Christ as their Saviour. Pastor Duffy was also thrilled to baptize them.

As the pastor dismissed the service, when he was standing in the baptistry, he told the crowd that, as usual, Chief Brockman would be in the vestibule to shake hands with them.

As the crowd filed out the front door, passing through the vestibule to do so, they paused to greet the tall, handsome lawman. Among them were the new converts, who expressed their appreciation for his preaching and let him know they were very glad to be saved.

One family among the new converts especially touched John's heart. They were the last to approach him. Edgar and Celia Martin, who were in their late forties, introduced themselves, then introduced their lovely blond-haired, blue-eyed daughter, Lisa, who was nineteen.

When John shook Lisa's hand, tears welled up in her eyes. "Chief Brockman, thank you so much for making salvation so clear in your sermon. I have never heard it that way before. All I've ever heard about how to get to heaven was that I had to do all kinds of religious things plus lots of good works, and then maybe, if I did enough of them, I would make it to heaven. You made it so clear that salvation is totally in Jesus and is by grace through faith in Him, and Him alone."

Edgar explained to Chief Brockman that today was the first time they had visited this church. They had come this morning because they had heard that the man called the Stranger, who was now chief U.S. marshal of the Western District, was preaching at First Baptist Church that morning.

John's eyebrows arched. "Oh, so you know about me as the Stranger, eh?"

"Yes sir," said Edgar. "I heard much about the Stranger when I was living in Texas many years ago, and when I heard that he was preaching here, I wanted to meet him. And Celia and Lisa wanted to come with me."

All three of the Martins rejoiced that they were now on the way to heaven and that they were planning to become members of Phoenix's First Baptist Church.

Smiling broadly, John said, "I am very glad for you. I wish my family could meet you." He told them about Breanna, Paul, Ginny, and Meggie. Then he bragged a bit, saying that his twenty-two-year-old son, Paul, was the same height as he was — six-feet-five inches — weighed almost the same as him, and that his facial features looked very much like his. He then told the Martins that Paul was one of his deputy U.S. marshals and a tremendous law officer.

Edgar Martin said, "Chief, believe me, Celia, Lisa, and I would like to meet your family."

"I would like that too. But if it doesn't happen here on earth, all three of you will get to meet my family in heaven."

Tears moistened the eyes of Edgar, Celia, and Lisa as they spoke their agreement that they would look forward to that.

Edgar asked, "When are you heading back to Denver, Chief?"

"I'm scheduled to head back tomorrow morning on the nine o'clock train from Phoenix."

Edgar met John's gaze. "Would you be willing to do me a big favor that would cause you to take a later train to Denver tomorrow?"

John replied with a slight frown on his brow. "If it's something very important, I could do that, yes."

"I have a friend who lives some twenty miles south of here," Edgar said, "and he's dying of cancer. His name is Ralph Webb, and he's seventy-two years old. Ralph's doctor made it plain that Ralph will die soon. Now that I'm saved, I want both Ralph and his wife, Laura, to be saved."

John smiled. "I understand that, my friend."

"Could you go to the Webb home in the morning and lead Ralph and his wife to the Lord?" Edgar asked. "I can't go with you because of my job, but I'll draw you a map so you can find their house. You can drive my horse and buggy there, and I'll write a note for you to give to the Webbs, Chief, so they'll talk to you."

John smiled again. "I'll be glad to do it. I'll telegraph my office in Denver and let Paul and the other deputies know what I'm doing. Then I'll catch the first train available after I return from the Webb home."

Edgar thanked the chief for his willingness to do this.

The next morning, Chief Brockman drove the Martin buggy, following the map drawn for him by Edgar. When John handed the note to Laura Webb, she read it, then invited the man with the badge on his chest and a Bible in his hand into their home.

Using his Bible, John had the joy of leading both Ralph and Laura to the Lord. He told them that he would have Pastor Alex Duffy come and visit them so he could help them in their new Christian life. The new converts told him they would welcome Pastor Duffy.

As John was driving Edgar's buggy back to Phoenix, he caught sight of an Indian man lying on the ground some thirty yards from the road. The man's horse was standing over him in the shade of some trees.

John quickly drove the buggy to the spot and pulled rein. Before he even left the driver's seat, he could see that the man, who was obviously an Apache, was breathing but in much pain.

As John knelt beside the man, he figured him to be in his early thirties. "Hello. I am chief United States marshal John Brockman from Denver, Colorado. Do you understand English?"

The Indian managed a slight smile as he looked at the badge on John's chest. "Yes sir. I was raised speaking English as well as Apache. I am Chief Windino. My reserva-

tion is a number of miles west of here. I —
I was riding my horse in this area alone,
after visiting another Apache reservation to
the southeast. I — I hope you understand,
Chief Brockman, that the white man's army
in Arizona allows Indian chiefs to visit other
reservations."

"I have heard that, yes."

Chief Windino licked his dry lips, then
drew a short breath. "I was on my way
home when suddenly a coiled rattlesnake
appeared a few feet from where I am now
lying on the ground. I did not see the snake
at first, but my stallion did and shied away,
trying to escape the snake. I was thrown
from my horse, and when I hit the ground,
the snake lashed at me and bit my upper
left arm. This — this only happened a few
minutes ago."

John saw that Chief Windino had the
snakebite covered with his right hand. "May
I look at the bite?"

The Apache chief nodded and removed
his hand from his arm.

John gazed at the bleeding bite. "Chief, I
must get the poison out of there quickly or
you will die. May I do it?"

Windino looked at him with pleasant, dark
eyes. "Yes. Please help me."

Knowing much about rattlesnake bites,

John used the knife in the scabbard on the Apache chief's waist to make the necessary three-quarter-inch cut across the bite, then sucked the poison out, spitting it and some of the chief's blood in the dirt.

When John finished, he washed his mouth out with water from a canteen in the Martin buggy. He then poured water over the snakebite on Chief Windino's arm, cleaning it out as good as possible.

After this, John tore a portion of cloth from his own shirttail to use as a bandage. He quickly wrapped the cloth around Windino's arm, covering the snakebite.

The Indian chief's face had become pale. Sweat beaded his brow and ran into his eyes, which had a glassy sheen in them.

"Chief Windino, you need medical help as soon as possible. Will you allow me to take you into Phoenix to a doctor?"

Chief Windino hesitated to answer, as he was thinking what his tribe would think of him letting a white doctor treat him. He licked his lips nervously. "I should go to my own medicine man instead."

John understood why the Indian was fearful of having a white doctor treat him. "Chief Windino, I must hurry to save your life. Phoenix has to be closer to us than your reservation. You need help immediately."

Windino closed his eyes briefly, then opened them and slowly nodded.

"Good." John noticed that the man was already beginning to shiver, due to the rattlesnake's poison that had already gone into his body. "I was able to draw most of the poison out, but some of it is in your bloodstream. I will take you to a doctor in Phoenix who will have the proper medicine to give you, and he can stitch up the cut I had to make on your arm."

Tears were in Windino's eyes as he said weakly, "Thank you for saving my life. Most white men would have let me die." He swallowed hard. "Are you sure a white doctor will want to work on an Indian?"

John nodded solemnly. "I assure you, if he shows any hesitancy, I will persuade the doctor to take care of you."

Windino's lips almost made a smile. "You are indeed a fine man, Chief Brockman."

John bent down and picked Chief Windino up into his strong arms, placed him on the right side of the driver's seat of the buggy, then tied the reins of the Indian's horse to the rear of the buggy. Quickly climbing up onto the left side of the driver's seat, John put the Martins' horse to a trot and headed for Phoenix.

Having been to Phoenix several times,

John recalled where there was a doctor's office on Main Street, though he could not remember the doctor's name. When John drove the buggy into town, he spotted the sign in the second block, then recalled the doctor's name when he saw the sign: Dr. Lee Adler.

After parking the buggy at the hitching post in front of the doctor's office, John lifted Chief Windino down from the driver's seat and carried him toward the office door. As he stepped inside, the eyes of the young nurse at the desk widened at the sight before her. She could make out the badge on John's chest, which was just visible above the Indian's legs.

She stood. "What can I do for you, sir?"

"Ma'am, I am chief U.S. marshal John Brockman from Denver. I happened to find this young man, Apache Chief Windino, on the ground a few miles from town." He explained to her about the snakebite and his treatment of it. "I need Dr. Adler to see Chief Windino as quickly as possible."

"Dr. Adler is free right now, Chief Brockman." She headed for a door at the rear of the office. "Follow me."

John was glad to see that the nurse showed no prejudice against the red man. Seconds later, she led them into an examination room where the doctor was preparing the worktable for the next patient.

"Dr. Adler," said the nurse, "this gentleman carrying Apache Chief Windino is chief U.S. marshal John Brockman. Chief Windino has been bitten by a rattlesnake and needs your care."

Dr. Lee Adler, who was in his midfifties, smiled at them. "Of course, Chief Brockman. Please place him right here on this table."

Pleased that the doctor also showed no prejudice against the Indian in his arms, John smiled at him, then carefully laid Windino on the table. John took a couple of steps back and halted where he could watch the doctor go to work on the Apache chief.

"Doctor, do you need my assistance?" the nurse asked.

"No. I'll call you if I do. You can return to the office."

As the nurse passed through the door, Dr. Adler removed the makeshift bandage from Chief Windino's upper left arm and examined the cut.

John spoke up quickly and explained about cutting the snakebite and sucking out the poison.

Dr. Adler nodded as he did a quick but thorough examination of the snakebite. He turned to the chief U.S. marshal. "You indeed saved Chief Windino's life by making the cut on his arm and sucking out the poison. It takes a little time for the thick rattlesnake poison to work its way into the bloodstream, but if you hadn't come along and done what was needed, Chief Windino would be dead by now."

The Apache chief had tears in his eyes once again as he looked at John. "I want to thank you once more, Chief Brockman, for saving my life."

John smiled at him. "I'm just glad I came along when I did."

Dr. Adler went to work and stitched up the snakebite and cut on Windino's left arm. Finally he wrapped a real bandage around it.

John paid the doctor for taking care of Windino. As he walked the Apache chief out of the office, he held onto him tightly so he wouldn't stumble or fall.

When they reached the buggy, John helped Windino climb onto the same spot of the driver's seat as before. Then he climbed onto the seat himself, took the reins in hand, and put the horse and buggy into motion with Windino's horse still tied to the rear. They headed in the direction of the reservation, as directed by Chief Windino.

Nineteen

A few miles from Phoenix, John turned to Windino, who was slightly slumped over on the seat. "I'm interested in how you got to know English so well. Do you mind telling me?"

"Of course not, Chief Brockman," Windino said with a smile. "My mother was a full-blooded Apache, but she had been raised by a white man and his wife right here in Arizona. She had gone to school with white children and learned to speak, read, and write English. She returned to her Apache people when she was eighteen years of age, and a short time later, she married a young man named Hawkuah. My mother's name was Soft Moon. Both of my parents are dead now."

John nodded. "I see."

"I was born almost exactly two years after my parents were married. As I grew up, my mother taught me to speak, read, and write

English. Does that answer your question?"

"It sure does," replied John.

Windino looked at John with appreciative eyes. "Chief Brockman, I want to thank you again for saving my life."

John smiled. "I would do it again if you needed it."

Windino shook his head in wonderment. "You are a very special man."

John let several seconds pass, then looked at the Apache chief. "Do you know who Jesus Christ is?"

"I have heard that Jesus Christ is the virgin-born Son of God."

"Do you believe it?" queried John.

Windino thought on it for a moment, then replied, "I have no reason to doubt it. Certainly, the God who made this world could do that kind of miracle."

"Have you heard about Christ's death, burial, and resurrection?"

"I have heard that He was nailed to a cross made of wood and that He died on that cross. And I have heard that three days later He arose from the dead."

John guided the buggy off to the side of the road and pulled rein. He reached under the seat and lifted his Bible so Windino could see it. "Do you know what this is?"

Windino nodded. "It says Holy Bible on

the cover. You are a Christian, aren't you?"

"I sure am. I want to read to you from this book about Jesus Christ."

Windino nodded but remained silent.

John then told the Apache chief the story of Calvary, pausing often to read Scriptures to him on the subject. Using more Scriptures, John gave Windino the full gospel story, then showed him passages on salvation and the new birth, explaining to him his need to be saved and warning if he did not receive the Lord Jesus Christ as his Saviour, he would go to a never-ending, burning hell when he died.

Windino looked John in the eye. "I mean no disrespect to you or your beliefs, Chief Brockman, but as an Apache chief and the leader of one of the Apache reservations, I must stay with my Apache religion."

John could tell by the look in Windino's dark eyes that he meant what he said. John closed the Bible with a silent prayer that the Lord would use the Scriptures he had given Windino to eventually bring the chief to Himself.

John placed the Bible back beneath the seat. "We will move on then." He put the horse into motion, and they headed on toward Windino's reservation.

Windino was still slumped over on the seat

when the buggy rolled onto the grounds of his well-populated reservation, and Windino showed the chief U.S. marshal where to stop. Many Apache warriors, rifles in hand, surrounded the buggy. A crowd of women, children, and older men gathered around, curious.

Windino raised a hand and spoke to the warriors in the Apache language. Then they lowered their weapons and took a few steps back.

John looked at Windino. "What did you say to them?"

"I told them to keep the peace, that this white man with me saved my life today. I will now tell them what you did to save my life."

John sat in silence, watching the faces of the Apaches surrounding the buggy as their chief spoke to them in their language. The only words John understood were when Windino told the people the name of the white man who saved his life: chief United States marshal John Brockman. When Windino finished, most of the men, all of the women, and all of the children gave a rousing cheer while smiling at John and waving their hands in the air.

John noticed that a number of Apache warriors, who stood back from the rest of the crowd, were scowling at him with hatred in their dark eyes. Keeping his gaze on them, John said from the side of his mouth in a low voice, "Chief Windino, why are those men over there looking at me angrily?"

Windino replied, "There are still warriors on every Apache reservation in Arizona Territory who hate white people and often attack and kill them." Windino took a deep breath. "I am sorry for this, Chief Brockman, but there is nothing I and the other Apaches who do not hate white people can do to change them."

Two warriors who were standing close to the buggy stepped up and lifted their hands toward their chief, ready to help him down.

Windino was about to let them help him from the buggy when John reached down and lifted his Bible from under the seat. "Chief Windino, I would like to give you this Bible. Will you accept it?"

The Apache chief smiled and nodded. "I certainly will."

"Good. Will you do me a favor and read it when you get to feeling better?"

"Yes, I will."

"You no doubt noticed when you were sometimes looking at the pages as I was reading to you that many passages are underlined."

"Yes. I did notice that."

"Of course, I would like it very much if you would read the whole Bible, but the passages underlined in both the Old Testament and the New Testament are about heaven and hell. And in the New Testament, those underlined parts show the gospel of Jesus Christ and God's plan of salvation. Please pay attention especially to those underlined passages in the New Testament. Will you do that?"

Windino smiled. "I will, Chief Brockman, I promise. Thank you for giving the Bible to me. Because you saved my life, I feel I owe it to you to do as you ask me."

John grinned warmly. "Good! I appreciate that. And Chief Windino . . ."

"Yes?"

"I would like to come back someday and see you again. Will you allow me to do that?"

Windino's face was beaming. "You will always be welcome to come and see me!"

"Thank you," John said, his smile broadening. "Well, I must get back to Phoenix so I can catch the next train to Denver."

Windino shook John's right hand white-man style, thanked him once again for saving his life, and allowed the two warriors to help him down while another warrior untied Chief Windino's horse from the rear of the buggy.

Federal marshal Danford Pierce was at his desk in his office when one of his deputies knocked on the door. "Sir, Chief Brockman is here to see you."

"Please send him in," Danford said.

Shortly, John entered the office and greeted Marshal Pierce.

Danford smiled. "John, welcome! It's good to see you. Please come in and have a seat."

As they sat together, John gave him the details about saving the life of Apache Chief Windino. John went on to tell Pierce about taking Windino home to his reservation in the Martin buggy and how most of the Apaches were friendly to him but that some of the warriors scowled hatefully at him. He then shared Chief Windino's comment on the scowls.

Marshal Pierce nodded. "Chief Windino has it right. There are still Apache warriors on all the reservations in Arizona who hate white people and will kill them when they find a way to do it without endangering themselves before the guns of the U.S. Army."

"Not only that," John Brockman said, "but by the reports I'm getting from you and the other federal marshals in Arizona Territory, more and more outlaws are showing up all over this territory."

"That's right, Chief. You know about that eight-man Dub Finch gang down in Texas, don't you?"

John nodded. "They're named after their bloodthirsty leader, they've robbed and killed people in Texas for years, and they've never been caught. What about them?"

"Well, the Dub Finch gang is now reported to be in Arizona."

The chief shook his head. "Oh no! Those seven men that Dub Finch has following him are vicious, heartless killers, just like their leader! I sure hope that gang will be caught and arrested soon, before they rob and kill more people. Do you know where in Arizona they've been seen?"

"Not exactly. All I know is that people in eastern Arizona have reported seeing them. What towns or particular areas the Finch gang has been seen in or around, I do not know."

The chief U.S. marshal rubbed his chin thoughtfully. "Danford, I want you to let me know by telegraph if the Dub Finch bunch brings trouble to Arizona and where they are located."

"I sure will, boss. You can count on that."

"I know I can," John rose to his feet.

"Well, my friend, I've got to get to the railroad station so I can board the next train to Denver."

The two men shook hands; then John left the federal marshal's office and headed down the street toward the railroad station. When he arrived, he bought a ticket for the next train headed for Denver, then went to the Western Union office. He sent a telegram to Paul at the chief marshal's office in Denver to let him know that his train was scheduled to arrive at seven thirty that evening. John had left Blackie at a Denver stable when he caught the train for Phoenix. He told Paul in the telegram that he would head straight for home on Blackie when he arrived in Denver.

Soon John was back at the railroad station and had boarded the coach to which he had been assigned. He made his way to an unoccupied seat near the rear of the coach, eased onto it, and scooted next to the window. Soon the conductor came through, announcing that the train would be leaving on time. A few minutes later, the train chugged out of Phoenix, heading eastward.

Letting out a sigh, John looked out the window, taking in the beauty of the desert country of Arizona. *This has been quite an exciting, exhausting day.* He adjusted his position on the seat and leaned his head on the back to rest. As he closed his eyes, he let his thoughts go to Ralph and Laura Webb. *Two people were snatched from Satan's grasp today. What a tremendous blessing, Lord.*

Then John's thoughts went to the day before and the souls that were saved when he preached at the First Baptist Church of Phoenix. His thoughts centered on the Martin family, and a smile curved his lips. *What a precious family, Lord. Edgar, Celia, and Lisa. And what a joy to see Edgar burdened so quickly after he got saved for his friends Ralph and Laura Webb and their need of Jesus as their Saviour.*

John's mind then went back to the Martins and their lovely daughter, Lisa. *Hmm, what a sweet girl. She's such a pretty little thing and just the right age for my boy.* John shrugged his wide shoulders. *But Lisa lives in Phoenix and Paul lives in Denver, and the two have never even met each other. Well, stranger things have happened, and with our wonderful God in control, there's always a way.*

He decided that rather than tell the whole family, he would tell only Breanna more about Lisa so they could take it to their heavenly Father. *It may not be Your will at all, Lord, but You did let the thought of Lisa being the one for Paul enter my head.*

As the train moved along the tracks heading due east, John continued to meditate on the possibilities ahead in Paul's life.

When the train was about two hours out of Phoenix, a loud male voice from a few rows ahead said, "You shut your mouth! It's none of your business if I've been drinkin' whiskey ever since we left Phoenix!"

Looking forward in the coach, John saw a husky man who appeared to be in his late thirties with a whiskey bottle in his hand, standing some six rows directly ahead of him. The big, angry man was looking at a much smaller and older man across the aisle, who was still seated but was looking up at him.

The husky man didn't notice the conductor entering the coach from its front door as he bellowed at the older man, "One more word outta you about my drinkin', and I'll knock your teeth down your throat!"

"Hey!" The conductor hurried toward the troublemaker. "You sit down and be quiet, mister! I want no more trouble out of you!"

Being under the influence of the whiskey, the husky man made a fist with his free hand and struck the conductor solidly on the jaw, knocking him to the floor of the aisle. Women shrieked and men gasped.

A smaller man about the big man's age left his seat a couple of rows farther up and moved toward him with his fists clenched. "You fool! You'll get thrown off this train for hitting the conductor!"

"Oh, yeah?" countered the big man and punched him hard, also knocking him down.

"You big bully!" cried out an elderly woman from a seat near the big man.

"Shut up, woman!"

By this time, Chief Brockman had stepped up to the drunk man. "*You* shut up, mister! Sit down and stay there!"

Anger flushed the man's face as he caught sight of the badge John wore, and his enormous chest and shoulders seemed to swell even bigger. Rage was mastering him as he said, "You big enough to make me, lawman?" He swung his fist at John's jaw.

John adeptly avoided the punch and smashed a left to the big man's jaw that made his knees wobble. John quickly followed that punch with a powerful right to his left jaw, knocking him down and out.

As the crowd in the coach saw the drunk man lying still, they knew he was unconscious. They cheered the man with the badge on his chest who had put the big bully on the floor, out cold.

By this time, the conductor was on his feet, rubbing his jaw. "Thanks, Chief, for what you just did. I'm going to the engineer right now and have him stop the train." He glanced down at the big unconscious man on the floor, then looked back up at the tall marshal. "Will you help me put him off the train?"

"Sure will," replied John.

It was just after eight thirty that evening when John Brockman arrived at his ranch, and as he neared the house, he saw that the parlor windows were lit up and the front porch lantern was burning. He could make out the Langford horse and buggy to the side. *Bless Whip and Annabeth. They're here to welcome me home. And I'll get a hug from Lizzie too!*

The tall figure of his son moved down the steps of the porch and raised a hand. "Howdy, Papa!"

Pulling rein, John said, "Howdy yourself, son!"

Paul stepped up close as his father dismounted. "I'll take Blackie to the barn. That way, you can go on in and visit with everyone waiting for you."

John smiled. "Okay, son. I appreciate that."

Father and son hugged each other, then Paul turned toward the house, cupped a hand beside his mouth, and called out loudly, "Mama! Papa's here!" Paul took Blackie's reins and headed toward the barn. "See you in a few minutes."

John walked toward the porch steps. At the same time, the door burst open, and the light shone on Breanna as she came onto the porch with all the others following.

John was welcomed home with a hug and a kiss from Breanna, followed by hugs and cheek kisses from Ginny and Meggie and a hug and a cheek kiss from little six-year-old Lizzie Langford as she told her "uncle John" she loved him. He then was hugged and welcomed home by Whip and Annabeth.

The group headed for the parlor, and everyone chose their seats and sat down. Breanna was next to her husband on one of the two-seat overstuffed sofas. Just as everyone was getting settled, Paul came in and eased onto an overstuffed chair facing his parents.

Breanna turned to her husband. "Okay, sweetheart, we're all waiting to hear how the services went at Phoenix's First Baptist Church."

John beamed at her, then at the rest of the group. "Well, I've got some wonderful things to tell you."

Everyone listened closely as John told about the souls that were saved under his preaching on Sunday, especially Edgar and Celia Martin and their lovely nineteen-year-old daughter, Lisa. "Lisa sure is lovely with blond hair and blue eyes, just like my sweetheart, Breanna."

John's eyes kept flicking toward Paul as he was giving this information about Lisa. John explained that the Martins had spent some time talking to him after they were baptized in the morning service.

Breanna was quick to pick up on the way John kept looking at Paul as he was telling about the Martins' daughter and that there was something going on in his mind regarding Lisa. *Guess I'll just have to wait until John is ready to share it with me,* she thought.

John went on to tell them about the joy he had of leading Edgar Martin's friends, Ralph and Laura Webb, to the Lord and about saving the life of Apache Chief Windino. John told them about giving Chief Windino the Bible and that Windino had promised to read it, especially the passages about salvation, heaven, and hell that were already underlined.

Tears misted John's eyes. "I'd appreciate it if everyone would pray that the Lord would use the Scriptures to convict Chief Windino of his lost, hell-bound condition and bring him to salvation."

They all assured him that they would do so.

"Papa, I wish I could meet Chief Windino," Paul said. "He sounds like quite a guy."

"Well, son, maybe someday you and I can go to Arizona and see Chief Windino. He told me I was welcome to come and see him again."

Paul smiled. "Okay. Maybe someday, huh?"

John grinned. "Yes. Maybe someday."

Whip looked at his boss and stood. "Chief, you look pretty tired. Annabeth, Lizzie, and I will go home now so you can hit the bed and get some rest."

The Brockmans walked the Langfords out to their buggy, thanked them for coming, and watched them drive away into the night.

When the family went back into the ranch house, Paul and the girls heard their mother ask their father if he was hungry. When John replied that he was indeed hungry, Paul offered to pray with his sisters as his parents usually did at bedtime so Papa could have something to eat. John and Breanna thanked their son for the offer, then hugged all three and sent them upstairs.

As John and Breanna moved down the hall toward the kitchen, Breanna rubbed John's back. "Honey, I have some leftover roast beef from dinner. I could make you a sandwich and heat up some potato soup. And for dessert there's cherry pie."

John smiled down at her. "Sounds good to me!"

When they entered the kitchen, John took Breanna into his arms. "I missed you so much while I was gone, sweetie. I love you so much."

"I love you too, John!"

They kissed each other soundly; then Breanna went to work to fix her husband's late-night meal.

John enjoyed his supper, right down to the luscious piece of cherry pie and hot coffee. He wiped away the last crumb from his lips with his napkin. "You certainly know how to please a tired, hungry man. Thank you, darlin'."

"My pleasure." Breanna gave him a tender look.

John drank most of the coffee, then set it down. "Honey, I need to share something with you."

"Of course. What is it?"

"Well, this may sound strange, but when I was on the train returning home, the Lord seemed to put something in my mind."

"Oh? What's that?"

"It was concerning Lisa Martin. The thought came to me that Lisa is just the right age for Paul."

Breanna smiled. "I noticed the way you kept looking at Paul as you were telling all of us about Lisa, and I picked up that there was something going on in your mind regarding her. I told myself right then and there that I'd just have to wait until you were ready to share it with me. So you're ready now, aren't you?"

"Yes, my sweet, I am. Lisa could be the very young lady that Paul has been asking the Lord to send into his life to become his wife. She's such a sweet and pretty little thing. I have no doubt that she would be a wonderful wife for our boy."

Breanna's brow furrowed. "Honey, I don't see how this could work out since they live so far apart. Lisa lives in Phoenix, and Paul lives in Denver. How will they ever meet?"

John chuckled. "You know, sweetie, the exact same thought came to me as I pondered the situation. I told myself that with our wonderful God in control, there's always a way."

"I can't argue with that. And since it seems that the Lord put this in your thoughts, I will certainly be in one accord with you in this matter. We know for a fact that with our wonderful God, all things are possible."

John yawned and stretched out his arms. "I'm really tired. Let's get a good night's sleep, but we'll pray about it together first, okay?"

"We sure will!" Breanna rose to her feet.

John stood too, and after Breanna had placed the dishes and coffee cup on the cupboard, they left the kitchen arm in arm and headed up the stairs.

TWENTY

As the days and weeks passed, Deputy Paul Brockman was proving to be even more of a tremendous federal marshal. He was continuously capturing outlaws and outdrawing well-known gunfighters who wanted to gain prestige by challenging and killing the young son of the famous Stranger, whom they felt they could outdraw and kill because of their greater experience.

The gunfighters all knew that by the code of the West, the law couldn't touch a man who challenged another man to a quick-draw shootout, since it was considered a fair fight as long as the one being challenged was wearing a gun belt with a revolver in the holster.

On Wednesday evening, May 8, when the Brockman family sat down at the kitchen table to eat supper, John asked Paul to lead them in prayer to thank the Lord for the food. Once Paul finished praying and the family began devouring the meal, John ran his gaze over their faces. "I told you that I'd let you know when I heard from Marshal Danford Pierce in Phoenix about the Dub Finch gang."

"Did the gang finally start robbing and killing in that part of Arizona, Papa?" asked Paul.

John shook his head. "No. In Marshal Pierce's telegram that I received this morning, he said there has been no sign of the gang since they were last seen in eastern Arizona in mid-April. He figures they must have just been passing through, heading westward."

"Well, from what I know about the Finch gang," said Paul, "they'll be robbing and killing somewhere in the West soon."

"No question about that," John agreed.

Early on Monday afternoon, May 20, Paul Brockman stepped out of the federal building, where he had been in conversation with his father and Whip in his father's office.

As Paul turned right to head up the boardwalk, he caught sight of a man about his age sitting in the saddle of a white horse across the street.

The man was staring straight at him.

Paul moved on up the boardwalk, keeping

the rider on the white horse in mind, and when he was about to cross the street at the corner, he looked back. Both horse and rider were gone. Paul shrugged and moved on.

The next day, when Paul came out of the federal building in the late morning and started down the boardwalk, he saw the man on the white horse again, directly across the street as he was the day before.

The man met Paul's gaze, then looked away. Paul headed on down the boardwalk. When he was three blocks from the federal building, he suddenly noticed the man on the white horse riding past him on the dusty street. He did not turn his head to look at Paul, but Paul could see him flick a glance his way.

Seconds later, the man pulled the horse to a stop some fifty feet ahead of Paul. He slipped from the saddle and quickly tied the reins to a hitching post. Paul kept up his normal pace. The rider, who had a gun belt low on his waist, stepped up onto the boardwalk, and fixed his eyes on Paul as he was drawing closer.

Paul whispered, "Lord, if this is what I think it is, please help me."

The mean-looking man stepped directly in front of Paul, who came to a halt.

"Deputy Paul Brockman, I'm challengin' you to a quick-draw gunfight!"

People nearby on the boardwalk stopped, and others who were coming toward the two men hurried to gather around.

Standing some twenty feet from his challenger, Paul frowned. "What's your name?"

"Jack Chedrick!"

Paul knew the name, and he could tell that many of the people in the gathering crowd knew it also from the way they were looking at each other. Chedrick was a gunslinger well known all over the West. He had taken out many a man who was known to be exceptionally fast on the draw.

"I've heard of you," Paul said levelly, "but I don't want to kill you. Get back on your horse and ride."

"I ain't doin' no such thing, Brockman! Your old man, when he was known as the Stranger, hunted down my father, Harold Chedrick, in Wyomin'. He captured him and took him to the Laramie County sheriff's office in Cheyenne. My father was then hanged by the law."

Paul said with an edge to his voice, "Harold Chedrick would not have been hanged if he didn't deserve it. Only murderers get hanged."

The crowd was getting larger as Jack Che-

303

drick's face flushed with anger. Through clenched teeth, he said, "If the Stranger hadn't hunted my father down and taken him to the sheriff in Cheyenne, he would have lived. Now I'm gonna kill the Stranger's son to pay him back for it. I'm not gonna murder you. I'm gonna give you a fair chance. Let's step into the street, and you go for your gun."

Paul knew that for the crowd's safety, he had to step into the street. As he did, the well-known gunslinger did the same. Standing in the dust, they were still some twenty feet apart, facing each other.

The crowd whispered that Jack Chedrick was *faster* than lightning on the draw. They could see that Chedrick was absolutely confident he could outdraw the Stranger's lawman son.

Paul saw it too and said again, "Get back on your horse and ride."

The challenger shook his head, showing that he felt insulted by the young deputy's command. "I told you to go for your gun!"

"Listen to me, Chedrick. If we draw against each other, I dare not just wound you, because your gun could go off and hit someone in the crowd! I'll have to kill you! Now get back on your horse and ride!"

While the spellbound crowd looked on,

Chedrick's hand suddenly went down for the gun in his holster.

Paul's hand went down much faster, and in a split second, the street thundered with the roar of his weapon.

Chedrick let out a deep, gusty moan as the .45-caliber slug tore into his chest, ripping through his heart. His face paled as the gun slipped from his hand and he fell backward.

Paul's father and Deputy Langford came running up, then skidded to a halt, accompanied by a young man named Harley Thayne.

Holstering his gun, Paul looked at his father. "How did you and Uncle Whip know this shootout was about to take place?"

Before John could answer, one of three men kneeling beside Jack Chedrick called out, "Paul! He's dead! I'm sure he was dead before he hit the ground!"

Paul nodded solemnly at the man.

John laid his hand on Harley's shoulder. "To answer your question, son, Harley was in the crowd and saw that there was going to be a shootout between you and Jack Chedrick, and he ran to the federal building to tell me about it."

John took a deep breath, looked down at the lifeless form of the famous gunfighter, then looked back at Paul. "Thank God, you're all right, son."

"Amen, Chief," said Whip. "Paul, we saw what was happening as we were running down the street. You sure outdrew him. I think you're faster than ever!"

In early September that same year, John Brockman was in his office at the federal building with Whip Langford, discussing the two fierce outlaws that Whip and Timber had pursued and caught the day before. The outlaws were now in the county jail, waiting to go on trial for their crimes.

"Well, Whip, with their criminal records, which include murder, I have no doubt they'll be sentenced to hang."

"I would say so, Chief." Whip was about to say something else when a knock sounded on the office door.

The chief recognized the knock of a new deputy who was manning the desk in the front office. "Yes, Avery. Please come in."

The door swung open, and young Avery Campbell stepped in with a yellow envelope in his hand. "A telegram was just delivered from the Western Union office, Chief. It's from Marshal Danford Pierce in Phoenix, Arizona, whom I understand you know well."

Taking the envelope from the deputy's hand, John said, "I've been expecting to hear from him concerning the Dub Finch gang. I wonder if they've shown up in Arizona again."

Whip's eyes widened. "Maybe Pierce and his men have caught that lowdown gang."

John opened the envelope and took out the telegram. He quickly ran his gaze over the telegraph's lengthy message as the other two men looked on.

When he finished reading it, John looked up at Whip. "Yep. The vile Finch gang is back in Arizona. All eight of them. Marshal Pierce says they're in south-central Arizona and that for the last three days, they've been robbing and killing in towns south of Phoenix, all the way down near Tucson. Marshal Pierce says he's going to lead a group of his deputies on the trail of the gang."

"Good for him. I hope they catch up to them."

"Me too!" Avery responded. "I've heard a lot about how mean, heartless, and bloodthirsty they are."

"You heard right, Avery," John said. "Dub Finch and his gang must be stopped. Marshal Pierce and the deputies will do their best to track them down and bring them to justice."

"Great!" said Whip. "I sure hope they do!"

There was a tap on John's office door. He called out, "Come on in."

The door swung open again, and as Paul entered the office, Deputy Campbell said to John, "Chief, I'd better get back to my desk."

John nodded. "Sure. See you later."

"Papa, do you have any orders for me? Anything you want done right now?"

"Don't think so, son. Why don't you finish up that paperwork I assigned you to do for the governor? I know there's no big hurry, but as long as you don't have any outlaws to chase at the moment, you can go ahead and get it taken care of."

Paul nodded. "Will do, Papa."

"Chief," said Whip, "speaking of paperwork, I need to go catch up on some myself."

"Okay."

Whip patted Paul's shoulder. "See you later, nephew."

"Sure enough, Uncle Whip," Paul said with a hearty grin.

When Whip had gone out and closed the door behind him, Paul said, "Well, I'd better get going too."

"I want to tell you something before you go." John held up the telegram. "I just received this telegram from Marshal Danford Pierce in Phoenix."

Even as the word *Phoenix* came out of his mouth and he was looking at his son, John thought of Lisa Martin. He and Breanna were still praying about the possibility of Paul and Lisa meeting and the Lord causing them to fall in love.

John brought his mind back to the telegram. "Son, Marshal Pierce sent me this telegram to let me know that the Dub Finch gang has once again shown up in Arizona."

Paul's eyebrows arched. "Oh, really?"

"Really," said John. Then he went on to tell Paul the full contents of the telegram.

When Paul had heard it all, he said, "I sure hope Marshal Pierce and his deputies can track that gang down and indeed bring them to justice."

"Me too," said John. Then he smiled. "I just remembered something. When I was in Phoenix with Marshal Pierce in April, I told him that with the way you're being so successful now, wearing a deputy U.S. marshal's badge, that you could run his office and do a great job."

Paul blushed. "Papa, I'm not sure I'm *that* good."

John chuckled. "You sure are!"

There was another knock on the office

door. John looked at the clock on the wall. "That has to be David Barrett. He asked for an appointment now. He said he has something very important to talk to me about."

Paul grinned. "I've got a feeling I know what it's about."

John smiled and headed for the door, saying over his shoulder, "I'm pretty sure I know what it's about too."

Pulling the door open, John smiled at David. "You're right on time for our appointment."

David stepped into the office. "I always try to be on time for appointments."

Paul moved up to David. "Howdy, pal!"

"Howdy yourself!" David chuckled.

"See you when it's time to go home, Papa."

"Sure enough," said John.

Paul exited the office and closed the door behind him. As he headed down the hall, he thought of his sister Ginny, who was now working at Mile High Hospital. *Well, sis, it looks like you and David will soon be setting a wedding date.*

A few more steps and Paul reached the office where the deputies did paperwork. No one else was in the office at the time. Sitting down at his desk, he thought again of Ginny and David. *Dear Lord, I sure will be glad when You bring that Christian young lady into my life whom You have chosen to be my wife.*

In John's office, the chief and a nervous David Barrett sat down together.

"Chief Brockman, I would like the honor of asking Ginny for her hand in marriage. Do I have your blessing?"

John was a bit emotional in a good way. "David, I gladly grant you permission to marry Ginny. Breanna and I think very highly of you, young man. You are God's answer to our prayers for our daughter."

David smiled broadly with a mist of tears in his eyes. "Thank you so much, sir! I love Ginny very much. She and I plan to set a date for the wedding later."

When David left the office, John sat at his desk and looked out the window. As he ran his gaze toward the distant blue sky, he pictured Ginny in his mind. He thought of the day she was born and what a precious, beautiful baby she was. It seemed like only yesterday that she was a baby, and now she was old enough to get married.

"My Ginny will sure be a beautiful bride." John stared at the sky. "And I know she will be a loving and dutiful wife, and without a

doubt, she will be a very good mother someday."

Tears filmed John's eyes as he thought, *It
probably won't be more than a couple of years
after they're married that I'll be known as Chief
Grandpa!*

His mind went to Breanna. *My Ginny was
taught by the best of all. Breanna has been
such an excellent example to our children.*

On Monday, September 16, Chief Brockman received a letter from Leroy Woodard,
one of the deputy marshals under Marshal
Pierce in Phoenix.

Dear Chief Brockman,
Marshal Pierce and a dozen deputies
have caught up with Dub Finch and his
gang. When they were putting them
under arrest, Finch led his gang to draw
their guns and fight back. In the shootout, three of Finch's gang members were
killed and one slightly wounded. Also,
Marshal Pierce was wounded.
Marshal Pierce is now in the Phoenix
hospital, and the doctors are saying that
he will live, but he won't be able to
return to his duties as head U.S. marshal
in Phoenix for several weeks.
Because of what Marshal Pierce knew

about your son's knowledge of running a federal marshal's office and because of how Paul has already proven himself to be an excellent lawman, Marshal Pierce would like your son to come and head up the office in Phoenix in his place until he can return to run the office again.

Outlaw leader Dub Finch and his four remaining gang members have been taken to the federal prison at Yuma, Arizona. A federal judge has sentenced them to be hanged at the prison at sunrise on Monday, October 14. Because of the gang's record of murdering so many people, the judge wants them to do hard labor at the prison while living with the formidable fear that they will each die at the end of a rope.

Sincerely,
Deputy U.S. Marshal Leroy Woodard
Phoenix, Arizona

Chief Brockman waved the letter after he finished reading it. "Well, this is good! Those bloody killers won't be murdering anybody else!"

TWENTY-ONE

After having been sent by his father to take some important papers to Sheriff Walt Carter, Deputy Paul Brockman approached his father's office and tapped on the door.

"Come on in!"

When Paul entered the office, he saw his father sitting at his desk with a letter in his hand. "Papa, Sheriff Carter said to thank you for those papers. They will help him a great deal."

John smiled. "I'm glad. Sit down, son. I have something here to show you."

Paul eased onto one of the two wooden chairs in front of the chief's desk and eyed the letter his father was holding. "Who's that letter from?"

"Deputy U.S. marshal Leroy Woodard in Phoenix." John extended the letter across the desk to Paul. "I want you to read it."

Paul took the letter and pored over it. Overwhelmed by what he read, Paul said,

"Well, I'm plenty glad that Dub Finch and the four remaining gang members are now in Yuma Prison facing the gallows. But I'm sure sorry that Marshal Pierce was wounded. I'm glad he's going to be all right, though."

"Me too," John said. "Ah . . . what about the rest of the letter?"

"Well, I'm very honored that Marshal Pierce wants me to come to Phoenix and head up his office for him until he's well enough to return. Is it all right with you?"

John smiled. "It is definitely all right with me. I am so proud that Marshal Pierce wants my son to fill in for him."

Touched deeply by his father's words, Paul rose from the chair, rounded the desk, bent down, and gave his father a great big hug.

That evening when John and Paul arrived home, Breanna and the girls welcomed them gladly.

After Ginny hugged her father, she looked up into his eyes. "Papa, I've already thanked you dozens of times for letting David and me get engaged, but I want to thank you once more. David and I are so in love."

As Ginny let go of him, John took hold of her left hand and eyed the engagement ring on her finger. "It still seems like you're just a baby, honey. But I guess if you were, that ring would fall off, wouldn't it?"

Ginny giggled. "It sure would!"

"No date set yet for the wedding, though?"

"Not yet, Papa. We're still praying about that."

John nodded. "All right." He reached into his shirt pocket, pulled out an envelope, and said to Breanna and the girls, "I received a letter today from deputy U.S. marshal Leroy Woodard in Phoenix. Let me read it to you."

When John finished reading the letter, Breanna was joined by Ginny and Meggie in telling Paul how proud they were that Marshal Pierce wanted him to temporarily head up his office in Phoenix.

Not wanting her family to know just how reticent she was about Paul's new assignment, Breanna pasted a happy smile on her lips and joined her daughters in hugging Paul, adding that they would miss him while he was gone.

Paul had his arms around all three. "I will miss you all too. I'll sure need your prayers as I become the temporary boss at Marshal Pierce's office."

They all assured him they would pray; then John led the family in prayer about it.

That night after Paul, Ginny, and Meggie

had gone to their separate rooms, John and Breanna entered their own room. While John was getting ready for bed, Breanna got into her nightclothes, then sat in front of her dressing table. One by one she removed the pins from her thick, blond hair, and the luxurious mass descended down her back.

Picking up her hairbrush, she slowly pulled it through her hair, staring off into space with her thoughts on Paul. At one point, she didn't even realize she had stopped brushing her hair and the hand holding the brush was dangling in the air.

Stepping up behind her, John took the brush from her hand. "Here, honey, let me do that for you."

Breanna looked at her husband in the mirror and smiled at him. "Thank you."

"What's troubling you, sweetheart?" John began brushing her hair.

The smile slipped from her face, and tears spilled down her cheeks.

John laid the hairbrush on the dressing table, placed his hands on her shoulders, and gently squeezed them, never taking his eyes from her image in the mirror. "Honey, what is it? What's bothering you?"

Breanna turned on the chair and rose to her feet. John let go of her shoulders in the process, and when she was facing him, John placed his hands on her cheeks, using his thumbs to wipe away the tears. "Come on, my sweet. What is it?"

Breanna sniffed. "It's Paul, darling. You know as well as I do that outlaws make the lawmen leaders targets more than anyone else who wears a badge. Think of all the years you've had to live with this."

"Oh, it's Paul's temporary position as head of the federal marshal's office in Phoenix that's bothering you."

Breanna nodded, more tears surfacing. Her voice barely above a whisper, she said, "I know I shouldn't worry about Paul. Worry is a sin. I know I should trust the Lord more, but it is so frightening to see our son being put in this dangerous position."

"Honey, I know that every day you pray for me in my position of chief U.S. marshal here in Denver as I have to face so much evil in this world. Why is it more difficult to do the same with our son as he takes on the temporary job in Phoenix?"

Breanna smiled slightly and tried to explain her feelings. "It's because I carried him beneath my heart for nine long months. I became accustomed to his every little movement, and in giving birth to him, my heart was enlarged to make room for my love for him. If necessary, I would gladly lay down my life for him. Nothing can compare with a mother's love for her children. Does that make sense, John darling?"

He thumbed away more tears from her cheeks. "Of course it makes sense, sweetheart. I can never grasp the love of a mother, but as Paul's father, I know I very deeply love him and how concerned I am for him. And if necessary I too would lay down my life for him in a heartbeat. But being a lawman has been our son's dream for many years, and I cannot come between him and his dream. He is positive that God wants him to be a lawman to serve, protect, and help others."

Breanna nodded.

John went on. "It would break Paul's heart if he knew the agony that this is causing you. He wants to make this world a better place to live in. In a way, it's his calling, sweetheart. Can you understand what I'm saying?"

"Oh yes, darling. Please forgive me for being so selfish and only thinking of my feelings in this matter. Above all, I want our son to be in the center of God's will, for only there will he truly be happy and fulfilled. I must trust the Lord to take care of our son, just as I trust Him to take care of my husband. Thank you for helping me to see it more clearly."

Breanna placed her arms around her husband's neck and rested her head on his chest, hearing the steady beat of his heart. Silently she thanked her heavenly Father for John and for the way he was always watching over her, as a husband was supposed to do.

John encircled her in his strong arms. "I'm glad I could help you, sweetheart. Anytime you need my help, I'm always here for you."

Breanna's mind went to Philippians 4:7, and the "peace of God, which passeth all understanding" lodged in her heart.

John planted a tender kiss on his wife's lips, then released her from his arms. Breanna let go of John's neck and looked into his eyes. "There's something I want to ask you."

John nodded. "Mm-hmm?"

"An idea came to my mind when Paul made it clear that he was going to Phoenix to help Marshal Pierce. I thought we should tell him to look up the Martins while he's in Phoenix. You know . . . so he could meet Lisa, and ah . . . they could fall in love. Should we do that?"

John smiled down at her. "You know, honey, the same idea crossed my mind.

However, the more I thought about it, the more I realized that it would be best if we just leave it up to the Lord. If Lisa is the one He has chosen for Paul, He can cause them to cross paths when they're both in Phoenix. I figure Paul will attend First Baptist Church while he's there. So the Lord can sure bring them together if it's His will, as we feel that it is."

Breanna's eyes were shining. "Yes! I like it! We will simply leave it to the Lord to make it happen."

Early the next morning, Paul went to the railroad station in Denver and bought a train ticket for that very day to travel to Phoenix. Next he went to the Western Union office and sent a telegram to Deputy Woodard, advising him that he would arrive in Phoenix by train at seven thirty that evening.

Later that morning, Paul's entire family, including Uncle Matthew and Aunt Dottie, plus Pastor and Mary Bayless, and Whip, Annabeth, and Lizzie Langford, were at the railroad station to see him off. They were gathered on the platform, right next to the train Paul would be boarding. People passed by them, looking on curiously at the large group.

With Paul's parents standing close by, his sisters clung to him as Pastor Bayless led them in praying for Paul in his new temporary responsibility as head of the U.S. marshal's office in Phoenix. John kept a close eye on Breanna and saw that she was holding up well. He prayed silently, thanking the Lord for sustaining her.

When Paul had hugged everyone, he went once again to his mother. "Just have to hug my mama one more time."

Breanna smiled. Then in her heart calling on the Lord for strength, she wrapped her arms around this stalwart son of hers, who was so much like his father, and whispered in his ear, "Go with God, my son. I know He will always be near to you."

Paul tenderly kissed his mother's cheek. "I know this is what the Lord wants me to do, Mama. Don't be afraid for me. The Lord will take care of me."

"I won't be afraid, Paul. You couldn't be in better hands."

The train conductor's strong voice made the last call for all passengers to board the train.

Breanna raised up on her tiptoes and planted a soft kiss on Paul's cheek. "Better hurry now. You don't want the train to leave without you. I love you."

"I love you too, Mama." Paul waved at his father, his sisters, and the others, and he hurried to the railroad coach to which he had been assigned and boarded the train.

Seconds later, Paul appeared at a window as he sat down. When he smiled and waved to the group, they all smiled and waved back. Moments later, the engine chugged, throwing billows of black smoke toward the sky, and pulled away from the station. As the train vanished from sight, silent tears glided down Breanna's cheeks, but God's grace reigned in her heart.

When Paul arrived at the Phoenix railroad station and stepped off the train, he spotted three men in federal deputy marshal uniforms in the crowd, moving toward him.

The three lawmen drew up, and one of them extended his hand. "I know you're deputy U.S. marshal Paul Brockman because Marshal Pierce told me you look a whole lot like your father."

As they shook hands, Paul smiled. "I've been told that a few thousand times."

Grinning while still gripping Paul's hand, the federal lawman said, "I'm Deputy Leroy Woodard."

Paul tightened his grip. "I read the telegram you sent to my father. Glad to meet you."

Woodard then introduced Paul to Deputies Mack Holman and Dan Slater. After Paul had shaken hands with each of them, Deputy Woodard said to Paul, "We've rented an apartment for you, just a block from the office." And they headed that way.

The next morning, Deputy Woodard introduced Paul to more deputies, then showed him around the office, filling him in on the basics of how things were done there. Paul told him it was exactly as things were done at his father's office, so he would be able to handle it correctly.

Deputy Woodard then took Paul to the hospital, explaining that Marshal Pierce wanted to see him.

When they stepped into the hospital room that Danford Pierce occupied, the marshal was lying flat on his back in the bed. A big smile curved his lips as he looked up at Paul. "My, oh my! You've really grown up since we last saw each other. And I do mean *up!* You're as tall as your father, aren't you?"

"Yes sir. Six feet five inches."

"And, boy, do you ever look like him!"

Paul grinned. "Yes sir."

Deputy Woodard stood by as his boss and Paul Brockman talked about Paul's duties.

Finally they were finished. "Thanks for coming, Paul," Marshal Pierce said. "I know you can handle the job."

As the week went by, Paul demonstrated to Deputy Woodard and all the other deputies that he indeed could run the office as well as handle outlaws that caused trouble in Phoenix.

On the following Sunday, September 22, Paul Brockman was out of town with two other deputies, trailing three outlaws who had robbed a stagecoach the day before. Paul had planned to attend First Baptist Church that day.

At the First Baptist Church of Phoenix that morning, Pastor Alex Duffy announced from the pulpit that the Edgar Martin family would soon be leaving Phoenix for San Diego, California. He explained that Edgar had been offered a good job there by a friend whose business was doing well. The Martins would be buying a covered wagon and planned to hook up with one of the wagon trains heading westward across Arizona to California.

After the service, many of the church members approached Edgar, Celia, and Lisa and told them that they would miss them when they moved to San Diego.

Paul's work at the federal marshal's office kept him from being able to attend the midweek service at First Baptist Church on the following Wednesday night. On Sunday, September 29, once again, he was in pursuit of outlaws with other deputies, and they did not catch them until nearly midnight.

On Wednesday morning, October 2, the Martin family joined up with a small wagon train of only six wagons, which had camped just outside of Phoenix the night before, and were on their way to southern California.

Later that morning, a telegram came to the U.S. marshal's office in Phoenix from George Henderson, the warden of the federal prison at Yuma. The deputy on duty in the front office brought the telegram to Paul to read.

When the deputy left to return to the front desk, Paul sat at Pierce's desk, opened the envelope, and read the telegram. All five of the Dub Finch gang had escaped from Yuma Prison the day before, taking two guards with them as hostages and threatening to kill the guards if anyone followed them. The names of the four gang members with Dub Finch were Jack Devlin, Curly Bender, Buck Gentry, and Kurt Jagger.

The dead bodies of both guards had been

found early that morning, lying near the road, despite the fact that no one from the prison had followed them. Warden Henderson thought the vile Finch gang may be headed eastward across Arizona and wanted to let Marshal Danford Pierce know about it.

Paul left Pierce's office and shared the message of the telegram with the deputies in the front office. He told them they would need to let all the deputies know the news so they could be on guard in case the Finch gang showed up in or near Phoenix. Everyone hated the thought of Finch and his gang coming their way.

Paul was about to go back to Pierce's office when he and the other deputies saw a man enter the building. Paul recognized him instantly. He headed toward the man, and as Pastor Alex Duffy spotted him, he said, "Aha! Deputy Paul Brockman! You've grown up since I saw you last, but you sure do look like your father!"

As they shook hands, Paul said, "It sure is good to see you again, Pastor Duffy. I've been planning to come to church, but it's been one thing after another since I got here, keeping me busy when your doors are open."

Pastor Duffy smiled. "I understand, Paul.

I'm sure you'll be at First Baptist as soon as it's possible."

"You can count on that."

The pastor said, "You'll be writing to your parents while you're here, won't you?"

"Of course." Paul nodded.

"Well, I thought your father might like to know that one of the families who were saved when he preached here last April is moving to San Diego, California — the Martin family. So Edgar, his wife, Celia, and their daughter, Lisa, are traveling there right now in a wagon train. Please tell your father what I said. Okay?"

"Sure. I remember Papa telling our family about the Martins. He will be glad to hear that they were good members here."

Pastor Duffy patted Paul's arm. "Well, I've got to go. See you at First Baptist whenever you can come."

"You sure will," Paul replied, "as soon as possible."

Early on Friday morning, October 4, just a day after Paul turned twenty-two, Paul was sitting at Marshal Pierce's desk, having arrived only a few minutes earlier, when a deputy ushered two men into the office. They introduced themselves as Lawrence Citron and Marcus Rusk, who were residents in Phoenix.

Lawrence cleared his throat and began to speak. "Marcus and I have been in western Arizona for several days. And while we were heading home yesterday on the road that leads to Yuma, some soldiers from Fort Huachuca told us that the five-man Dub Finch gang escaped from the Yuma Prison on Tuesday and that they were headed eastward."

Marcus continued the story. "When we stopped last night near the road to make camp, we happened to see a campfire several yards farther down the road. Lawrence counted five men around the fire."

Lawrence nodded. "That's right. And we sneaked up close in the dark and heard one of the men call their leader Dub. The five of them were talking about their escape from Yuma Prison, saying that they were going to stop in Phoenix tomorrow, rob the Phoenix National Bank, and then head for Mexico."

They had Paul's undivided attention. Lawrence Citron and Marcus Rusk told him that they quickly went to their horses, saddled up, and galloped toward Phoenix. They'd just arrived, so it would be later that the gang would hit the Phoenix National Bank.

With this information, Paul gathered four

of the deputy U.S. marshals and six soldiers from Fort Huachuca who were in town. He told them what he had learned from Phoenix citizens Citron and Rusk about the planned holdup of the Phoenix National Bank. Paul's plan was for the four deputies to hurry home and put on civilian clothes so they could pose as customers in the bank. They would have revolvers hidden under their jackets or suit coats. After Paul finished laying out the plan, the four deputies hurried home, then returned quickly, dressed and armed as planned.

Forty minutes before the bank's opening time, Paul took the ten men to the bank. Flashing his badge at the locked glass front door, Paul quickly gained the attention of one of the vice presidents. When the man opened the door, Paul told him why he, the deputies, and the soldiers were there. They were quickly taken to bank president Harry Miller's office. Paul laid out the plan to Miller, and he agreed with it.

"I'll put two of my older male employees who have been with the bank for a long time on the bench just outside the front door," Harry said. "They can appear to be resting for a while, since folks often sit there. Then they can warn anyone about to enter the bank and send them away."

Paul and his men liked the president's plan. The rest of the employees were told of the pending robbery and of the plan, and though they were nervous about what was going to happen, they were ready to duck and hide when the lawmen and the soldiers aimed their guns at the robbers.

TWENTY-TWO

The Phoenix National Bank opened at nine thirty as usual, with the two silver-haired bank employees sitting on the bench just outside the front door.

Some twenty-five minutes after the bank had opened, the two men on the bench recognized Dub Finch — whose photograph they had seen in newspapers — as he and his four gang members approached the building.

Dub was a muscular, thick-bodied man of forty-five. His ebony eyes carried a calculating and greedy look to them. His homely face was rough-whittled from the timber of trouble he had made for himself in life, and one glance at his features made it clear that he could be plenty mean.

From the hairy reaches of Finch's stocky neck to the crown of his large head, his skin was dark, like burnt oak. His five-foot-eleven-inch frame weighed better than two-hundred-and-sixty pounds, with massive bones that seemed too thick to ever be broken. His shoulders were exceptionally broad, his deep chest and muscular tree-trunk upper arms made men eye him with awe.

When Finch and his men entered the bank, they sensed nothing out of order as they moved up to the tellers' counter, where four well-dressed men were doing business.

As they whipped out their guns, Dub Finch shouted, "This is a holdup!"

Suddenly, deputy U.S. marshal Paul Brockman and six soldiers in army uniforms rose from behind the tellers' counter with their cocked guns pointed directly at the robbers at the same time that the tellers swiftly ducked down and the other bank employees and officers ducked behind their desks.

Aiming his own gun directly at Finch's big face, Paul shouted, "Drop your guns, every one of you, and get your hands in the air — or else!"

The five stunned escaped convicts and robbers, realizing they were outnumbered, looked at each other wide eyed. They were stunned even more when the four customers turned out to be deputies dressed as civilians who whipped out their guns and cocked them.

Paralyzed by the horror of their helpless situation and with their hair bristling coldly at the napes of their necks, the four men with Finch looked at their leader. Finch swallowed hard, dropped his gun on the floor, and raised his hands over his head. He said to his men, "Do the same. We haven't got a chance."

As the guns clattered to the floor and the other four robbers raised their hands over their heads, the bank officers and employees looked on with smiles as Paul Brockman and his four deputies handcuffed the robbers and, along with the soldiers, guided them at gunpoint out the door.

Bank president Harry Miller followed them out the door. "Thank you so much, Marshal Brockman, deputies, and soldiers. Your heroic actions today prevented bloodshed and robbery." Harry turned to his two older employees still sitting on the bench. "And thank you, men, for your help. You can come on back into the bank now."

When the bankers had gone back inside, Paul thanked the soldiers for their help. Then he and his deputies, along with the soldiers, took the Dub Finch gang to the Maricopa County jail in Phoenix and had the sheriff lock them up.

Jack Devlin was locked in a cell with Dub Finch, while Curly Bender, Buck Gentry, and Kurt Jagger were locked in an adjacent cell. As Paul stood in front of the two cell doors with his deputies and the soldiers, he looked at the outlaws and said, "You will be taken back to the Yuma Prison, where this time you will hang."

All five gang members glared at Paul through the bars of their cell doors with hatred in their eyes, and Paul knew they would like to kill him.

When Paul returned to his office with the soldiers and deputies, one of his men asked, "Marshal Brockman, how do you plan to get those five gang members back to the prison?"

"I'm not sure at the moment, but I'll figure out a way to do it."

One of the solders spoke up. "Marshal Brockman, we would escort you and the gang all the way to Yuma, but right now, the army here in Arizona is just too busy handling Indian troubles all over the territory. We simply don't have the time to make the nearly two-hundred-mile trip from Phoenix to Yuma."

Deputy Leroy Woodard said to Paul, "If we had enough men to help you take Finch and his pals back to the Yuma Prison, we would do it, but we need every deputy here at the office to handle other outlaws."

Paul nodded. "I understand, Leroy. I'll work out some way to get the Finch gang to Yuma; then I'll let you know what it is."

With that, Paul went to Marshal Pierce's office, closed the door, and sat at the desk. While pondering the problem, his mind suddenly went back to the iron wagon he'd seen at Fort Logan. He snapped his fingers. "That's it!"

Going to the outer office, Paul told the deputy at the desk that he would be back shortly. He had some important business to take care of.

As Paul hurried along the boardwalk of Phoenix's main thoroughfare, he headed toward a wagon builder's shop that he had noticed several times. He wanted to see if the wagon builder could put an iron cage on a wagon made of iron. His plan was to lock the five outlaws in the cage and drive the wagon to Yuma Prison himself.

As he drew up to the shop, Paul noticed on the sign that the wagon builder's name was Max Younker. He also noticed that Younker had several husky draft horses in a corral next to the shop. When Paul stepped inside, Max was at a worktable, repairing a wagon wheel.

Max smiled at the man with the badge on his chest. "Hello, Marshal. You're the one taking Marshal Pierce's place, aren't you?"

Paul smiled. "Yes. My name is Paul Brockman."

"What can I do for you?"

Paul told the wagon builder what he needed and why.

"I commended you, Marshal, for what you're doing, but it would take me several days to build the iron cage. Up till now, I've only made wooden wagons."

Paul rubbed his chin. "I really would like a wagon totally made of iron. This gang of killers I'll be hauling to Yuma Prison are dangerous men."

"I understand. Tell you what," Max Younker said. "I know an elderly ex-soldier at the west edge of town who has one of those army wagons made completely of iron and with just such an iron cage. He's been trying to sell it. His name is Clarence Lewis, but everybody calls him Sarge because he was a sergeant in the army for many years."

"Sounds good! You tell me exactly how to find Sarge Lewis, and I'll see how much he wants for the iron wagon."

"Please let me know if you're able to obtain the wagon."

"Sure will," said Paul.

Max then gave Paul the directions to Sarge Lewis's old cabin. Paul went immediately to the location and there saw the iron wagon next to the cabin. It was exactly like the Fort Logan iron wagon, including the measurements of the wagon bed and the cage.

Paul knocked on the door, and after a few seconds, he heard the slow shuffle of feet inside. When the door opened, a silver-haired old man with thick glasses looked at him. "What can I do for you, Marshal?" he asked in a weak voice.

Paul told Sarge Lewis who he was, then explained why he needed Sarge's iron wagon with the cage on it.

"I sure am glad that the Dub Finch gang has been caught and will be taken back to Yuma Prison to be hanged."

Paul nodded. "How much do you want for the iron wagon?"

Sarge smiled. "Because of what you will be using the wagon for, I'll give it to you for free."

Paul's eyebrows arched. "Really, sir?"

The old man nodded. "Really, son. You take it and keep it."

Paul thanked him, then said, "I will hurry back to Max Younker's shop to see how much he'll charge me to use two of his draft horses to pull the iron wagon to Yuma. I'll be back as soon as I get the horses."

The old man smiled. "I'll be right here, son."

When Paul arrived at Max's shop, he told the wagon builder that Sarge Lewis had given him the wagon for free. Max said, "Because of what you are doing, Marshal Brockman, I will give you two of my huskiest draft horses for free."

"That's very generous of you, Mr. Younker."

"No doubt you will want to take the iron wagon home to Denver."

Paul nodded. "Since Sarge Lewis gave it to me, I'd sure like to."

"Well, you sure can't pull it to Denver yourself. You'll still need those horses to get the wagon home."

Paul thanked Max for his generosity. Then he led the horses in their harness to the old cabin and hitched them to the iron wagon. Sarge Lewis looked on, smiling. Paul thanked him again for the wagon and drove back to the office. He found that the six soldiers were still there with the deputies.

Paul showed them the iron wagon with the iron cage built into its bed and the two strong horses, explaining how he got them. "Fellas, since no soldiers or deputies are available to go with me, I'll just have to drive the wagon to Yuma myself, with the Dub Finch gang locked up in the cage."

"Marshal Brockman, some of us have recently been in western Arizona. I need to warn you of the danger you're going to face on the trip to Yuma. Many Apaches who hate white people are running wild in that part of Arizona. It's bad enough anywhere in the territory, but it's worse in that direction. At least there are a few U.S. Army camps set up along the way to Yuma to protect white travelers crossing Arizona, but the camps are many miles apart and can only protect a few of those travelers."

Paul nodded. "I appreciate your bringing this up, Sergeant. I have known about the army camps for a little while, and of course I know about the Apache trouble in western Arizona. As a born-again Christian, I will simply trust the Lord to watch over me as I make this trip."

The soldiers and the deputies commended Paul for his courage.

Paul turned to the deputies. "I am going to the hospital now to inform Marshal Pierce of my plans." He looked at Deputy Woodard. "Leroy, I'm going to recommend that Marshal Pierce put you in charge of the office while I head to Yuma."

"Marshal Brockman, I will gladly do it if Marshal Pierce assigns the job to me."

Paul smiled at him. "I was quite sure you would accept the responsibility."

Later that day, Paul arrived at the hospital and entered Marshal Pierce's room. He found the marshal sitting up in the bed, braced by pillows at his back. "Wow!" Paul exclaimed. "You're looking much better!"

"Yes," said Pierce. "Praise the Lord, I am indeed feeling better. My doctor told me this morning that since it has been almost a month since I was shot and I am doing so well, he's going to let me go home in another day or two."

Paul told him of his plans, then suggested Deputy Woodard as his choice to head up Marshal Pierce's office while he made the Yuma trip. Marshal Pierce wholeheartedly agreed.

"Paul, when you arrive in Yuma, will you send a telegram to Deputy Woodard at my office so he'll know you made it all right? And also let him know approximately when you will return to Phoenix."

Paul nodded. "I sure will, sir."

Late that afternoon, Paul sent a telegram to his father at the federal office in Denver. Paul explained about the Dub Finch gang's escape from Yuma Prison, how he and the other ten men captured them, and that he was going to take the five-man gang back to Yuma Prison in an iron wagon with an iron cage, just like the one they saw together at Fort Logan. He asked for prayer, as he would be driving the iron wagon alone all the way to Yuma.

That evening, John Brockman gathered his family in the parlor of their ranch house, along with Ginny's fiancé, David Barrett. Whip, Annabeth, and Lizzie Langford and Pastor Robert and Mary Bayless also joined them.

As John solemnly read Paul's telegram to them, a sliver of well-known fear ran down Breanna's spine. *This is Satan's work,* she thought. *He wants me to doubt my Lord and discourage me. Well, it isn't going to work, devil! I depend on my Saviour to protect Paul, and all of the promises of God in Him are yea and amen. Get thee behind me, Satan!*

When John finished reading Paul's telegram aloud, they had a special prayer meeting for Paul, then and there.

When the guests were about to leave the Brockman home, David and Ginny approached Pastor Bayless, and David said, "Pastor, Ginny and I will be ready to set our wedding date soon, and we will come to your office to see if the date we choose is all right with you."

Pastor Bayless smiled. "I will look forward to meeting with you when you are ready to set the date."

In Phoenix the next morning, Paul Brockman entered the county jail, and while the sheriff and six deputies looked on, Paul handcuffed Finch, Devlin, Bender, Gentry, and Jagger with their hands in front of them.

Finch and the others glared at Paul as he led them outside the jail, accompanied by the sheriff and the six deputies. When the outlaws saw the iron cage built into the bed of the wagon, their stomachs turned over within them.

Paul ordered the outlaws to climb into the cage through the opening at the rear of the wagon, and they stiffened with rebellion, but the angry looks on the faces of the six armed deputies and the sheriff were enough to make them obey. The iron door of the cage was closed by Paul, who used a sturdy padlock to secure it. He slipped the key into his pocket.

Paul put water and food in the boxlike iron sections alongside the wagon bed — some for the prisoners and some for himself and the horses.

The sheriff and the deputies wished Paul the best and watched as he drove the iron wagon away from the jail.

The wagon left Phoenix behind, and Paul was moving the horses at a mild trot along the dusty road, heading due west. The five outlaws sat on the hard, uncomfortable floor of the iron cage and looked angrily at Paul's back through the small squared openings between the iron bands that made up the cage.

Dub Finch scooted closer to the wagon seat where Paul held the reins and continued to glare at him, his heavy lips set in a thin, bitter line. The agitation on his face preceded a convulsive wrestling of his big, thick shoulders as he growled, "You ain't never gonna get us to that prison at Yuma, Brockman! We're gonna find a way to get loose and kill you before we even get near there!"

Paul would not give Finch the satisfaction on responding to him. He simply kept his eyes on the road with every intention of delivering the gang to the prison.

After a couple of minutes, Finch shouted, "Hey, dumb head! Did you hear what I said?"

"Yeah, I heard you." Paul didn't turn

around. "You'd better just keep your mouth shut and save your breath."

Finch looked around at his men, who were obviously feeling hopeless about escaping the hangman's rope. Biting his lower lip, Finch took in the rolling desert, its rocks and cacti.

Paul figured that by driving at least ten hours a day, they would arrive in Yuma, which was some one-hundred-and-eighty-two miles from Phoenix, within two days.

The iron wagon rolled along the desert road, and soon the five outlaws in the cage were lying on its hard floor, snoozing. As Paul held the reins, he happened to look down at a large, flat rock alongside the road, and he saw a huge lizard sunning itself on the rock.

Paul's thoughts went to his prayers offered to the Lord in the past months concerning the future wife God had chosen for him. He wondered when "Miss Right" would come into his life. *Lord, I sure would appreciate it if You would send her to me soon. She's out there somewhere, I know that. And thank You that one day, by Your leadership, she will come into my life.*

Early on Sunday morning, October 6, the wagon train that Edgar, Celia, and Lisa

Martin were traveling with was moving westward on the road that led to Yuma and on to San Diego. The Martins' covered wagon happened to be the last in the row of six covered wagons.

It was early enough that morning that a rosy freshness of the sunrise still slanted along the bronze slopes of the desert, and here and there blossoms of ocotillo shone red. Long shadows of the tall cacti made their appearance on the sandy ground.

As the Martin wagon followed the others, lovely Lisa was in her bed asleep in the rear of the wagon.

Celia, who was sitting on the driver's seat next to her husband, turned to him. "I sure wish we could be in church this morning. I miss it."

"Me too, honey," Edgar said, gripping the reins. "But at least we've been told of some good churches in San Diego. I can hardly wait to get there and find the one that the Lord will lead us to join."

"Me too!" Celia smiled broadly.

Suddenly, there was a wild, whooping sound off to the left, along with the rumble of pounding hoofs. Edgar's head whipped that direction and gasped. "Celia, it's Indians! Apaches! They're coming at us on galloping horses — and they're lifting their rifles!"

Celia looked past her husband, who was quickly picking up his rifle, and saw the attacking Indians. With her heart pounding, she looked into the covered part of the wagon and saw that Lisa was still asleep.

The Apaches began firing their rifles as they drew closer, and as Edgar told Celia to duck down low, he fired in return, as did the other men in the wagon train.

Bullets were striking the canvas of the Martin wagon, and Celia was weeping as she twisted from her low position on her seat and looked back at her daughter.

Lisa's eyes were wide with terror as she gasped, "Oh, Mama! We're going to be killed!"

Twenty-Three

The men in the covered wagons had their horses galloping hard as the Apaches drew nearer, firing their rifles.

One wagon hit a large rock on the side of the road and turned over. A man and a woman were thrown onto the ground beside the road. The tongue of the wagon had broken, and their two horses went galloping away with the wooden wagon tongue bouncing on the ground behind them.

The Apaches drew rein and quickly shot the man and the woman, killing them instantly. Then the warriors put their horses to a full gallop and went after the other wagons.

While the five wagons were racing away as fast as possible, the Apaches drew close to the last wagon in line. Suddenly both Edgar and Celia were hit by bullets, and as they buckled on the seat from the hot lead in their bodies, the Indians also shot their galloping horses. The horses immediately collapsed, and the wagon turned over, throwing terrified Lisa Martin out of the rear of the wagon and onto the ground.

The entire band of the Apaches agreed to let the other wagons go, then quickly turned around and rode back to the Martins' overturned wagon. Dismounting, they saw the young lady lying on the ground, looking at them with fear showing in her tear-filled eyes. They also saw the couple lying a few feet from her on the ground with bloody bullet holes in the clothing of their upper bodies. Both of them appeared to be dead.

Lisa Martin lay weeping as she looked at her lifeless parents, expecting the Indians to kill her.

Just as the Indians were raising their rifles to shoot her, pounding hoofbeats were heard, and a larger band of Apaches rode up and drew rein. Their leader spoke sharply to the Indians about to shoot the young lady on the ground.

Lisa didn't understand the Apache language, but when the guns were lowered, she knew the chief had commanded them not to shoot her. She was surprised to see the chief speaking to them again, showing anger.

It seemed that he was asking them questions. They answered him in soft words, and after he said spoke to them again, he moved to the spot where Lisa lay. She was still weeping over her dead parents as the chief knelt beside her.

"Young lady, I am Chief Windino. I am very angry that some of the men from my reservation attacked the wagon train you were with. I assume this man and woman lying on the ground over here are your parents."

"Y-yes sir." She wiped tears from her eyes, surprised to hear him speak English.

"I am very sorry for what my men did to your parents, but I want to tell you that *you* will not be harmed. I will take you to my reservation, and I will have some of the women take care of you until I can get you to the nearest army camp where the soldiers can help you."

Lisa was sniffling and still wiping tears. "Thank you, Chief Windino."

A few minutes later, when the Apaches were preparing to ride away, one of the warriors looked at Lisa with blazing hatred in his eyes. Her heart trembled within her, and she silently prayed, asking the Lord to protect her from that Indian and any other who felt the same way toward her.

Lisa then set her eyes on the bodies of her parents on the ground. Tears streamed down her ashen cheeks as she considered her predicament. *Whatever am I going to do? Papa and Mama were my only living relatives. I have no one to go back to in Phoenix, nor do I have any reason to continue on this trip to California. I have hardly any money or any means of supporting myself.*

Sorrow overwhelmed Lisa as she sat behind Chief Windino on his horse. *I hope Chief Windino is true to his word and will take me to the nearest army camp. Please, Lord. Please, please help me.*

Lisa took a shaky breath and whispered, "Dear Lord, I am so glad to know that Papa and Mama are in heaven with You. I am alone here on earth, but I am glad to know I am in Your care."

Chief Windino put his horse in motion, and his men followed as he headed in the direction of the Apache reservation.

Less than half an hour later, Paul Brockman was coming along the road, driving the iron wagon with the murderous outlaws in the cage. He guided the wagon around a slight bend in the road and came across the two overturned wagons and the bodies of their occupants lying on the ground. He drew the iron wagon to a halt, jumped down from the driver's seat, and hurried toward the overturned wagons. Passing the first one, he ran to the second and examined the man and the woman on the ground.

They were dead, and their horses were gone.

He then rushed back to the other over-turned wagon, noting that both horses lay dead. He knelt down and examined the woman first, finding quickly that she was dead. He rose to his feet and went to the blood-soaked man. Just as he knelt to examine him, Paul was stunned to see that the man was barely breathing and looking up at him.

Before Paul could speak to the wounded man, Edgar Martin spoke weakly. "My wife is dead, isn't she?"

Paul nodded sadly. "Yes sir."

Edgar closed his eyes for a few seconds, biting his lower lip, then opened them. "You — you look very much like chief U.S. marshal John Brockman, who lives in Denver."

Paul swallowed hard. "Sir, I am Chief Brockman's son. My name is Paul."

Edgar's voice grew weaker as he told Paul his name, then how he, his wife, Celia, and their nineteen-year-old daughter, Lisa, were saved under the preaching of his father last April at the First Baptist Church in Phoenix.

Paul's eyes filmed up with tears. "My father told our whole family about you and your family being saved and baptized that Sunday morning."

Edgar managed a slight smile. "Your father is some kind of man!" He then told Paul of the Apache attack, saying that he passed out two or three times during the attack. The next thing he knew, the Apache chief, who spoke English, was telling Lisa his name was Chief Windino.

"I know of Chief Windino, sir. I was about to ask about your daughter. Where is she?"

Edgar feebly licked his lips. "Chief Windino said some things to Lisa I could not understand. My — my brain was fading on me. But then I clearly heard him tell her he was going to take her to his reservation. I passed out then, and when I came to, Lisa and the Indians were gone."

Paul nodded. "I see."

Trembling severely, Edgar grasped Paul's wrist. "I was so scared that the Apaches would torture Lisa and kill her. P-please, Paul, I beg you! Do whatever it takes to rescue Lisa from the Apaches! Get the army to help you!"

Paul's mind was racing. Edgar's breathing was now very shallow. Paul was about to try to encourage him by telling him that Chief

Windino was friendly toward white people when suddenly Edgar gasped, drew a deep, ragged breath, and let it out. His eyes closed.

Paul carefully examined him, checking for breath and a pulse in his neck and his wrists. But there was no breath and no pulse.

Edgar Martin had died and gone to be with the Lord and his wife in heaven.

At that precise moment, a unit of ten U.S. Army soldiers rode up and dismounted. The leader introduced himself as Lieutenant Felix Armendall. Paul told the lieutenant who he was and where he was from. Then, pointing at the prisoners in the iron wagon, who were now awake and sitting up, he explained who they were and what he was doing. All of the soldiers had heard of the Dub Finch gang.

Paul told the soldiers about the Apache attack on the wagon train and how he had come upon the victims in two of the wagons, with one man still alive, who had told him the story before dying just now.

"Lieutenant Armendall," Paul asked, "can you and your men see that the bodies of the four people lying on the ground are buried?"

The lieutenant nodded. "Absolutely. It's the least I can do."

"Thank you, sir. I need to go to Chief

Windino's reservation immediately to see about Miss Lisa Martin. I sure hope she's all right."

"That's mighty kind of you, Deputy Brockman. Tell you what. My men and I will escort you to Chief Windino's reservation. It's only about twelve miles from here. Chief Windino is quite friendly, even to us soldiers, though some of his warriors are not. It's because of those unfriendly warriors that we'll escort you there. I'm quite sure that if Miss Martin is all right when we get there, Chief Windino will let her go with you."

Paul smiled. "I appreciate your offer to escort me there, Lieutenant."

"Glad to do it. And later today, my men and I will see that the people from both wagons are given a proper burial."

While the soldiers were mounting their horses, Paul climbed up onto the driver's seat of the iron wagon. Ignoring the Finch gang glaring at him, Paul put the team into motion. As Paul drove the iron wagon, Lieutenant Armendall rode beside him as the rest of the soldiers followed behind.

When they arrived at the reservation, the lieutenant had his men flank the wagon on both sides as he trotted his horse just ahead of it. Paul drew rein as several Apache warriors moved up and signaled for the wagon and the soldiers to stop.

The lieutenant greeted the warriors in a friendly manner. "I would like to talk to Chief Windino." Even as the words were coming out of his mouth, he saw the chief coming toward him. Apache women and children were also gathering around the soldiers and the wagon.

Full of fear, the outlaws in the wagon's cage stared at the Indians.

The crowd looked on as Chief Windino welcomed Lieutenant Armendall. From his saddle, the lieutenant pointed at Paul. "This young man would like to talk to you, Chief Windino."

The chief nodded, then moved toward the wagon. He gazed up at Paul and said, "Please come down so we can talk."

Paul smiled at him and quickly hopped to the ground.

Chief Windino stepped up to Paul, smiling. "I must ask, are you related to chief United States marshal John Brockman of Denver, Colorado? You look so much like him."

Paul nodded. "Yes, I am Chief Brockman's son, Paul. My father told our family of how he had saved your life last April when you had been bitten by a rattlesnake."

"He certainly did, and because your father saved my life, I feel much warmth toward him."

Paul told the chief about finding the parents of Miss Lisa Martin on the road where they had been attacked and shot by some Apaches. He then informed the chief that Miss Lisa's father, barely alive, had told him that he heard Chief Windino tell his daughter that he was taking her to his reservation. After telling him this, Mr. Martin died.

"I see," Windino said, a sad look on his dark face.

Paul's brow furrowed. "Chief, is Miss Lisa here on the reservation now?"

"She is. Miss Martin has not been harmed. At this moment, she is in one of the wickiups with two older women who are trying to console her over her parents' death. She thought, of course, that her father was already dead. I'd planned to deliver her to a U.S. Army base soon. I will take you to the wickiup right now so you can meet her."

Paul noticed that several of the Apaches who had gathered around were eyeing the men inside the cage on the iron wagon. Chief Windino followed Paul's gaze. "Who are the men in the cage?"

Paul quickly told Chief Windino the story of the condemned outlaws and how he was taking them back to the prison at Yuma, from which they had recently escaped.

Windino nodded and rubbed his chin.

"Chief Windino, I've come to see if Miss Lisa will let me take her with me on my way to Yuma rather than your taking her to an army base. And after the outlaws are delivered to Yuma Prison, I will take her with me to Denver, find her a home there, and see that she is taken care of."

The chief smiled. "Deputy Paul Brockman, I commend you for being willing to do this for the young lady. Come. I will take you to meet her."

Moments later, Paul waited outside the wickiup the chief had entered. He could hear Windino telling Miss Martin about Deputy Paul Brockman being there and why.

When the chief finished telling the story, the flap that covered the wickiup's opening was pulled open. The lovely blond-haired, blue-eyed Lisa Martin stepped out behind the chief. Two older Apache women remained at the opening, looking on.

The chief stepped to one side, allowing Lisa to get a full look at Paul. As she drew up close to Paul, a smile graced her drawn features.

Seeing her grief and almost feeling it himself, Paul took a step closer to her and clasped both of her hands in his. "I am so very sorry, Miss Martin, for your loss. I am here to help you in any way I can. I heard Chief Windino tell you that I am willing to take you to Denver with me after I deliver the outlaws to the Yuma Prison and that I will find you a home there and see that you are taken care of."

Lisa remembered her plea to God, asking Him for help, and a smile curved her lips. "You are an answer to my prayers."

Paul's heart fluttered at Lisa's presence and her words.

Lisa took a brief moment to explain why she and her parents were moving to San Diego, then wiped tears from her eyes. "My parents are now in heaven with the Lord, Deputy Brockman, and it is because of your father's preaching that they became Christians, as well as myself. And now, here you are, Deputy Brockman, offering to take me to Denver, find me a home, and see that I am taken care of."

"You can call me Paul, Miss Martin."

Lisa found her heart beating quicker as she talked with Paul. "All right. Then you can call me Lisa."

"All right, Lisa. Then you *will* let me take you with me, first to Yuma, then home to Denver?"

"I sure will!" Lisa wiped away more tears from her eyes. "Never have I felt so alone in all my life. I have been asking the Lord to help me, and now He has. I'll try to never be a problem to you. And any assistance you can give me in finding a place to live and some kind of employment will be greatly appreciated." Lisa's eyes were sincere as they looked into Paul's eyes.

"It is my pleasure to be of help, Lisa. Finding you a place to live or a source of employment won't be a problem. Having you with me on this arduous journey will be a true blessing. While I'm driving the iron wagon with five outlaws in its cage, it will be great to have you to talk to. And we can get to know each other better." Paul gave her a cheeky grin, and Lisa smiled back.

"Lisa, we'll have to stop at Phoenix on the way to Denver, since I was filling in there at the U.S. marshal's office for the wounded man in charge, federal marshal Danford Pierce."

"Oh, you were?" said Lisa. "I knew about his being wounded in some kind of battle with outlaws."

"Yeah. The outlaws that wounded him are the ones I'm taking back to Yuma."

"Oh, I see. Well, good! Paul, I am excited about going to Denver with you. I would love to become a member of the church in Denver where the Brockmans are members."

"Well, that will be no problem. And you'll love Denver's First Baptist Church as much as you love your church in Phoenix."

Lisa nodded, then put a finger to her temple. "Just before Chief Windino put me on his horse to bring me to the reservation, he asked if I had belongings in my family's wagon. I told him that I did, and he had one of his warriors get my leather bag of clothing out of the overturned wagon and carry it on his horse for me. I'll need a few moments to go back into the wickiup and get it."

Paul felt his heart banging his rib cage as he kept his eyes on the beautiful Lisa Martin while she was talking. "Sure. No problem."

TWENTY-FOUR

Already feeling a strong attraction for Lisa Martin, Paul Brockman glanced at the Apaches still gathered around them and let his gaze settle on Chief Windino briefly. Then he turned back to Lisa. "Before we head for Yuma, I want to have a talk with Chief Windino in private."

Lisa nodded. "Of course. I'll go back into the wickiup and get my bag. You can find me right here."

Chief Windino stepped up to Paul. "It would be nice to have a private talk with you before you leave, Deputy Brockman. My wickiup is just a short distance from here. Please come with me."

Lisa watched Paul walk away with the chief, then turned and found that the two older women were still at the opening of the wickiup. One of them smiled and, knowing some English, she said, "You can come in and get your bag of clothing, Lisa."

Paul followed the chief inside his wickiup. There he saw a small table with two crude wooden chairs. Windino pulled one of the chairs back and invited Paul to sit in it. The chief then sat opposite him and said, "What is it you wish to talk to me about?"

Paul leaned forward and placed his elbows on the table. "My father told me he had talked to you about receiving the Lord Jesus Christ as your Saviour while showing you many Scripture passages on the subject, most of them being underlined so they were easy to find. He told me you said you couldn't leave the Apache religion because of your being a chief and the head of this reservation. My father said he gave that Bible to you and asked you to read it."

Windino nodded. "Yes, he did, and I have read those underlined passages many times, along with many other Scriptures." He paused and took a short breath as his eyes filmed with tears. "Deputy Brockman, I want to be saved. I want the Lord Jesus Christ as my Saviour. I realize now that if I cling to the Apache religion, when I die, I will go to hell. Would you help me?"

Paul's own eyes filled with tears. "My Bible is out in the iron wagon, so could we use yours?"

Windino smiled. "We sure can!" He left

his chair, hurried to a small, old chest of drawers, opened the top drawer, and took out the Bible John Brockman had given him.

As Windino returned to the table, Paul asked him to sit beside him. The chief handed the Bible to Paul, then moved his chair beside Paul's and sat down.

With Windino looking at the pages, Paul went over some of the marked passages, making sure the chief clearly understood them and that he believed Jesus Christ was the only way of salvation, which was purchased for him on the cross of Calvary when He shed His blood, died, was buried, and arose from the dead in three days.

With this totally clear, Paul had the joy of leading Chief Windino to the Lord. The chief wiped tears of joy from his cheeks.

"My father is going to be so happy when I tell him you're now saved," Paul said. He showed the chief in the Bible that his first step of obedience to the Lord, now that he was saved, was to get baptized.

"You should go to Phoenix and visit with Pastor Alex Duffy at First Baptist Church, Chief Windino. Pastor Duffy can help you learn more about your new life in Christ and will baptize you in a church service."

Windino assured Paul that he would go meet with Pastor Duffy real soon.

They left the wickiup and walked to the spot where Lisa was waiting with her leather bag on the ground beside her. As they stepped up to her, Paul said, "I've got some wonderful news. Chief Windino just received the Lord Jesus Christ as his Saviour!"

A big smile spread over Lisa's face. "Oh, Chief Windino, I am so happy for you! One day we will see each other in heaven."

Windino agreed with her wholeheartedly. Then Paul gave the chief a manly hug, saying he was glad that they would get to be in heaven together forever.

The soldiers were still there. Paul went to them and thanked them for escorting him to the reservation. As the soldiers were riding away, Paul helped Lisa onto the driver's seat of the iron wagon while Dub Finch and his outlaw companions glared at them between the small openings of the iron straps of the cage.

After placing Lisa's leather bag in one of the compartments on the side of the iron wagon, Paul climbed up onto the driver's seat next to the lovely blonde. Then waving at Chief Windino and the crowd of Apaches standing there looking on, Paul put the horses in motion, and they were soon heading west on the road toward Yuma.

As the iron wagon topped a slight hill and

the reservation passed from view behind them, Lisa turned to Paul. "Will we be in danger while we're driving to Yuma?"

Paul nodded. "We very well could be, with vicious Indians roaming about and robbers riding the road between Phoenix and Yuma. I've got my Colt .45 in my holster and a rifle down here at my feet, under the seat. I will put them to use if I have to. The main thing for us to do, though, is to trust the Lord to take care of us."

A small shiver of fear ran down Lisa's spine as she thought of her recent ordeal.

Noting the fear on Lisa's face, Paul reached his right hand over, placed it on her left hand, and gave it a reassuring squeeze. "Let's remember that we are cradled in God's hands. We must trust Him to protect us."

"I agree, Paul." Lisa gazed into his eyes. "But I'm only human, and I can't help thinking of the horrible Indian attack on the small wagon train my parents and I were traveling with and that they were both killed." Tears trickled down her cheeks, and she hastily wiped them away.

Paul squeezed her hand again. "I'm so sorry, Lisa. I can't even begin to imagine what you're feeling and the pain in your heart. But . . . but I am here for you, and I will protect you the best way I know how."

"How about we pray right now?" Lisa said.

"Oh no!" came the voice of Dub Finch from the cage behind them. "Not that religious stuff!"

Paul drew the wagon to a halt and looked back through the small, square openings in the cage straps. "This isn't 'religious stuff,' Finch. This is true Bible Christianity! We're going to pray now, and don't any of you interrupt us."

Paul put his right arm around Lisa's shoulders, and as they bowed their heads and closed their eyes, he led in prayer, asking the Lord to protect the two of them all the way to Yuma and then all the way to Denver.

When Paul closed his prayer in Jesus' name, a sweet sense of peace came over Lisa's heart. The five outlaws were staring at them as she thanked Paul for praying and trusting the Lord as he did.

Paul gently snapped the reins and put the horses back in motion.

As the wheels of the iron wagon tossed up dust from the dry road, Jack Devlin said, "You two are nothin' but religious fanatics."

With the reins in his hands, Paul looked back at Devlin. "I'm telling you, we are not religious. We are saved and will never go to hell! Heaven is our home when we leave this world because we have received the Lord Jesus Christ as our Saviour. I tried to talk to you men about this the first night we were on the road to Yuma, warning you that if you die in your sins, you will go to a never-ending, blazing lake of fire called hell, but all you did was make fun of me."

"Well, if your Christianity is so great," Dub said, "why did you put us in handcuffs when we left Phoenix, and then the next day you put these ankle chains on us!"

"That's got nothing to do with my being a Christian, Finch," said Paul. "It's got to do with the fact that all five of you are cold-blooded murderers. You got the handcuffs and the ankle chains because of what *you* are."

"Well, whatever you say, Brockman," spat Kurt Jagger, "we don't believe all that Jesus Christ stuff you preached at us! We want nothin' to do with it. That Bible you believe is full of nonsense! We don't believe it." The other four quickly spoke their agreement.

Paul ran his gaze over their faces. "Well, let me tell you this. Every one of you will find out that the Bible is absolutely true when you hang at Yuma Prison. When you die at the ends of those hangman's ropes and plunge into the fire of hell, you'll wish you had listened to me and made Jesus Christ your Saviour!"

The outlaws said no more to Paul.

Later, when darkness fell over the desert and they stopped for the night, Lisa volunteered to cook their meal.

"That's mighty kind of you, Lisa," Paul said. "One of the compartments on the side of the wagon contains bacon, beans, and biscuits I bought before leaving on the trip."

Paul released the horses from the iron wagon, tied them to a nearby tree, and gave them food and water.

The prisoners ate inside the cage, and after the meal was over, Paul walked them at gunpoint to a low, bushy spot nearby, where they could relieve themselves. Then he returned them to the iron wagon and locked them once again in the cage.

Paul thought about having Lisa sleep on the driver's seat of the wagon, but since he would be sleeping underneath the wagon, this would put her too far from him. Wanting to keep propriety correct yet have Lisa close to him during the night so he could protect her if needed, he placed his bedroll under the middle of the wagon, telling her she could sleep in it. He then made a pallet with extra blankets for himself a few feet away at the rear of the wagon.

The next morning, as the iron wagon continued westward, Paul, Lisa, and the prisoners suddenly saw a band of eight angry Apache Indians galloping toward them on their horses, whooping their hatred loudly and clutching their rifles in the air.

Paul lifted his rifle from beneath the driver's seat with his free hand and cried out, "Lord, help us!"

Lisa gripped her hands together. "Yes, Lord! Please help us! Those Indians mean to kill us!"

All five of the outlaws in the cage were frozen with terror but uttered not a word.

As the wild Indians were drawing closer, a dozen U.S. Army soldiers rode their horses out of a wooded area alongside the road and began firing their rifles at the Apaches.

Seeing that they were outnumbered by the soldiers, the Indians quickly turned their horses about and galloped away. Lisa breathed a prayer of thanks to the Lord, as did Paul. The Dub Finch gang was obviously relieved.

Paul stopped the iron wagon, and when the soldiers gathered around on their horses, he thanked them for coming to their rescue. As the soldiers rode on, Lisa wiped away tears. "Paul, I'm glad the Lord saw to it that these soldiers were camped at this spot on the road to Yuma."

"Amen, Lisa! We have a wonderful God, don't we?"

"We sure do!"

Paul, Lisa, and the outlaws arrived in Yuma late in the afternoon on Tuesday, October 8. The trip had taken longer than Paul figured because of the interruptions along the way. The one interruption he was so thankful for was when he had to take time to go to the Apache reservation and meet with Chief Windino in order to take Lisa with him — where he also had the joy of leading the chief to the Lord.

When Paul drove the iron wagon onto the Yuma Prison grounds, Dub Finch and his gang members were looking very solemn. As Paul pulled the wagon up to the guard tower, two guards came through the gate and stepped up to the wagon.

Paul introduced himself and explained why he was bringing the Finch gang back to the prison.

One of the guards opened the gate. "Go ahead and drive the iron wagon inside the walls of the prison, Deputy Marshal Brockman."

While Paul was doing so, the other guard hurried toward the warden's office to tell him about the remaining five members of the Dub Finch gang being brought back to the prison.

The first guard closed the gate, then moved over to where Paul had stopped the wagon. "Follow me in your wagon, Marshal. I'll take you to the warden's office."

Moments later, as they were drawing near the building that housed the warden's office, Warden George Henderson came out the door with the other guard at his side.

Paul jumped to the ground, shook the warden's hand, and introduced Lisa Martin.

"Miss Martin, I am so sorry for the loss of your parents," Warden Henderson said, then turned to Paul Brockman. "And thank you, Marshal, for your courage in bringing the five remaining members of the Finch gang across dangerous country back to the prison."

The warden called more guards to come to the iron wagon. "Marshal, can you unlock the cage, please?"

When the pale-faced outlaws had made their way out of the cage, Warden Henderson stepped up to them, his eyes narrowed. "You have just under a week to do hard labor here at the prison before you are hanged as the judge has scheduled it —

Monday, October 14."

Fear was in the hearts of the escapees, but they tried not to show it. Paul removed the ankle chains and handcuffs. Then the Finch gang looked at Paul with fiery eyes as the guards took them away at gunpoint.

The warden took Paul and Lisa into his office. There the warden handed Paul a telegram that had come for him two days ago from Deputy Leroy Woodard in Phoenix. Paul read the message, which stated that he could go directly on home to Denver because Marshal Pierce would be back on the job on Wednesday, October 9.

When Paul told Lisa the news, she clasped her hands together. "Oh, Paul, I'm so glad that we can now head straight for Denver."

After leaving the prison, Paul drove the iron wagon down Yuma's Main Street with Lisa at his side as he kept his eye out for a nice hotel. When he spotted the Western Hotel, he pulled the wagon onto the hotel's parking lot.

Paul and Lisa obtained separate hotel rooms, then had supper together in the hotel's restaurant.

The next morning, as Paul helped Lisa up onto the driver's seat of the iron wagon, he told her that it would take them about nine days to make it to Denver.

As they traveled eastward, talking about the things of the Lord, both Paul and Lisa were secretly becoming more attracted to each other. Each night, they prayed together for the Lord's protection. Paul let Lisa sleep in the cage of the iron wagon, and he slept on the driver's seat.

Each day, Paul prayed silently while driving the wagon, telling the Lord he felt that Lisa was "Miss Right" for him.

Paul was unaware if it, but Lisa was silently praying also, asking the Lord to guide her. She felt that she was falling in love with the handsome, kind, unselfish Paul Brockman, who so loved his Lord and Saviour. *Lord, Paul would make me a perfect husband.*

As they traveled day by day, Paul and Lisa ran into a few problems. On the third day after leaving Yuma, Paul had to interrupt a stagecoach holdup. He stopped the wagon when he saw what was happening and hastily snuck up on the three robbers, his gun drawn and cocked. Surprising them, he made them drop their guns, then arrested them.

With Lisa at his side on the driver's seat, Paul carried the robbers a few miles in the cage and delivered them to the marshal of the next town, which was only five miles from the spot of the robbery.

After Paul and Lisa had been back on the road for some three hours, Paul heard Lisa sniffle and looked at her. Tears filled her eyes.

"Lisa, what's the matter? Why are you crying?"

She looked at him through her tears and said, "Oh, Paul, these are happy tears. I'm so grateful for all you've done for me. It means so much that you are willing to take me to Denver and see that I find a place to live, a place to make a living for myself."

Holding the reins in one hand, Paul reached over and took hold of Lisa's left hand. He looked deeply into her teary eyes. "I have to tell you this, Lisa. I am head over heels in love with you. I know it beyond any doubt."

She sniffled slightly, blinked at her tears as she stared into his eyes. "Paul, I feel exactly the same way about you!"

Paul quickly pulled the wagon off to the side of the road. "For the last couple of years, I have been asking God to send Miss Right into my life. And I know that He has. Lisa, *you* are Miss Right. I know it."

They shared a tender kiss; then the lovely blonde said, "I know the Lord has sent Mister Right into my life, Paul. *You* are my

Mister Right."

Paul stroked her cheek. "Well, since we both know what the Lord has done, I want to ask you a question."

Lisa blinked. "What is it?"

"Will you marry me, Lisa?"

She gave him a potent "Yes!" and they shared another tender kiss.

As the days passed and Paul and Lisa drew closer to Denver, Paul told her all about his family and how the Lord had worked in their lives.

While the iron wagon was crossing a bridge over a wide river, Lisa said, "Paul darling, we have a lot of plans to make. And — and" — fear crept into her voice — "what if your family doesn't like me?"

Paul looked at her and frowned. "Are you kidding? They are going to love you! I guarantee you, Papa, Mama, Ginny, and Meggie will be absolutely overjoyed to have you in the family. Sweetheart, just put those negative thoughts out of your mind, and let's enjoy making our plans for a wonderful future!"

Lisa patted his hand. "I'm sorry, darling." Her face beamed with love for this man that God, in His wisdom, had given her. "I'm sure you know your family well, so I'll stop worrying and we can start fully enjoying our lives together."

"Yes!" Paul said, and the iron wagon was once again rolling through the dust of the road. "We, ah, should set a date for our wedding soon."

"That's fine with me."

"We're making pretty good time, Lisa. Looks like we'll be arriving in Denver next Thursday, October 17."

She smiled at him. "The sooner, the better."

"You can join First Baptist Church in Denver on Sunday, October 20."

"Yes!" she said excitedly.

"And, honey, speaking of setting our wedding date, we should give it a little time before getting married so you can get acquainted with my family, some of our close friends, and Pastor Bayless and his wife, Mary. I'll find you a place to stay until then."

"I appreciate that, darling."

"I've been thinking about the wedding date," Paul said smiling at her. "How about we ask Pastor Bayless to perform our marriage ceremony on Sunday afternoon, November 24?"

Lisa smiled. "That's enough time from now. Yes!"

When they entered the next town, Paul

pulled the wagon up in front of a general store, which had a sign saying they had a jewelry department. He took Lisa inside and bought her an engagement ring and a wedding ring.

When they were once again seated on the driver's seat of the wagon, Paul placed the engagement ring on Lisa's finger, saying he would keep the wedding ring until the wedding. He got another tender kiss.

Paul and Lisa arrived in Denver late in the afternoon on Thursday, October 17. Paul drove the iron wagon toward the federal building. "Soon my father will be heading home from the office, so I want us to talk to him right away."

Lisa smiled. "That sounds great, Paul."

A few minutes later, in his office, Chief Brockman was just rising from his desk, getting ready to go to the corral behind the federal building to mount his horse and head for home. There was a tap on his door, and John recognized it. Smiling, he rounded his desk, calling out, "Come on in, son!"

Paul opened the door and stepped into the office, leaving the door open behind him. He was beaming. "Howdy, Papa!"

They hugged each other; then John took a step back. "Well, how did the trip to Yuma go? I'm so glad to see you!"

"It went fine, Papa. If the hanging went as scheduled, Dub Finch and his four remaining gang members were hanged three days ago."

John nodded. "Well, they won't be killing anybody now."

"Right," Paul said. "I'll tell you the whole story of the trip later. But right now, I want you to know about something absolutely marvelous that happened to me on the trip."

John's eyebrows arched. "Oh? Tell me."

Paul smiled at his father, then turned toward the door and called, "Okay, sweetheart! Come on in!"

John's eyebrows arched again, and his eyes widened as he saw the lovely blonde enter his office. "Well, hello, Lisa!" He smiled at her. "It is good to see you!"

"Papa, could we sit down and talk?"

"We sure can," replied John, with Paul's word *sweetheart* to Lisa echoing in his brain. He knew then and there that the Lord had answered Breanna's and his prayers.

John went to Lisa and gave her a fatherly hug. When the door was closed and all three were seated, John was told the complete story from both Paul and Lisa about her parents' death, how the two of them met, how Paul had taken Lisa all the way to Yuma with him, and that they had fallen in love.

Paul smiled at Lisa. "Show my papa your engagement ring, sweetheart."

John was delighted to learn that Paul and Lisa were engaged. *Thank You, Lord!*

Paul then told his father the full story of the Dub Finch gang, the trip in the iron wagon, and how he had been able to lead Chief Windino to the Lord.

John was elated at the news about Chief Windino. He said, "Well, let's head for the ranch. Lisa, you can sleep in one of the spare bedrooms of the ranch house tonight."

Lisa smiled warmly. "Thank you, Chief Brockman."

TWENTY-FIVE

Breanna Brockman and her daughters were sitting on the front porch of the ranch house with the guests Breanna had invited for supper, waiting for John to arrive. Seated with the Brockman family were Whip and Anna-beth Langford and six-year-old Lizzie, as well as Pastor Robert and Mary Bayless and Ginny's fiancé, David Barrett.

They were all chatting when Meggie pointed toward the front gate of the ranch. "Mama! Look! Papa's home, and Paul is driving one of those army iron wagons, and there's a lady sitting beside him!"

Moments later, as John drew up to the house on Blackie and Paul and Lisa drew up in the iron wagon, John smiled at the group and dismounted. Paul drew rein, smiling at the group also, then hopped from the wagon and helped Lisa down from the driver's seat.

John, Paul, and Lisa headed for the porch,

where the entire group was now on their feet. But Breanna was quicker as she moved down the porch steps. The trio stopped at the base of the steps, and John cheerfully said to his wife, "Wow! Looks like a celebration of sorts."

"No, sweetheart." Breanna hugged her husband. "Just our family and these special friends having supper together. I hadn't told you about it because I wanted you to be surprised. Supper is ready now."

Then Breanna took a step toward her son and gave him a huge welcome-home hug. "Paul, I'm so glad you're home!" Leaning back in his arms, she asked, "Who is this lovely young lady?"

"Mama, this is Lisa Martin."

Breanna's mouth dropped open in total surprise. While Breanna was struggling to get a grip on herself, John told their guests about the Apache attack on the wagon train the Martins had been traveling with on their way to California, in which Lisa's parents were shot. He explained that her mother was killed instantly and how Paul came along after the attack while taking the murderous Dub Finch gang to Yuma Prison in the iron wagon. John explained that just before Lisa's father died, he told Paul that Chief Windino, who was not part of the attack, had taken Lisa to his reservation.

John proceeded to tell how Paul had gone to the reservation so he could take Lisa with him to Yuma, then how Paul had led Chief Windino to the Lord while he was there.

John turned to Lisa, who was standing very close to Paul, and said, "Lisa, dear, everyone here is going to be excited by what I am about to announce."

Paul and Lisa looked at each other and smiled.

Breanna's heart began to pound. *Lord, have You done it?*

John ran his gaze over the group. "Breanna and I know that our son has been praying for some time, asking the Lord to send the right young Christian lady into his life for him to marry. Well, those prayers have been answered."

Eyes brightened in the group.

In her heart, Breanna prayed, *Lord Jesus, when I learned that this was Lisa Martin with Paul, I was sure that Your hand was in it!*

"Show everybody your engagement ring!" John told Lisa.

She lifted her left hand and moved it back and forth so everyone could see the ring on her finger.

This brought much excitement, and Breanna was the first to hug Lisa, telling her how happy she was; then Breanna hugged Paul. The rest of the group moved in, and both Lisa and Paul received plenty of hugs as they were congratulated on their engagement.

While the hugging was going on, Breanna stepped close to John and said quietly, "We were right about Lisa being God's choice, weren't we?"

John grinned. "We sure were."

When the excitement settled down, and the hugs were finished, Ginny looked at Paul and Lisa. "Have you set a date for the wedding?"

"Well, little sis, Lisa and I have planned to ask Pastor Bayless if he would perform our wedding ceremony at the church on Sunday afternoon, this coming November 24."

Instant gasps sounded among the group. Everyone looked toward Ginny and David, who were standing side by side.

Ginny looked up at David, and he said, "Go ahead. *You* tell them!"

"David and I had set that exact date and time with Pastor Bayless for *our* wedding."

Paul and Lisa looked at each other, surprise showing in their eyes. Paul said to Lisa, "Sweetheart, we'll change our wedding date, then."

Pastor Bayless spoke up quickly. "That's

not necessary, Paul. I will be glad to perform a *double* wedding that day!"

Joy abounded in the hearts of Paul and Lisa, David and Ginny, and everyone else.

Breanna rushed to Paul and Ginny and hugged both of them at the same time. Then she looked at Lisa. "Oh, sweetie, we're so happy you are going to be a part of our family!"

Lisa blinked at the tears that formed in her eyes. "Thank you, Mrs. Brockman. It was so hard to lose my parents in such a horrible way. But I'm so grateful to have a new family to fill the emptiness in my heart."

Breanna hugged Lisa, kissed her cheek, then looked around at the group and said, "Hey, everybody, supper is going to get cold if we don't get to the dining room and eat it!"

Ginny said, "Meggie and I will take the main part of supper out of the warm oven right now, Mama."

During the meal, John said, "Paul and Lisa, I just wanted you to know that Breanna and I bought David and Ginny a house in Denver for their wedding present. And we'd sure like to do the same for you two."

Paul and Lisa warmly thanked Paul's

parents for this.

Paul then explained to the group that the iron wagon, which was exactly like the one he and his father had seen at Fort Logan, belonged to him, as did the draft horses. Looking across the table at his father, Paul said, "Papa, could we leave the iron wagon and the horses here at the ranch since we'll be living in town when we get married?"

John smiled at his son. "Of course you can. That will be fine."

The next day, John and Breanna took Paul and Lisa house hunting in Denver, and they found a lovely three-bedroom frame house for sale, which had a cozy parlor and an ample kitchen. An extra-large yard surrounded the house, and a nice white picket fence enclosed it all. Paul and Lisa loved it, and John and Breanna bought it for them.

When the sale was completed, Lisa hugged John and Breanna at the same time and said, "Oh, this place is just so wonderful! How can we ever thank you enough?"

Breanna hugged Lisa back. "Just be happy in it, honey, and in your marriage! That will be all the thanks we could ever want or need."

John wrapped one arm around Breanna and the other arm around Lisa. "That's for sure, Breanna darling!" Then he looked at

Lisa and Paul. "Just be happy in your marriage, and you'll be happy in this house!"

That evening, the Langfords took Paul and Lisa to a restaurant in Denver. Whip and Annabeth were delighted to learn about the house that John and Breanna had bought for Lisa and Paul, which they could move into after the wedding. Until then, the Langfords invited Lisa to stay in their home. Lisa gladly accepted the offer. Paul thanked them for their kindness.

The next Sunday morning, Lisa walked down the aisle during the invitation after Pastor Bayless's sermon. He introduced her to the church and asked her to give her salvation and baptism testimony. She was quickly voted in as a member.

The pastor then announced the double wedding that would take place in the church on November 24. After the service, Lisa stood with Paul in the vestibule and was warmly welcomed by the church members.

As the weeks passed, Lisa came to love everyone in the Brockman family very much — including Dr. Matthew and Dottie Carroll as well as friends David Barrett and Whip, Annabeth, and Lizzie Langford.

On Sunday, November 24, the double wedding took place. When the wedding reception was over, and Paul and Lisa were about to leave to go to their house, Lisa said, "Paul darling, there is something I want to ask you."

He looked down into her lovely blue eyes. "What is it, sweetheart?"

"It's about the iron wagon."

Paul blinked and slanted his head to the side. "What about it?"

Lisa smiled. "Since we have an extra-large yard at our beautiful home, I want to bring the iron wagon from your parents' ranch to our place and put it in the yard."

Paul's eyebrows arched. "Honey, why would you want that iron wagon in our yard?"

Reaching up and putting her arms around her husband's neck, Lisa squeezed him tight and giggled. "If it wasn't for that trip you took to Yuma in the iron wagon, you and I would never have met. I want the iron wagon as a keepsake so I can look at it every day!"

Paul laughed heartily and bent over to kiss her. As he looked into her eyes, he said, "Honey, if you want that iron wagon, you've got it!"